OLD SOUL

a novel

Carol LaDuca

ISBN 9798742204220

Cover design by: Carol LaDuca
Library of Congress Control Number: 2018675309
Printed in the United States of America

PROLOGUE

I'm an old soul, an indigenous old soul from the Americas—and a spirit. As this story unfolds you may wonder how I, of Central American genetics, came to mentor a young Iroquois from the northern region. We indigenous peoples of the Americas are all connected—cut from the same cloth, so to speak.

Most humans barely give us spirits a passing thought. It's like we don't exist. They tend to think it's better that way, less confusing. I'll give you a for instance. For instance what does a human usually do in a déjà vu moment? In our experience he brushes it aside as if it were a fly alighting on his arm. Ninety-nine point nine percent of the time the flicked feeling goes pouf as if that sensation didn't really happen. It's too much to ponder for most humans so they banish the feeling and get on with whatever it was they were doing. They miss the point. We were trying to connect.

This is the story about the point one percent who understand that the material world and the spiritual world are as related as the shore is to the sea. We are in constant motion with one another, we ebb and we flow. We cannot be separated.

I have agreed for one last time to mentor a soul about to come back. I've been mentoring for centuries and had hoped to retire. It's a difficult job because it's so unnerving to the spirit who has been chosen to return, in this case Kateri McCann. I had promised her great-great (I can't even remember how many times great) grandmother that if a Mohawk spirit would become Kateri McCann I would mentor her. At the time I thought what are the chances of that happening? I was exceedingly honored then but now I'm so old I don't really know if I can be of much help.

I've been observing the spirit of Kateri for a few weeks now. She is definitely a pip and probably will do well in the material world. But I have to caution her about the challenges humans inevitably foist upon their progeny. They screw up so badly it makes me shudder. Yet she's excited to return to earth. Her last adventure was so long ago she can hardly remember the details. She's an incredible energy. I'm invigorated just being in her aura. Although she pooh-poohs all my warnings about the messes humans make and the sorrows these messes will impose on her, she thinks she can handle it and make a difference this time.

I'll be with her throughout this journey. My fingers are crossed she'll hear me as she traverses the turning points in her life. We will soon find out.

Mathilde, mentor

PART 1

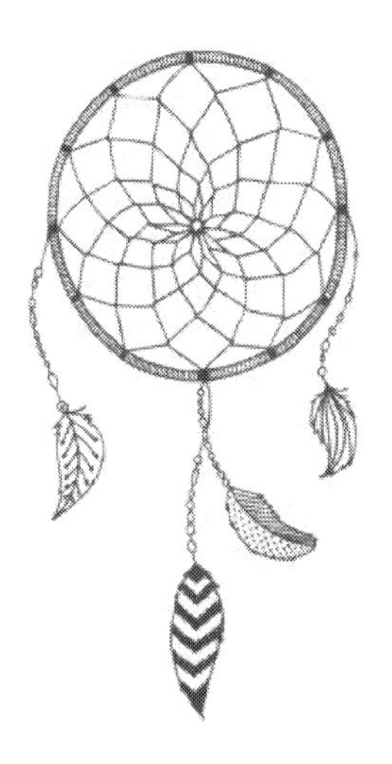

If you want to touch the past, touch a rock.
If you want to touch the present, touch a flower.
If you want to touch the future, touch a life.

Unknown

BECOMING KATERI

I was born before, so this conception is my second time around, an old soul who comes by from time to time. Before this recent 1963 birth I knew so many things. I saw the past as if it were a looping video and I could visualize a future including faces and feelings of things yet to come. Between the past and the present I hibernate in infinity wondering of a future that may happen at any moment.

That moment neared in May of '63. Images of dark eyes and lean bodies, pick-up trucks and angry voices began to rouse me from my dormancy. Each conception is different. This time I am overcome by a sense of bittersweet as I plunge into the darkness of gestation.

I am becoming human. I am becoming Kateri McCann.

My actualization began two generations ago in a confluence of diversity and xenophobia when four unlikely strangers united to become my grandparents: a Native American, an Englishman, a charismatic Irishman and his exotic ingenue wife.

Of the four I am fondest of my Akhosotha, that means my grandmother in the language of the Mohawk but I always call her by her easy name, Oona. Without even knowing I would be in her future she was already waiting for me. It doesn't matter one iota to Oona that I will be conceived on a mattress that was tossed into the back of a pick-up truck by an eighteen-year-old on his senior prom picnic hoping he'd get lucky with my mother, and did. Oona is all about natural things. She and I have already bonded.

Oona has straight black hair that falls to her waist at bedtime. It's mostly braided but sometimes caught up in a pillow of spun silk at the nape of her neck. Either way it accentuates her high cheekbones and soft brown eyes. I think she's beautiful.

By the time she has become my Oona she has grown grandma arms—soft, plump cushions of love that fall from her shoulders. They are waiting for me. I will snuggle there, fall asleep there, I will push and probe her doughy skin and bury my fingers in its folds with great amusement. I can't wait to see Oona. It's my favorite comfort even now as I wait. I will inherit her spiritualism.

Grandpap Will Thompson and Oona are an unlikely match. Will is a lanky Englishman with blond bushy brows shading ocean blue eyes. A traveler and passer-through-of-far-fetched-places and a student of indigenous cultures, Will never meant to stay in one place or to end up here in Turner Mills but Oona become the last stop on his wanderlust and she is never going to leave this place. To her, this land is sacred despite the cunning of capitalists who secured rights to build a soot-belching factory on what was once native land. Oona says, "Make up your mind, Will, I'm staying put." Grandpap stayed put.

Jobs are so plentiful in Turner Mills in the late '40's that all Grandpap has to do to get hired is to show up at the plant's main gate. He's hired on the spot as a smelter. His handsomeness becomes even more rugged as the red dust from the plant settles in the crow's feet that form when he squints. He comes home dirty smelling of sweat and smelt and swings Oona off her feet because he's crazy in love. She chastises him saying, "Put me down Will Thompson, for God's sake," and handing him her ladle says, "here, taste this soup." He laughs and swings her around once more. Even in his constant state of steel plant dishevelment I know why my grandmother loves him. He'd do anything for her, twice, if she asked. His dream is to move Oona out of the shadow of the fire-spitting behemoth at the end of the street and into the sunny, soft rolling hills a few miles south. He's saving for that day although it never comes.

His workman hands are rough. He'll draw them across the baby skin of his first granddaughter in attempts to amuse me and I'll coo despite their scratchiness. Grandpap's eyes are sapphires that catch the sun whenever I say "up" but it's those hands, those big bear claws, coming out of his sleeves and reaching for me that makes me feel cherished. They can do anything—swing Grandmother, make steel and make my own hands disappear into his. They may be the only safe hands I will ever know. I pretend Grandpap is my real father. He makes not having one okay, better than okay, he makes me feel loved.

Kip McCann is my real father but there'll be no Kip McCann in my real life. There'll be no boisterous Irish family to answer my childhood how-comes like how come I talk so loud, how come I laugh so much and how come I have all this red hair. Instead I'll start my days being loved by a tribe of aunts and uncles and a slew of cinnamon-colored cousins and have a happy childhood. My mother, Connie Thompson, will marry Kip McCann but before you can say Jack Robinson, she will be the ex-Mrs. Kip McCann.

When I am six she'll re-marry a very nice man named Carl Warner. We'll become the Warner family and I'll wonder why my name didn't change, too. I'll stay Kateri McCann. God knows Carl will be a good dad, actually a great dad, but as far as I'm concerned, Carl is the other kids' father—and there were three more to claim him after me. I'll always love him in my own way but I will never get myself to say that other F word: Father. He'll always be Carl.

Then there's The Judge, my McCann grandfather. The Judge is the only name I will ever call him. The shoe fits. He will judge me, my mother Connie and my father Kip, all three of us, as unworthy. Unworthy of what I ask you? Unworthy of his precious McCann family name, or his precious aunts, uncles and cousins. The Judge gives poignant meaning to the notion of Original Sin and I happen to be the face of it.

The Honorable Mortimer McCann's fiefdom is Family Court where he presides over the misconduct of families from his lofty bench. It's an elected position so The Judge is always on the handshake and kissing babies he doesn't even know. He is charismatic, gregarious, bodacious, energetic. What's not to like about The Judge? He doffs his fedora at every female he passes, calls everyone by first name, has a Purple Heart for dragging fellow Marines to safety under fire in Japan, can get you a job with the County and can get your brother one, too. It goes without saying that he's the pillar of God's special house in Turner Mills, the Cathedral. But The Judge has a secret that will be his undoing. Me. I am the bump in the belly of Connie Thompson, the girl from the wrong side of the tracks, the girl who tricked his firstborn into eating the apple, who tempted Kip McCann into putting a mattress in the back of his pick-up truck on prom picnic.

I wonder if The Judge would have been so quick to pretend I didn't exist if he had known I'd be born with his charisma, his gregariousness, every bit of his bodacious-ness, his energy and his red hair. I could be a fly in the ointment of his ascending political career.

And there's his wife, my other grandmother. When you look at someone as beautiful as Margaret Mary O'Sullivan McCann you see a work of art, a Mona Lisa, and you expect every layer of her to be as beautiful as the layers that became DaVinci's finale. But the layers beneath Margaret Mary's beautiful face with its lilting Irish laugh are painted with dark swaths of xenophobia. My mother Connie would say "swaths of hatred" but that's such strong language to use on my grandmother. You would think Margaret Mary couldn't possibly hate people she doesn't even know, especially newborn babies like me, just because they weren't Irish. Huh, you would think.

There's something strangely disquieting about this exotic grandmother. I'm having trouble pinpointing what I sense. Obviously she's beautiful and obviously with a name like O'Sullivan she's Irish. Yet her skin tones are darker and richer than that of a fair-haired colleen and her hair is coal black. Widespread eyes accentuate the high structure of her cheekbones. Black, well-shaped brows come to a point over her pupils and make her seem inquisitive. These are the eyes that make men swoon. True, she could be what's called Black Irish, a descendent from the Spanish invasion of Ireland's southern coast but that's not the sense I get. Margaret Mary seems familiar. I've known her or the likes of her somewhere before and this feeling intrigues me as much as it bothers me.

The Judge fell hard for these Irish eyes in the 1940's, just like my mother Connie did for his son Kip in the 1960's. In The Judge's case, when Mortimer was in law school he caught a glimpse of Margaret Mary O'Sullivan on the Main Street trolley on her way to work. It was neither her red lipstick nor her stiletto heels that made his heart stop in mid-beat. He had fallen instantly and hopelessly in love with her eyes. They were black-irised and limpid and as deep as a Pierian spring. They captured The Judge and he had to possess them, and did, in 1944 when she became Margaret Mary O'Sullivan McCann.

A generation later the same thing happened to Connie. She was in biology class, of all places, when she became possessed by a pair of black-irised, limpid eyes belonging to a kid named John Patrick McCann, called Kip by everyone except Sister Mary Francis, the grammar school principal, who always used his given name and he always corrected her saying, "It's Kip, Sister, Kip." Margaret Mary had given her firstborn an ominous inheritance—striking, fathomless eyes—and Connie Thompson was about to leap with abandon into Kip McCann's Pierian spring.

Senior prom was approaching. Kip had finally gotten around to asking Connie Thompson to be his date. From that moment on Connie and her mother, my Oona, went into full prom preparedness. The Village Dress Shoppe for the gown, Baker's for the matching shoes, Penney's for nylons, and to complete the outfit, they borrowed cousin Ginny's crinoline and her bunny-fur wrap. Petite and bubbly, blonde and blithe, Connie looked beautiful. Grandpap did a double take when she descended the stairs. He couldn't believe this child, his baby, had somehow morphed into a princess.

Grandpap did another double take when Kip showed up at the front door with a cymbidium orchid in hand. Yesterday, it seemed to Will, when Connie's young man came by to discuss prom details, Kip was just another gawky kid at the back door asking for his daughter. Today, right now, Grandpap saw the most handsome eighteen-year-old ever to get into a tux. Warnings about wolves went off in his head.

"No later than one," he reminded Connie, "and don't you dare drink. Here's a dime," he whispered as she came close for a kiss, "phone me if Mr. Wonderful-In-A-Tux should try anything, you know what I mean."

"I know Daddy, don't worry, Daddy, it's just a dance. I'll be fine." The two sped off for The Judge's house so Mrs. McCann could take some Polaroids.

Kip's brother, Beaner, was waiting on the front stoop of their Cedar Street house for Kip and his girlfriend to pull up. Since Beaner had never seen his brother in anything but jeans and a black tee shirt he was surprised at what a tux could do for a kid. He was even more surprised when Kip opened the passenger door of the truck and a pouf of pink petticoat, pink lace and pink ribbon tumbled out containing a beautiful princess. Stunned, Beaner wondered what such a beautiful mortal was doing with his obnoxious big brother.

Kip and Connie got home, not at one, but at three a.m. "I'll pick you up at nine for the picnic in state park," he said as he squeezed in a last kiss before her front door closed completely. "Everybody's going," he added, "it'll be a blast." Kip McCann jumped the three steps from her porch to the sidewalk, went home and put an old mattress in the back of his truck.

Connie was up before seven rummaging through everything in her closet after only four hours of sleep. At last she found an outfit for the picnic: these pink plaid pedal pushers with that pink bolero blouse tied at the midriff, those new Grasshoppers, and the brand new, still-had-the-tags-on bikini, the one her mother reluctantly let her buy at Renninger's Department Store. "Honest, it's not too skimpy, Mama, everybody's wearing these now," she had pled.

Will was not liking this. "Don't worry, Daddy," Connie assured him as he looked over his newspaper at her bare midriff from the kitchen table. "Kip doesn't drink and he's a real good driver, besides there are ten couples going. We'll be home early, I promise. It's just a picnic."

The hot sun, the beer, the bikini, the exhausted, happy teenagers and the mattress in the back of the pick-up truck were about to tell a different story.

* * *

It's May 18, 1963. My images are beginning to fade. It must be time. I hate this part. Gestation. I want to see more future. I need to know what will become of me. I'm distraught. Oh, God.

GESTATION

It's dark in here. Gestation is not my favorite part of this whole born-again process. I can't tell whether it is day or night and half the time I don't know who's out there talking with my mother. Yet this stage of my sweet new beginning is, in hindsight, the best days of my life.

Although I no longer visualize the faces of the people with whom I'm sharing genes, I now can hear their conversations, after all I'm only a thin skin away. It's like eavesdropping. They can't see me so they think I can't hear them but I can. It doesn't make sense that a zygote can hear but I assure you, I'm extremely tuned into every detail of my becoming.

I'll probably forget everything I'm learning by eavesdropping after I'm delivered but right now I'm hearing an earful. I hear my father tell my mother that Beaner was waiting, watching out the bedroom window when my father pulled into the driveway at 3:30 a.m. the night of the prom. According to Kip, Beaner saw him put the mattress in the bed of his truck. Moreover, according to Kip, the next morning, right after Kip left to pick up Connie for the picnic, Beaner happened to share that bit of news with his father as they ate breakfast. The Judge went ballistic. Beaner didn't think his dad was going to get that spastic over a mattress and he worried all day for Kip, or rather worried that Kip might beat him up behind the garage when he found out he told.

To circumvent this bad scenario, Beaner spent all afternoon Saturday and into the night hanging around Farley's Delicatessen at the top of Cedar hoping to intercept Kip on his way home from the picnic to warn him that their dad was about to kill him. When Kip turned down Cedar at eight that night, there was Beaner jumping up and down, waving him to stop.

"He knows about the mattress," Beaner blurted into the truck window. "And he's waiting for you."

"I had to get rid of that thing before my dad checked my truck," Kip told Connie at school on Monday. "I threw it in the field behind Mooney's house. 'What mattress?' I told my dad when he quizzed me. 'I didn't have a mattress. Beaner's seeing things.' "

For some period of time after the prom picnic Connie and Kip are pretty much inseparable, at least I think it's Dad that Mom's with. He has a particular rush to his breathing that I can now recognize. They speak to each other in very quiet voices. I have to listen carefully to catch any of it.

They are in love, of course. I hear him say how he adores her blue eyes, her tiny waist, her contagious laugh. I hear the snap of a hair band and feel a gust of breath as he buries his nose in her hair and him saying how he loves to let her silky strands slip through his fingers. He plots to take her places where they can be together again. Private. She helps him think where.

It seemed that this idyllic life of love went on for a long time. They found a knoll they could hide behind in the back of Kent Park near Commercial Street and they'd spread a beach towel on the grass and lie there studying clouds, imagining shapes, among other wonderful things. They'd drive to the dunes at Juniper Lake with a six pack of Stroh's in her beach bag and lie in the sand and talk of a future. They'd hang out on the couch at Annie's house, Connie's best friend since kindergarten, when Annie's mother was working or volunteering at the church. Being an accomplice to their match making often made Annie upset. And for the first time in Connie's life, my mother was lying to Grandpap, saying she was going to Annie's to study for midterms.

Kip's lies, on the other hand, had been going on for so long nobody paid attention. "I'm going to Mooney's to help put shoes on the Fairlane," or "new brakes," or "a new distributor." Margaret Mary never caught on.

One day I awoke to violence. I was tossed from side to side, from up to down. I thought I was being evicted. I could hear my mother sobbing as I bounced around my little room. I thought she was dying. I thought I was dying with her. I had forgotten about this part of the process. She was retching. Retching and sobbing. She had just discovered the dark side of love.

My Oona wasn't one to talk to her daughters about sex and as a result had never warned Connie about how easy it is to make babies. Connie and Annie got all their sex information from Judy Janiga whose older sister had gotten pregnant and was sent away to a home for unwed mothers. She was gone for months and months. When she came back to the neighborhood she came with neither a baby nor a boyfriend. She went into the Janiga house and never seemed to come out again. Mr. and Mrs. Janiga stopped walking around the neighborhood after dinner like they used to and Judy said everybody in her house was always sad after that.

Connie knew from Judy's description that the home for unwed mothers was where young girls who got pregnant were sent until they had their babies. Since somebody always wanted to adopt a newborn it was hoped all these new babies would find a home. To save face, families would sometimes make up outlandish stories about their pregnant daughters like "she's gone to help my sister in Paducah" or "she's taking a semester in Europe." That idea was ridiculous since no middle class families in those days had enough money to send a daughter to Europe for seven months. She thought Oona would be sending her to that home for sure, but she didn't.

The day of the first retching Connie ran over to Annie's. "Oh my God, Annie, I threw up my breakfast. I think I'm pregnant."

"You're not pregnant," Annie said, "how could you be? You have to have sex to get pregnant." Then Annie became unusually quiet. "Jesus, Mary and Joseph," she said as the obvious began to register, "you had sex with Kip."

"I'm in love. I'm totally in love," Connie sobbed.

"Have you told him you're pregnant?" Annie asked. "He seems to love you a lot. He's all over you all the time."

"No," Connie sniffled.

"Well, then, tell him he's about to become a father and you two should get married. A lot of people get married at our age."

"Not a lot of people get married at seventeen, Annie," Connie reminded, "only the girls who get pregnant."

"Not only the girls who get pregnant," Annie tried to reassure. "What about the girls who marry the guys going to Vietnam? A lot of them are seventeen."

"You're not helping at all," said Connie, "I'm seventeen and want to be a senior in the fall. Kip is eighteen and wants to be a freshman in college in the fall. I'll bet you anything, Kip won't marry me."

"Never say never," Annie tried to help. "The two of you might be so right for each other that neither rain nor sleet nor hail can keep you apart."

"Yeah, right," Connie mumbled. "I gotta go home."

Connie took the long way home from Annie's that day. We walked and walked. I liked the rhythm of it. While we walked my mother talked to herself and I can hear. She wondered whether she should tell Kip first, or my grandmother or Grandpap. She wondered if she'll be sent to the home for unwed mothers and if she'd be able to tolerate it. She wondered what will become of me if she goes there. She wondered whether Kip will marry her and doubted it based on what happened to Judy Janiga's sister. She wondered if she didn't eat anything much whether she could hide the inevitable bump. Finally her head throbbed from all this wondering and we went home.

The Thompson house was unusually quiet when we entered the front hall. My grandparents were out back talking over the fence with the neighbors and my mother's three sisters were out somewhere. Connie looked long and hard at the phone on the table at the foot of the stairs then apprehensively picked up the receiver. Shaking, her index finger could barely turn the numbers. She began to dial. TR6057.

The phone rang in a house on the preferable side of the B&O tracks, tracks that separated the Irish side of Turner Mills from the other side. It interrupted the excitement happening at the McCann home. The Democratic Party had just selected the charismatic Mortimer McCann as its candidate. A photographer had just arrived, sent by the party chairman, to take a dynamic photo of this handsome Irish candidate with his glamorous wife, three stunning sons, ages eighteen, sixteen and ten and a most beautiful little girl of six.

He had just arranged the group in the shape of an obtuse triangle with Mr. McCann in the most prominent position and the others flanking him in their order of importance. Kip was told to sit on the arm of the couch as the oldest son might, the younger boys between their mother and father and little Charlotte on her father's lap. When the phone rang Kip abandoned his post to answer it.

"Kip," my mother whispered into the mouthpiece. "Kip, you need to come over. Right now. I need to talk with you."

"I can't come over now," the voice at the other end responded. "My dad's got a photographer here setting up a family portrait for Dad's election propaganda, I mean campaign. I gotta stay home."

"It's not about your father's campaign anymore, Kip," she blurted out, "I'm pregnant."

"Yeah, Dad. I'm coming," she heard him talking over her to someone in the room. "Give me a minute." Click.

The phone went dead. I don't know who hung up on whom but I'm pretty sure this wasn't going well. I put what will become my ear closer to mother's naval, just in case I could catch more information but none came. We were both deadly quiet. Then it got choppy in here. My mother was sobbing.

In the McCann household just minutes before the phone rang, the photographer was clucking to himself over this easy assignment. Every person in his portrait would be gorgeous. How often does that happen? He might even claim this portrait as one that might get him much better assignments. He was particularly taken with Mrs. McCann's eyes and those of her oldest son. The photographer could tell how the two faces with those almost black, light-grabbing eyes would play dramatically against the four fair haired, blue-eyed Irish faces and anchor the portrait, giving it lots of dimension. Without a doubt this would be the best family portrait he had ever taken. "If I can get the kid and his mom into my studio for a real portrait," the photographer fantasized, "I might win myself a serious prize."

Kip hung up the receiver and returned to his perch on the couch. Nobody noticed anything different except the photographer. A minute ago the oldest boy's eyes looked liquid and deep, effervescent just like his mother's. Now they looked...what? Vapid? Flat? Cold? He couldn't be quite sure. High hopes for better assignments hinged on this kid and his mother. All of a sudden there was nothing to photograph, just another Kodak moment of a smiling family good enough for a political brochure.

The flash went off a couple of times with minor adjustments between shots and the photographer called it a wrap, thanked the family for its cooperation, looked once more at the oldest son, wondered what happened, bet it was about that phone call, shrugged and left.

Kip was out the door right behind him. Within minutes he was on Garfield

Street at Connie's side door. "Where can we talk?" he whispered as she stepped out onto the asphalt driveway. She pointed toward the back of the house, then around the side near the lilac bush. He took her by the elbow and hurried her along.

Unlike their other hideaway meetings, urgent for bitten lip and tangled tongue, coddled breast and short, hot breaths, this meeting gave Connie a sneaky feeling crawling up her back, more like that of being called into the principal's office for something not her fault. A red flag went up as her soft blue eyes began to fill.

"I'm pregnant," she said for the second time today, finally owning its reality.

"Are you sure..." Kip cut in.

Connie was about to say she was sure, that she had been vomiting mornings, that she was afraid to tell her mother, and that, yes, she would marry him but before she could finish her thought, Kip finished his sentence.

"...that it's mine?"

The water that had filled her orbs and made her eyes seem even bigger and bluer than they were, now flooded over their banks and raged down her cheeks. "Why you little shit," my mother cried pounding my father's chest with her fists, "just whose kid do you think it is?"

Kip's back slid down the side of the house into a slump on the ground. "This can't be happening to me. This isn't happening to me. We can't let it happen."

"Are you fucking out of your mind," my mother retorted. "It's not happening to you. It's happening to us. You can't pretend there's no baby in here because there is. *Daddy!*"

Just then the word abortion slipped out of Kip's mouth.

"Are you talking coat hangers?" Connie gasped. "You want somebody to use a coat hanger on me?"

That got my attention. This guy, this father of mine, wanted to have me killed. I had to do something. I wanted to scream or to kick my mother so she could kick my father but I was too new for a fight, instead I gave my mother all I had—a bad case of indigestion and that got her attention. She refueled and her vitriol continued.

"I didn't mean coat hangers," Kip was now fumbling over his words. "Aren't there certain herbs or medicines you can take or phone numbers you could call to find doctors who'd do it?" It disgusted him even as the words spilled out.

"They're called poisons, asshole, and abortionists. I should take poisons so you can go back to your little life and pretend we never had a child together. You're not going to get away with murder you son of a bitch. Not while I'm still alive." Mother was really worked up. I remember hoping I'd inherit that don't-push-on-me gene, I was very sure I was going to need it.

"I didn't mean you should take anything that could poison you, God no, I'm just thinking of...of... us, you and me, our future."

The word 'future' caught in his throat. He had never thought of Connie as his future, she was his love toy, his baby doll, his free ticket to nirvana. But his future? He wanted to become a biologist, four years of college, two years of post-graduate, maybe even a PhD, that was his future, not Connie, and especially not her kid, well, his kid, too.

"Okay. Okay." Kip said at last. "We need time to think about this. Have you told anyone else?"

"Nobody," said Connie, "just Annie and she won't tell a soul."

"Are you sure?" Kip asked.

"Positive," Connie said with conviction. But Annie had already told her mother.

Mrs. Crantz didn't know what to do with the information Annie had just given her. Connie was as much a part of the Crantz home as Annie was of the Thompsons. The girls had been inseparable since they were in Mrs. Plumlee's kindergarten class. They lived seven houses apart and when the girls were five their mothers decided they could run between their homes unchaperoned. In that sense Connie was her baby, too. And now this dilemma. What should she do with this information. Tell Oona? Tell Will? Confront Connie? Get involved at all?

She kept going over the options as she peeled supper's potatoes. When she caught herself not paying attention to the peeling she discovered she had whittled the potatoes down to nothing and had to retrieve more from the pantry. She prayed for guidance.

Guidance came to her like a bolt from heaven. She had worked herself into such a knot that she was convinced The Judge and the Mrs. from the other side of the tracks were not going to have their precious son become a father at eighteen. She was sure they would know who to call to perform the abortion. "Abortion! O my God!" she exclaimed wiping her forehead in her apron, "they'll make Connie get an abortion. They're the most influential people in this town, they'll know exactly who to call." She stopped peeling and sat down. She had to think about this. She had to find a way to stop the abortion. Mrs. Crantz always found solutions to problems in her Catholic faith and she was determined to find one now.

When she wasn't working as a clerk in City Hall she spent her hours volunteering for the Altar and Rosary Society at the Cathedral. Although really a parishioner of St. Basil's in her own neighborhood, she loved the transcendent feeling that overcame her in this celestial cathedral with its Spanish marble floors and Pepini's life-size sculptures of the Stations of the Cross, fourteen tableaus in all. She liked it best when she was completely alone in the church arranging the flowers or preparing the altar linens. She made it a point to schedule her volunteerism when she knew the other ladies would be busy in the rectory.

It's times like this when there was no one else in the church and no sounds to hear but celestial silence under the mighty dome of this holy edifice, and her own breathing, that Mrs. Crantz felt closest to God. She'd look up into the artwork of the dome and find herself in the company of twelve apostles and three archangels. Then as her eyes and spirit transcended to even greater heights she'd find herself in the company of Mary during an artful Assumption Into Heaven and then...euphoria. Jesus in red robes emblazoned with streaming rays of gold emanating from behind his robes spoke to her in no uncertain terms telling her that she is such a good and faithful servant. Finally at the tippy top of the dome, the White Dove of Peace completed the seraphic scene showering those who chose to believe...with resolve.

Resolve. Mrs. Crantz finally knew what to do. Swiftly she headed for the telephone table in the front hall and picked up the receiver. "Monsignor," she said into it, "this is Rita Crantz."

THE ANATOMY OF A SECRET

Kip was completely distraught. He didn't mean to use the word abortion. He wondered how he even managed to think such a thing. He had never killed anything in his life. One Thanksgiving weekend when he was fourteen his father took him deer hunting at his uncle's farm in Tremble. "I was handed a rifle," he related to Connie, "and was told to follow my dad and uncle into the woods 'stealthily,' they said. It wasn't long before a four-point buck crossed our path, Uncle Bill motioned to dad 'this one is mine' as he raised his gun to his shoulder and took careful aim. I knew this incredibly handsome animal would be dead in a second so I shouted out 'I see him, I see him!' The buck bolted into the foliage. My uncle and my father looked at each other and said 'never again.' They traipsed me back to the farmhouse and told the women-folk to 'keep the kid' with them.

"Then there was the time Shadow got sick. I took him myself to Doc Perry," he continued unable to stop. "Doc said there was nothing to do, that Shadow's time had come and did I want him to put Shadow out of his pain. I said no, I'll nurse him, I'll feed him with an eye dropper if I have to, I'll do anything for Shadow and I won't let him die. Doc Perry just shook his head and said, 'Trust me, son, you don't want your dog to suffer.' I took Shadow home and laid on the floor next to him all weekend long. I bawled my eyes out most of the time and Shadow died in my arms." Connie was sniffling while my dad told his stories. I could feel her melting into his words.

"I don't know why I said you should abort your baby," then realizing his

Mooney needed a smoke. He waited until the truck went around the bend then hightailed it to the playground at the top of Cedar, the neighborhood hangout where he got on a swing and lit up a Marlboro.

"Hey man," a kid named Jonesie said as he approached the swings. "What's with you? You don't usually light up where the moms can see you."

"McCann just laid one on me," Mooney replied. "He got a girl pregnant. Connie Thompson, that really cute girl from the Other End...pregnant. I needed a smoke."

Ever since the archbishop had appointed him pastor of this grand cathedral, following the death of Father Burns who was loved by all and affectionately called the Padre of the Populi, Monsignor Wolfe celebrated daily morning Mass at 8:15 on the cathedral's main altar. When he was assigned this position as a young priest, twenty-some years ago, he was filled with unabashed pride telling his proud mother that her little boy, Gerald Wolfe, was the anointed one chosen to follow in the footsteps of the late great Burns. But in less than a year into the job he realized this wasn't his kind of place.

Although his was the biggest parish and the grandest church in the six county diocese with well over 250 families, these people, his parishioners, were (and he didn't mean to be snooty about it), working class. They were noisy and boisterous and most of them shanty Irish. They lived in warrens of little streets radiating from the cathedral and all named after saints or trees.

He began reflecting on his own upbringing, his idyllic days before seminary, riding ponies and playing polo on his family's estate in East Pleasantville. He better understood folks who had horse barns, who joined country clubs and whose daughters were debutantes. He didn't understand his flock, people who lived in houses with flats, one on top of each other. People who shared their tools, their lawn mowers, their sugar and spices and passed hand-me-down clothes from family to family. They were a generous people to each other and certainly to their church.

Every weekday morning after Mass when he was sure the ladies of the Altar and Rosary Society had snuffed out the altar candles, Monsignor would hang his alb and chasuble in the sacristy and slip a long, black cassock over his head and down his slender six-foot four frame for his morning walk. He'd reach for the biretta, his monsignor beanie, the one with the little red tuft on the top that indicated in priest jargon he was no ordinary monsignor, he was a

Right Reverend Monsignor. He'd work the beanie until he got the tilt just right then check the mirror for any hair that might have gone amiss. Satisfied, he'd swish across the marble floor toward the back of the church with his cassock swaying right and then left. With every footfall a peek of wingtip shoe would poke out from under the cassock as if to see he was still on course.

On this particular morning Monsignor had a funeral so he had missed his usual walk which meant his back would act up and would bother him for the rest of the day. It was nearly lunch time, no time for the walk. He retreated to his private chapel in the rectory and prayed for the humility required of him to relate to his blue-collared flock. This morning, after weeks and weeks of praying, he had come to an important decision. He had decided to do something he had never done before—make a real difference.

"I've been pastor here for twenty years and all I've managed to do is keep this place running," he told himself. He was convinced the Blessed Virgin Mary who smiled at him from a painting in the small alcove of his private chapel was asking him to take a stand for something.

"Now that John F Kennedy is president," the monsignor explained to the painting, "time is ripe for Catholics. We can and must elect Catholic mayors, Catholic governors, Catholic judges, maybe we can even get Catholics on the Supreme Court," he explained to her, "and that just doesn't happen in a vacuum. We have to make it happen and that's exactly what I intend to do. On Sunday," he added flushed with passion, "I'm going to ask my congregation, at all five Masses, to put our very own Mortimer McCann on the Family Court bench. Go to the polls and vote for McCann!"

He got up from his velvet-pillowed kneeler empowered, prepared to blur the line between church and state when the phone rang.

"Monsignor, this is Rita Crantz."

The last thing Msgr. Wolfe wanted to hear was another whine from the ladies of the Altar and Rosary Society. He put up with the The Ladies only because his pastoral predecessor, the beloved Burns, wanted to find a role for women in the church. Asking them to launder altar linens and arrange flowers for Sunday Masses seemed to satisfy the ladies and now Msgr. Wolfe had inherited them.

He had other things in mind when Rita Crantz's call came into the rectory and he was quite impatient to dismiss her.

"Monsignor," she was saying, "I'm very worried about a pregnant seventeen-year-old in my neighborhood."

"Mrs. Crantz," he reminded her, "you need to talk with Father Guzzo, your pastor. He's the best one to advise you through this most troubling situation."

"I will," said Rita Crantz, "but I thought I should mention it to you first, Monsignor. You see, the father of this baby is Kip McCann and he's planning an abortion."

"Kip McCann? Mortimer's son?"

"Yes, Monsignor, Mortimer's son."

Msgr. Wolfe didn't say *Holy Mother of God* into the receiver but he certainly thought it. "Abortion you say, Mrs. Crantz? I'll see what I can do, Mrs. Crantz. Don't bother Father Guzzo with this just yet, I'll have a talk with the McCanns, Kip...and Mortimer."

"Oh thank you Monsignor. I really didn't know who I should tell or how I should proceed. You've relieved my mind. I'll trust your judgment, Monsignor. Thank you oh so much."

Click. Problem solved.

"Why me, Lord?" Wolfe groaned, sounding more like Peter on the way back from Gethsemane than a right reverend monsignor. He needed that walk.

THE LIFE OF A RUMOR

Msgr. Wolfe strode up Park along the cemetery fence to the main gate like a man on a mission. At the gate he turned on his heel and strode back to the rectory. From rectory to main gate and main gate to rectory, Monsignor was not walking, he was pacing.

"I'll have a talk with Mortimer," he had promised Mrs. Crantz on the phone and so, on his third pass as he neared the midpoint between the cemetery gate and the rectory, he crossed the street and turned down Cedar where the McCanns lived.

He had never been on Cedar before and was amazed as he looked around. The houses seemed so tiny and packed together. These were his parishioners' homes, the Boyles, the Flynns, the Healys and Whalens. He knew that almost every house on this block had at least five children and he had baptized all of them and then a few years later had put the host on their tongues in First Holy Communion. He came to house number 47, the McCann house. Mortimer's car was in the drive.

Since no one ever comes to front doors in this neighborhood Mortimer thought it must be the Fuller Brush man. He was about to call for Margaret Mary but caught a glimpse of something too tall and too black through the window, not the Fuller Brush man who was short and dumpy.

"Monsignor!" McCann bellowed opening the door as wide as it would go with all the winter coats still on the hooks in the small vestibule, "what a surprise, what an honor. Come in, come in."

Msgr. Wolfe stepped in and quickly swept the room with a glance. "Can we go into your office?" he asked presumptuously, "I have something to discuss with you."

"My office," McCann roared, "you mean somewhere private...that would be the back stoop, Monsignor, follow me. Want a tuna sandwich?" he asked as they cut through the small kitchen on the way to the back porch, a landing essentially.

"No, no, I'm good. There's something I've been meaning to talk with you about."

McCann was thrilled. A few weeks ago Monsignor had hinted at some kind of support for McCann's upcoming election and now he assumed the monsignor could only mean one thing, Wolfe was about to throw his weight behind this parishioner, and perhaps, dare he dream, even petition the congregation from the pulpit to elect McCann judge, telling parishioners he's "one of our own."

The truth is, the monsignor *had* intended to throw his weight behind McCann. He had decided to be brazen from the pulpit and blur the lines between church and state. He was going to brave the backlash from the bishop. He had prayed about it every day for the past three weeks on the padded kneeler in front of Our Lady Queen of Heaven. He had decided that the time was ripe, now that John Fitzgerald Kennedy, a Catholic, was president. Even Gambino, the Mayor of Turner Mills, was Catholic albeit an Italian Catholic. The timing is now, the monsignor was certain, for the spread of Catholicism throughout the country, and the timing is now for God's chosen Catholics, the Irish, to lead the way.

Wolfe felt too tall on the back stoop so he chose to sit down on the landing. Even perched he looked awkward, his knees making a tent of his cassock, his long arms fumbling for a place to roost and his hands smoothing out imaginary wrinkles until they found their way into their comfort zone —a prayerful position. McCann on the other hand looked completely at ease draping his body along the stoop rail, one foot on the driveway and the other planted on the second step is if he'd stood there a thousand times with a beer in his hand.

"I'm curious, Monsignor, you don't usually make side trips on your daily walks. What brings you down Cedar?"

"Two things, actually," the monsignor replied, deciding to get right to the point. I need to talk with you about the upcoming election and about the abortion."

Mortimer didn't catch the monsignor's exact words. He heard 'upcoming election' and 'abortion' assuming monsignor meant the abortion *issue* not a specific abortion. Wanting to assure his pastor that he was in complete agreement with the Catholic position on this hot topic, he launched into his well thought out and practiced response on the matter. After all, he was as "devout as yourself" he told the monsignor and would, as a Catholic judge, always, without fail and without compromise, preserve the life of the unborn.

Mortimer thought he had made it extremely clear that under no circumstances would he, Mortimer McCann, violate the church's position on abortion in his work as a judge. In fact, wasn't the abortion issue the main reason, perhaps the only reason, why people like Rt. Rev. Msgr. Gerald Wolfe were willing to do whatever it took to get Catholics, better yet, Irish Catholics, in positions of power? To uphold the sanctity of life, isn't that what this is all about? What he couldn't understand was Monsignor's nonplussed reaction to his argument for the preservation of life.

"I'm listening to you, Mortimer," the monsignor said at last, "and I admire how convincing you're able to sound. But I didn't come here to discuss how I might help you get elected, I came to figure out *if* I'm going to help. Why I really came down Cedar was to see if there's still time."

"Time? Monsignor, time for what? What are you talking about?"

"The abortion. Time to stop the abortion. I hope I'm not too late."

Mortimer McCann's arm was no longer casually draped over the railing and both feet were now solidly on the drive. This conversation was becoming personal and sinister. He wanted to say *what the hell are you talking about* but managed to keep his words under control despite the blush of anger that was creeping up and out his collar. What he did manage to say was, "What abortion, Monsignor? Margaret's not pregnant and even if she was, one more child in this family would be a blessing."

"It's Kip. Your Kip. He's gotten a little seventeen-year-old from school pregnant," Wolfe blurted out. He, too, was now standing, looming large and looking like a punishing God. "That's not the worst of it," he continued. "They're about to abort the baby. I know this for a fact."

"Christ Almighty this is the first I've heard of it," Mortimer said in a slow exhale. The two men stood looking at each other for an eternity neither knowing what to do or to say. The potential judge, now cemented to the driveway with leaden feet, looked up at the imposing priest not knowing whether to feel accused, accursed or sucker punched. Monsignor Wolfe, now controlling the top of the stoop like Poe's raven, looked down on the politician debating whether or not to use the keys to the kingdom for this obviously flawed family.

Mortimer said he'd look into it; the Monsignor said he'd await the findings and the conversation ended politely. Monsignor said he had an appointment shortly and needed to hurry back to the rectory. He left Mortimer at the back stoop watching the back of the black cassock swish this way, then that, down the driveway, wondering if this meant there'd be no recommendation from the pulpit. The monsignor already knew.

Mortimer didn't go right back to his office that afternoon as he had intended. Instead he sat home in a state of confusion. He didn't know whether to strangle his firstborn or question his own fathering skills. He was furious that his son was trying to sneak an abortion past him. Thoughts of the grandchild never entered his mind but thoughts of elections did. Should he tell the party chairman what he had just learned or tell Margaret Mary the baby news?

Margaret Mary had already noticed an atmospheric charge permeating the house and asked on several passes through the living room where Mort sat staring at the brief on his lap, if everything was all right. Finally she asked who was at the door.

"Your Fuller Brush man," he replied without looking up. "I said we didn't need anything."

Mortimer was madly in love with Margaret Mary. She was still exotic at fifty one. Her laughter still warmed him like a good drambuie. It wasn't until after their second child was born, a colicky baby, that he realized her fragility. She'd get upset over seemingly nothing and he would spend hours cooing with her and calming her down. When their third child was born, eighteen months later, it got even worse. She wouldn't get up mornings to prepare the older children for their school day, so he did it. She couldn't pack lunches or go to the parent teacher conferences, so he did it. She couldn't shop for cocktail dresses to wear to the posh parties and fundraisers related to campaigning, so he brought home little black dresses that made her look Hepburn-esque. He knew her frailties as well as he knew her dress size and took care to protect her. Now this. Their firstborn, her favorite, impregnating a seventeen-year-old three months before the election. He needed to tell her the baby news.

"Margy love, sit here for a minute. I need to tell you something important," he called from the couch. Sensitive to the change in his voice she hurried into the room and sat straight up on the edge of the couch.

"Margy love," he repeated, "I have great news. We're going to be grandparents. You're going to be a grandmother."

The news was slow in making its impact. Margaret Mary wasn't sure that what she had heard was good news but Mortimer seemed to think so and she depended on his vibes for her vibes. A grandmother? Who was he talking about, certainly not one of their children, they were still babies.

"John Patrick," he said using her preference instead of the nickname he had dubbed on his firstborn. "Kip and Connie Thompson are going to have a baby. We're going to be grandparents..." then after a pregnant pause, added "or not."

"Or not!" she cried, confused, "what are you saying?"

Margaret Mary's eyes grew round and large and filled to the brim with water that finally popped out onto her high cheekbones. None of this sounded like good news to her.

"Did the Fuller Brush man bring you this news," she asked sarcastically. "Who was really at the door?"

"Monsignor Wolfe. And he said the kids are wanting to get an abortion."

"Did he hear this news in the confessional?" she wanted to know, "so that it's private and confidential, between him and Kip and now us, of course."

"No," he answered somberly, "he heard it from one of the ladies of the Altar and Rosary Society." Mortimer knew if he said anything else, even if he exhaled wrong, she would get hysterical. He didn't have time for this right now. He needed to think, he needed to find Kip, he needed to get out of here. "I've got a client at two," he said as he packed up the brief and left.

Kip was easy to find. The back door opened and in he walked. "Hi Mom," he said brushing through the kitchen like he had something important to do upstairs. Margaret Mary lit up a Parliament, her second one since the news.

"Not so fast young man," she said exhaling smoke quickly so she'd have enough breath to catch him as he tried to escape the kitchen. He knew this was going to be his moment of truth.

"What's this about an abortion?" she demanded.

He had two ways to go with this question. One, deny it completely because it was the truth, there would be no abortion, or two, return to the kitchen, sit down with his mother and spill his guts, his puking-ly, scared guts because he didn't have a clue what he should do next *except* not let Connie have an abortion. She wouldn't anyhow.

He returned to the kitchen and put his head down on the porcelain tabletop. "I don't know what to do, Mom," he muttered miserably. "I honestly don't know what to do."

"Well," she said kindly, "is it your baby?"

"Yes, I think."

"That's not good enough," she exclaimed getting herself worked up. "Never mind," she added trying to get her voice under control. "The point is a child will be coming into this world, our world, within a year, and it could be yours or it couldn't. Do you know what a child does to your life?" she continued now zeroing in on what her own children have done to hers. "They take away your freedom, they confuse you, they rob you of your future, they become your future and they don't do it well. They make you crazy."

"You're not crazy, Mom," he offered, more hopeful than convinced.

"No, I'm not," she assured him, "but do you think I wanted four kids?" she continued talking more to herself than to her son. "I only wanted you. You would have been enough. You are all I ever wanted. So if this is not your baby, get the hell out of her life. She'll do okay, poor people seem to have a knack for doing okay."

"Mom, she's not poor. The Thompsons are like us. They just live on the other side of the tracks. She's really nice, Mom, and so is her whole family. Honest, they're just like us. You might even like Connie, she's fun and curious and smart."

"Don't push your luck," his mother continued. "How can you expect me to like the girl who has just ruined my firstborn's future. We'll figure this out as a family. Dad will know what to do. Dad always knows what to do."

Kip was sure Dad would know exactly what to do, which meant cover this mess up. Elections are in twelve weeks and more than anything, Kip knew his dad wanted to be a judge.

Margaret Mary suggested a few more ways to deal with 'the situation.' The McCanns could pay for Connie's time at a home for unwed mothers although it would be a strain on the family's finances or Mortimer could find a nice family to adopt Connie's baby privately, or Kip could claim on a stack of bibles the baby is not his. Margaret Mary ran out of ideas.

Kip dragged his weary body off the chair and sullenly headed up the stairs to his room.

DECISION TO MARRY

Mortimer *did* know exactly what to do. He had thought about it all afternoon as he rocked back and forth on the swivel chair in his law office staring at the Planned Parenthood billboard that just got pasted up outside his office window. Finally a solution to the problem emerged. The kids should get married. Getting married would right the wrong and turn the prospect of death by abortion into the warmth of a babe in the cradle. His constituents might actually love that the family did the right thing.

The marriage could take place over Thanksgiving; his colleague, Judge Daly, would certainly agree to do the honors. Only immediate family would be invited to Daly's chambers for the ceremony, and he did mean immediate, it wouldn't even include his mother. He had to think this through. Continuing to stare at the Planned Parenthood billboard, Mortimer projected a best case scenario and unleashed this imagination: *Kip marries Connie, US drafts all eighteen-year-olds, son is sent to Vietnam, is gone two years, comes home, finds his wife has been unfaithful, son is traumatized from war, disgusted with wife, wants a divorce, I can help with divorce and son goes on with normal life.* He put his face in his hands so that the new family portrait, now framed and sitting on his desk, couldn't see him cry.

During supper that same evening Margaret Mary suggested to Mortimer that they take an after dinner walk around the block. Kip, Beaner and the other two kids looked up from their Banquet chicken pot pies as unbelievingly as if their parents had said the family was moving to Iceland. The

McCanns never walk around the block together. Margaret Mary usually has her smoke after dinner while Mortimer takes his own brisk walk to the cemetery and back. The two of them on a stroll? *Highly unlikely* the kids simultaneously thought darting glances to each other; only Kip could guess what this walk was all about. Him.

From Mortimer's perspective, the walk was productive. He told Margaret Mary of his plan to get the kids married off, perhaps as early as Thanksgiving when Kip would be home from college.

"What do you mean *home* from college?" she challenged. "He'll be *home* from college every night. He's going to the local university, remember?"

"I've given this a lot of thought," he said taking her hand as they walked. "Kip needs to be away from the scandal he has caused. I'm sure you'll agree the best thing for Kip, for us, for our family is that we do the right thing. And I think the right thing is to welcome this child, our grandchild, with open arms and loving hearts. Let's overlook what the neighbors will say behind our backs and delight in what God has in store for us. This baby forgives us the mistakes we've made as parents and gives us another chance to get it right. It's a blessing in disguise. You just wait," he added with the bravado of a trial lawyer, "it'll be the best thing that has ever happened to us."

Margaret Mary knew her Mortimer, knew that he had a plan up his sleeve.

"So what's the plan?"

"They'll get married in November," he said with conviction, "the child will be born legitimate even if it isn't his." He didn't add what else he was thinking which, if he had continued, would have been "and they'll get divorced the day after this baby is born."

Two days before Kip was to start college locally his father had 'big' news. Mortimer was able to pull some strings, "a lot of strings," he actually said, and managed to get Kip a seat in the freshman class at Sherburne College, 150 miles away and definitely not to Kip's liking.

"Because," the omniscient father quickly added before his stunned audience could object, "you don't want to stay around for the city-wide embarrassment, you know, your scandal."

Kip's shiny dark irises and pupils squeezed into slits of anger as they tried to figure out what the hell his father was doing with his life. There was no use arguing. His dad often made split-second decisions, a quality Kip usually admired in his father, but this was not one of his better ones. How had his life gotten this far out of his control, he wondered. Would it ever become his own again as it was before prom weekend? He seriously didn't think it could. Still staring into his father's steely, blue-eyed look of determination Kip came to an epiphany: his father, the man he had spent eighteen years adoring, was wrong, dead wrong, and the stare that began as son to father turned, in an instant, into man to man. Kip decided he would create his own fate and make his own decisions and he had just made one—he would marry Connie.

I was napping when Kip rang the bell at Mom's house. I vaguely heard it and normally such a routine noise wouldn't have awakened me but the swoosh of Mom's blood suddenly rushing through our bodies got my attention. I knew it had to be Dad at the door. He hadn't been here in a while. Mom and I had our ups and downs because of it but we finally got over it. I kept sending out vibes telling her, *Mom, you are Mohawk, you are the earth, you are strong, you are woman and you need to get me out of here healthy. I'll surprise and delight you with the woman I am becoming. Don't worry about us. With or without him we're fine, we're better than fine. We have all we need—life!*

I keep reminding myself that Mom's only seventeen and this is her first time around. I've done this before and this isn't the worst thing that can happen.

Mom's parents have had a few weeks to assimilate the news about me. There had been an interminable silence in the room when she finally told Oona and Grandpap. Her body tensed into what seemed like a contraction squeezing me into a painful wad as she braced for their anger at her sinning, her stupidity, her embarrassment to them, but none came. Oona was first to end the silence and I wish I had been visible, I would have hugged her so tight.

"Well, now," Oona said with all the tranquility of a clan mother, "I think we still have Janet's crib in the attic."

Yes! my spirit shouted. *Oona, you are the greatest! You are all we will ever need.* I meant it.

"I'll go up and look," Grandpap said next. My grandfather was okay with whatever calls Oona wanted to make about their daughters, this one included, because Oona infused our household with a calmness that wafted into every nook and cranny and Grandpap loved the serenity. With four girls, three of them teenagers, now one of them pregnant, in a four bedroom workman's cottage with one bathroom, life should have been chaotic but our home hummed with love. My grandparent's reaction to the stunning news Mom had just hit them with makes us do a double take. I'm now feeling lucky. This is a good place for me to be born.

Yep, it's Dad at the door. I can hear him saying, "Hi, Mr. Thompson, can I talk with Connie?"

"Does he know about us?" Dad whispers to Mom as she steps out on the porch and heads for the glider.

"He knows," she replied.

"And he let me in?" he asked surprised.

"They didn't talk about sending me away either," she responded.

"Then you did better than I did."

"Why, what happened when your parents found out?"

"I'm an embarrassment and a disappointment," he answered. "They want to send me out of town to school, away from where I can't do any collateral damage to my father's campaign. Away from you and junior there," he added poking Mom's belly.

I'll junior you! I wanted to blast. *You are going to be so amazed at this daughter of yours! I am going to be so like you, you won't be able to stand it. Wait and see.* I amused myself with my strong sense about whom I was becoming.

The glider stopped swinging and the porch got quiet. My father began talking, tentatively at first, and then his voice strengthened as he grew in his conviction. "I loved you in May when you made me a man," he was telling her. "I wanted to be with your forever. Then I became scared of you in July because you gave me reality, responsibility. So I ran. I blamed you for robbing me of what was left of my childhood and left me with facing myself. I would have kept on running and hiding from you if my dad hadn't made me feel like I did this thing to him. My dad is my hero. I love him like crazy, how could he turn on me...just like that," he said snapping his fingers. "In a heartbeat I became an impediment to his dream. He doesn't care about me, Connie, or about us, he only cares about Mortimer J McCann, the next judge. I'm having a child, he's having his dream and I'm the spoiler."

"You're angry," my mom said.

"Damn right I'm angry," Dad hissed.

"Your anger doesn't solve anything," she added.

"Oh yes it does," he went on. "It makes me realize what I should do about this life of mine that I'm carrying around like a monkey on my back and this life of mine that you're carrying."

"What are you talking about," she said. "I'm losing you."

"No," he said. "You're not losing me. You're getting me. I want to marry you, Connie. I want to make this right...for you, for me and for junior."

Stop calling me junior!

They decided between themselves that they would marry in November when my dad came home from Sherburne for Thanksgiving. He was sure he'd catch hell from his parents when he dropped this new bomb on them. He didn't care how they felt about it, he was taking charge of his life and it felt real and right. Connie would stay in high school until the baby was born and after the baby came they'd ask Oona to babysit so Mom could finish her senior year. She'd live at home. Kip would stay at Sherburne and he'd get a job as well. He said he needed a degree to become a responsible parent and maybe he should major in education since marine biology didn't look like it would work out in this latest plan for his life. They'd decide on the rest of the details by phone or "maybe," Kip suggested, "you could come down to Sherburne over Columbus break for the long weekend. We could make more plans then."

After their talk on the glider my mother got her groove back. I knew she was hopelessly in love with the guy. I still had my doubts about him. He kissed us and held us for the longest time before he had to get home and throw a few things together for Sherburne. He said he had no idea how to go away to college, didn't even know what to pack and wasn't looking forward to any of it. Mom said, "Consider yourself lucky. Nobody in your school is going to point at you and say 'Wow, there's a guy who's scared to go away to college' but everyone in my school's going to point at me as I become a teenage mutant elephant. I'd rather be you."

My dad said, "I know, I know," and they kissed and talked on and off like that for a long time. I got bored and fell asleep until the last smooch which was so full of suction and playfulness that it woke me up. Mom's saying she loves him, he's saying he loves her, he's promising to call from Sherburne and I'm waiting for the glider to stop jiggling.

"Aren't you forgetting something?" Mom called after him as he jumped off the porch. He patted his thighs to see if he had the truck keys in his pocket.

"Isn't there something you meant to ask me?" she prodded. He had forgotten to ask her to marry him. Officially.

He spun and leapt up the three steps to the porch as if they were one, tripping to his knees in front of the glider. He rearranged himself on one knee, proper like, asked for her hand and with all the decorum of a seasoned romantic said, "Miss Thompson, would you make me the happiest man on earth? Will you marry me?"

Not a bad recovery, I mused as I listened to all the commotion created by leaping and landing and tripping. He must have looked comical.

"Yes," she said, "I will."

Mom waited until she could see the taillights of his truck blending in with the rest of the traffic before bounding into the house with our news.

"Well?" Oona asked, already guessing what had just transpired on the porch by the look on her daughter's face.

"Where's Dad? I want to tell you both at once."

Janet was already eavesdropping from the top of the stairs. "Get down here, nosy, and I'll tell you, too," Connie called toward the stairs. Everyone who was home crowded into their tiny kitchen. "Kip asked me to marry him," she blurted out, "and I said yes."

You could have heard a pin drop in the Thompson kitchen. The first reaction came from Janet. "Can I be bridesmaid? Oh please, please. I've always wanted to be a bridesmaid. My best friend has been one already." Janet moved in closer to Connie, snuggling as if to firm up her standing as a favorite baby sister.

"If I have bridesmaids," Connie said stroking Janet's hair, "you will be my one and only junior bridesmaid but you'll just have to wait while Kip and I make our plans."

The brief diversion of the bridesmaid discussion gave Will and Oona a chance to absorb this news. Quite frankly they were surprised. The railroad tracks were the great divide in Turner Mills. You lived either between the tracks and the stacks or you were blessed because you didn't. Although the air was just as red and dusty on the preferred side of the tracks, the haves (mostly Irish) had drawn a line between themselves and their have-not-neighbors consisting mostly of a melting pot of peoples drawn to Turner Mills from Europe and Africa to make steel, to make a living, to make a life—Poles, Ukrainians, Blacks, Croatians & Slavs.

Oona was more than a little bewildered by this turn of events. She had heard through Annie's mother that Mrs. McCann was as xenophobic as a person could be and Annie's mother should know, she had connections in the big cathedral through the ladies of the Altar and Rosary Society.

"So what does Mrs. McCann think about her son marrying my daughter?" she wanted to know.

"I don't really know," Connie answered not getting the implication. "He hasn't told them yet. We just now decided we're getting married. He's gone home to break the news."

"Hmmm," Oona murmured not giving anyone in the room a clue to her thoughts.

"And he's going to marry me over Thanksgiving," Connie bubbled on. "Let's see. I'll be six months along. I guess it won't be a surprise to anyone by then. I wish we could get married before I pop out. It would be less embarrassing in school. But," she continued, "I bet all of Turner Mills knows the news by now anyhow. Oh, Mama, I'm so happy. There couldn't be a better ending. Don't you agree?"

"I can't believe my baby is having a baby and getting married all at the same time," Oona fudged the answer as she gave Connie a warm hug. The meaning of the hug went right over my mother's head and all Mom felt was its reassurance but I felt something different as Oona wrapped her arms around us. Her arms said to me: "I'll be your safety net."

Kip worded and re-worded in his head how he would tell his parents as he drove over the railroad bridge to home. How can you soften, "Hey folks I'm getting married," he wondered. He knew it wasn't a secret he could keep for very long. He shrugged as he pulled into the driveway and said out loud to his steering wheel, "Let's get this over with."

As was his custom at 5:30 p.m. each evening, Mortimer was packing his Fischer pipe with tobacco ready to light it up before easing into the couch to read the Observer. Margaret Mary was busy making dinner, a usual one, two large cans of Dinty Moore hash tossed into a 9 x 13 pan punctuated with six indents made by her fist into which she dropped six raw eggs, one for each member of the family. The eggs would cook up like big yellow eyeballs in the rectangular brown body of hash in thirty minutes and every diner would get an eyeball and part of the brown body on his plate. Kip opened the back door as she was putting the pan in the oven. As it slipped onto the oven grate he thought to himself, "Here's a good reason for going away to school."

"Is that you, Kip?" his father called from the living room. "Come here, I want to talk with you about something,"

"Me, too," Kip called back, "I have something for you to hear also."

"Go ahead, son," Mortimer deferred.

"No, no Dad, you go first, mine can wait."

"Well, all right. Your Mom and I were thinking," Mortimer began. "Margaret Mary," he called into the kitchen, "come in here for a minute. Your mother and I were thinking" he repeated, "in light of everything that has happened, I mean, the baby and all, um, I don't want to push you into anything but wouldn't it be the honorable thing for you and Connie to do is, well, get married? Make this baby legitimate?"

Kip shot a quick glance at his mother. She was not quite smiling but not upset either and Dad was pleasant as could be. "We were thinking," the father continued, "that you might get married over Thanksgiving. Mom and I could make some arrangements for Judge Daly to marry you in his courtroom. I wish there was enough time between now and Thanksgiving to have a bigger wedding but there just isn't. And I'm sure Connie will want to be married before the baby begins to show and people talk," his father concluded. "Well, say something."

"You are not going to believe this, Dad, Mom, but that's my news, too. I was just about to tell you that a half hour ago I asked Connie to marry me and she said yes. Not only that, Dad, but we're on the same page time-wise, we talked of getting married over Thanksgiving. It just makes sense. I guess I didn't give you guys enough credit. I thought you'd be mad, kick me out or something drastic like that. I'm so relieved. Honestly."

"When I was eighteen," Mortimer reminisced, trying to make an example of doing the right thing, "I enlisted in the Marines. I wanted to save the world from Hitler. When you are eighteen, Kip, you can make hard decisions. You can make yourself a man. Mine was the war, yours is the child. But, son," Mortimer lowered his voice almost to a whisper, "let's not tell your brothers and sister about this marriage decision. They're too young to understand. They'll get all confused. Let's just get you off to school and we'll figure out everything else later. Let's keep this to ourselves. Is that okay with you?"

Kip thought this last part strange. Why should they keep this news hush-

hush from his siblings?

"Promise?" Mortimer asked again.

"Sure, Dad."

"You'd better get packing," his dad was changing the subject. "I'll have to drive you on Sunday and I want to get an early start."

"You don't have to drive me, Dad. I'll take my truck."

"Freshmen can't have cars on campus. I know. It's a stupid rule but none-theless it's the rule."

"I won't stay on campus. I'll find an apartment."

"No, that won't work either," Mortimer added. "Freshmen have to live in the dorms for at least one semester. Another stupid rule."

Kip assumed he was being run out of Dodge and felt a massive amount of frustration creeping in. He didn't want to go away to college, he couldn't imagine being even a half hour without his truck and he couldn't see himself living in a dorm room with a nerd or a jock or a whiny kid who missed his mother. He reminded himself to stay cool. In three months he would marry Connie with his father's blessing and the two of them, well, three really, would get out of Dodge. Forever. He bit his lip and went upstairs to pack.

WEDDING PLAN BLUES

Connie would have phoned her best friend to tell her the latest news but she wanted to see the expression on Annie's face so we went there. "I have news to share," Mom sang out as she let herself into the Crantzes' back hall. "Where are you?"

"What? What?" we heard Annie respond as she came running to the hall wondering why her friend was in such high spirits.

"I'm going to be Mrs. Kip McCann. Soon. Thanksgiving," Connie said breathlessly.

Annie was trying to believe it but she couldn't quite wrap her head around this news from her best friend since kindergarten. This was adult news and they weren't adults. They were seniors in high school. Now Annie felt like she was the kid while her friend was graduating into a higher status—Mrs.

It was easier for Annie to comprehend a new baby becoming part of their friendship than a new man. A new baby meant Annie could grow into a relationship with the child from its first breath. A new man was competition.

"Help me plan my wedding," Connie begged her friend. "Who should we invite from our class? Should I wear a wedding gown or will I look like a 'bad' girl wearing white with a baby on the way? Will you be my maid of honor?"

Annie wanted to put her hands over her ears and scream *stop!* School was starting in a few days and her biggest concern up until this moment was whether or not to drop Spanish 3.

"Whoa, Connie, aren't you putting the horse before the cart?" was the only thing Annie could think of to say and, of course, it was the wrong thing. The two friends exchanged a quick glance and in that instant a telepathic charge went off. They both felt it. I even felt it. Something had changed and they realized it was their friendship. It scared them both half to death. Connie said she had to get home and bolted.

Kip's exodus on Sunday morning left two families in upheaval, three if you count the Crantzes. Connie didn't know what she should do next. She thought she was getting married but nothing seemed to be happening, The Thompsons didn't know whether they should start shopping for gowns and renting halls or just put the crib up. Period.

Margaret Mary didn't know if she should call the Thompsons and invite them over...no, not over, out; out to the Colony House for dinner. The McCann siblings didn't know what had just happened but the household's vibe told them to stay out of everyone's way and don't ask. Kip felt he had been blindsided by his father, and conversely, Mortimer thought everything had gone exceedingly well.

On the surface, the period between the beginning of the new semester and Thanksgiving was tranquil. Connie and Annie met their school bus at the corner every day as usual. The boys at school who always had a teasing rapport with Connie were unusually stand-offish and none of the girls said anything at all about the big news while everyone looked first at her waistline.

Kip was assigned one of the new dorms at Sherburne and his roommate was easy enough to get along with. His schedule allowed him to get a job at the bookstore.

Connie gave him a few days to settle in before she started calling his dorm floor. The hall phone would ring and ring. If anyone eventually picked it up he was likely to inform her that Kip's room was at the other end of the hall and, "I'm on my way to class right now, call back," or they'd just pick up the receiver and put it back down again without saying anything. She began calling every day and then several times a day. She became known on the floor as the phone stalker girlfriend. Every once in a while someone would actually make the trek to the end of the hall and call Kip to the phone. When they did connect she'd beg him to call her whenever he could and he promised he would but that depended on if he had enough dimes to make a long distance call and he usually didn't, he said.

October was nearing and Connie desperately wanted to know if they were still planning their Columbus weekend rendezvous. She had looked into the bus fare and Oona, reluctantly, said she could go. Kip finally called.

"I just talked to my dad," Kip was saying into the receiver wondering how to word what he was about to tell her. "Change of plans. Dad's taking my brothers on our annual fishing trip to the mountains and wants me to meet them at an exit on the interstate so I can go with them. My roommate lives near that exit and is going home that weekend. I can hitch a ride. Going fishing in the mountains is something Dad and I have done for years. My uncle and his kids are coming, too," Kip was now blathering on about how these annual trips to Pike Lake were so important to all the boys in the family and their dads. He told her he shouldn't miss it, that it would probably be the last time he could go. "I'm sorry honey," he said hoping to hang up before the sniffling started. "Now that I'm thinking of it," he added having a sudden inspiration, "this trip to the mountains is perfect timing. I'll be stuck with my father in a boat fishing for hours, and he and I can iron out all the details about our wedding. Then I'll call you as soon as I get back and we'll firm up all our plans. I'll get a roll of dimes so we can talk as long as we want."

Kip's plan made a lot of sense to him, not so much to his broken-hearted girlfriend. "Okay," she whimpered.

"Love you."

"Love you, too."

With each passing day Kip began liking his life at Sherburne better than his old one in Turner Mills. On a few occasions he even forgot about his 'predicament.'

One class in particular gave him a reprieve from his anguish. Anthropology. He had talked the professor into accepting him into class even though he was a freshman because he was super excited about his Irish heritage and had begun looking into his own Irish history long ago, had already gone back one hundred and fifty years in his research and had even written to a chieftain. The professor liked it when kids got as excited as Kip about anthropology and told him, "Sure, why not?"

So the days leading up to Columbus weekend flew by and Kip was taken off guard when his roommate said, “Hey, grab your stuff, my dad’s picking us up in a half hour.”

Kip met with his family exactly as planned at the interstate rest stop and the caravan of three cars containing one dad, two uncles and seven cousins, headed north after some high-fiving and some burgers. Hours later they pulled into their cabins, the ones the dads always rented and it seemed to Kip that maybe nothing from boyhood had changed.

That day they kept catching pickerel and although they didn't want to take the bony things back to camp, they were happy to have bites with a little fight in them. Luck changed and they caught enough tasty keepers to have a camp cookout. Cast iron fry pans appeared out of nowhere as did a braid of garlic and a bag of Idaho’s. Men who wouldn’t be caught dead in their kitchens at home were now gourmet chefs showing off to their kids. Everyone loved it.

On their final day Mortimer, Kip and Beaner got out on the lake early so they could get one last hour of fishing before checking out but Beaner became seasick even through the lake was barely rippling. Mortimer headed for shore telling Beaner to go play with the campsite’s two lab pups that had licked their hands and jumped up their legs on their arrival. Beaner was happy to play with the dogs.

Back on the lake, Mortimer and Kip were having fun pulling in brown trout. Eventually the fish stopped biting and the two sat rocking back and forth in the ripples saying nothing. Finally Mortimer decided this was as good a time as any to fill Kip in on the upcoming marriage.

“We have to talk about Thanksgiving,” Mortimer began.

“Yeah, Dad, I suppose we do,” answered Kip feeling his throat tightening.

“Well,” Mortimer resumed, “Judge Daly has agreed to marry you in his chambers on the 25th, the day before Thanksgiving. I had my jeweler friend make up a set of rings especially for you and Connie.” With that statement he pulled a small box out of his fishing vest and popped it open. There sat the smallest diamond ring Kip had ever seen, nothing at all like what his mother wears, and two thin little wedding bands.

“Looks like you’ve got everything covered, Dad,” Kip replied unimpressed.

“Not everything,” Mortimer added, “we need to have a little party to celebrate. We can’t just leave Daly’s chambers and go home. What do you think of our two families having dinner together at the Westlake? It’s an elegant club and if we can get the President's Room, our little party would be lovely and private. By the way, how many people are in the Thompson family? Immediate family?"

"There's six, Dad, but Connie has a best friend from childhood and I'm sure she'd like Annie to be there too."

"Okay that's seven."

"What about Grandma?" Kip asked thinking maybe his father forgot about inviting his own mother.

"Nah, let's just keep this to our immediate families," Mortimer casually replied.

Kip was beginning to see into his future as the boat drifted toward shore. He began thinking he might need more than one roll of dimes for the hall phone to talk Connie into his father's version of their wedding. He was pretty sure Connie would have a mind of her own on this matter and he was going to be pickle in the middle. He could see it coming.

That's exactly what happened. It took Kip more than a few days after the fishing weekend to get up the courage to call her.

"How'd it go?" was her first question when she heard his voice on the other end of the line.

"Not bad," he replied, "we caught a lot of fish."

"I don't mean the fishing," she was quick to say, "I'm waiting here going crazy. I don't know whether we're getting married or not, where the wedding will be, how many guests we'll be inviting. I have a thousand questions and no answers. Thanksgiving is only six weeks away. My parents ask me every day if I've heard from you. I need to know."

His head was pounding. How was he going to get through this conversation? The only thing he could think of was to take a page from the Mortimer J McCann playbook—put on your happiest voice your biggest smile and say, "I have great news!"

So he amped his voice into its excited range and said, "Honey, I have great news! My Dad's got the whole thing covered. We'll get married in Judge Daly's chambers on November 25th at 2 o'clock. Then, listen to this, it's awesome, my dad has reserved the President's Room at the Westlake Club for a small reception. Just our two families and, of course, Annie. The reception will be intimate and our families will have the opportunity to get to know each other. Oh, and honey, I also have a nice surprise. It comes in a little box and I'm going to hop on the Greyhound bus next Saturday and deliver it to you in person."

Connie was ecstatic and Kip was surprised how well the Mortimer J McCann approach had worked.

"Next Saturday? What time will you get here? Are you coming directly to my house?"

"No, I have a better idea. I made a reservation at the Crown Hotel for just the two of us, I mean three of us. I'm not even telling my parents I'm coming to town. Can you make an excuse for an overnight at Annie's or something and meet me downtown? I'll only be able to stay for one night and I'll have to be back on the bus at two on Sunday. Every girl needs a proper engagement and I intend to make ours something you'll always remember."

They said goodbye on a high note. Each of them thought the conversation a success. She for her reasons, he for his. He put the receiver back in its cradle then picked it up again. He dialed O and asked the operator for the number at the Crown.

November 25th came too soon for Kip and not soon enough for Connie. My mother had long since given up trying to hide me under billowy blouses and unzipped bell bottoms. There was no more talk with Annie about wearing white or even a wedding dress. I am growing like a weed in here. Nothing fits Mom and the marriage is coming up. Me, Mom and Oona take the bus downtown to Harris' maternity department for something 'respectable' to wear to the ceremony. Mom tries on three or four things and each time says she looks fat. She plops down on the chair in the dressing room and cries.

Don't cry, Mom, I try to tell her. *It's only a dress. It's only a wedding and it's certainly not about how fat you are. It's about a marriage and me. ME. I'm your blessing, Mama. Can you hear me?* But she's too upset to listen. We eventually get back on the bus with a Harris bag in our possession. "It'll do," she told the kindly sales lady.

A STRING OF PEARLS

There's no one in County Hall on the 25th of November as Mortimer guides Margaret Mary by the elbow and she clickety-clacks in high heels through the echoing halls with three kids goose-necking behind her. Although she still isn't quite sure that Kip is this new baby's father, and that perhaps they should have made more of an issue out of denying its parentage, she acceded to her husband's plan as she always does. So she clickety-clacked along with him until they reached Daly's chambers. Since they were early they chose some seats, automatically selecting chairs on the right, the groom's side as if this were a church. After the children had looked around the room at pictures of all the former old judges and John F. Kennedy hanging on the walls, they got bored and started poking at each other. Mortimer was reading something he had pulled out of his pocket paying no attention to the others. Margaret Mary scolded, "Quit it" to her children several times to no avail. Twenty minutes later five more people arrived dressed in their Sunday best. Everyone nodded a hello and the newcomers took seats to the left.

Margaret Mary couldn't contain her surprise over the ethnicity of the newcomers to the room, after all Connie was blonde and blue-eyed and although she had a proper English name, could have passed for Irish. "What do you suppose?" she said to her husband in a stage whisper that reverberated around the room. "These people can't possibly be Connie's family. Why, they're Indians for God's sake! Kip isn't marrying an Indian, is he?"

"Can you keep it down, Margaret?" Mortimer shushed but it was too late.

Everyone in the room was now staring at one another, half the room not believing what they thought their ears had just heard. The McCann children were the most excited about their mother's whisper. They stopped poking each other and stared in amazement at the girls across the aisle. They had never seen real Indians before and they began looking around for feathers.

The Thompson children looked to Oona and Will, visibly upset with being pointed out as Indians. Oona sat stone-faced and stern. Will reached over and took her hand, patted it. Their children knew enough to let the insult pass.

Connie and Kip and Annie waited outside the chambers so they could make somewhat of a grand entrance when it was time. Still sitting with his family, Beaner, his brother's best man, didn't have a clue what his duties included. "When do I get up? Where do I stand? When do I give Kip the ring?" he asked his father. Mortimer told him not to worry, he'd let him know.

"Now," Mortimer said elbowing Beaner when Judge Daly entered the room from behind an enormous mahogany door, twice as tall as the judge. Beaner got up and tripped his way past his parents as Judge Daly pointed out exactly where to stand. Annie peeked into the courtroom and Judge Daly gave her the now sign. "It's time," she said turning toward Connie and Kip.

Annie entered the courtroom first, pretending it was St. Basil's Church, walking oh so slowly toward the judge. Kip and Mom, arms entwined, followed. Kip decided Annie was walking too slow and, attempting to pick up the pace, stepped on the back strap of her left sling. Annie turned and shot him a glance that said "this is how you're supposed to walk, dummy." Fortunately twenty steps was all it took to traverse the room. Connie looked beautiful; she had woven fresh flowers into her hair and wore a blue dress with sparkles on it that lit up her eyes; Dad was in a suit. As the bride and groom walked past their families Charlotte sang out in her little girl voice, "Ohh, you look so beautiful Connie, like my Barbie doll!" Everyone including Judge Daly laughed in agreement. Five minutes later Kip and Connie were man and wife, Mr. and Mrs. John Patrick McCann, and family—me.

It was a little awkward after the ceremony. Mortimer and Margaret Mary tried to be gracious by introducing themselves, shaking hands and exchanging pleasantries with Oona and Will while the children from both families eyed each other cautiously. After a few politenesses, Mortimer announced that everyone should head to the Westlake Club for an intimate dinner together.

Connie's sisters wanted to ride to the Westlake with the bride and groom so Oona and Will asked Annie to ride with them. Mortimer, Margaret Mary and the three younger McCanns, already a carful, followed them out of the chambers.

"Oh, by the way, we'll all need to enter the Club by the side door known as the Ladies Entrance." Mortimer informed the group. "I know how silly it sounds in this day and age but women aren't allowed in the main entrance," he went on. "It's a men's club. Ladies are only guests here." Will squeezed Oona's hand for the second time today.

As quiet as Connie's sisters were in the judge's chambers, they were now bubbling with hostile excitement in the car, eager to tell the bride the 'Indian' episode that had preceded the ceremony. In their excitement they totally ignored their new brother-in-law and gave Connie a detailed accounting of the elder Mrs. McCann's stage whisper that they all had heard, adding that Oona had squinted her eyes until they were just slits like she does when she's really mad and that Will had to hold Oona's hand to keep her from getting up and bopping Mrs. McCann on her pageboy with her purse. The more the girls talked the wilder the episode became. Connie was just as bad. She encouraged every little detail out of her sisters and with such an enthusiastic audience the girls began exaggerating.

By the time they had gone the ten blocks up Roosevelt Avenue to the Westlake, Kip had a stranglehold on the steering wheel. This was his mother they were bashing. When he couldn't stand it any longer he turned toward the backseat and said, "That's my mother you're talking about for chrissakes."

Connie stopped listening to the girls for a second and looked over at her new husband as he swung the wheel left into the parking lot. The artery at his right temple was thumping. "Oh, oh," she said to herself, "he's really mad."

"Oh, honey," she said to him, "they're just making this up."

"No we're not!" they retorted.

Connie turned toward the backseat and glowered at her sisters, the same look Oona wears when she means shut up. They shut up.

The President's Room was festooned with gourds and pumpkins either falling out of cornucopias or nestled in tiers on the Kittinger side tables. The mahogany mantelpiece, over which hung a giant painting of George Washington, flickered with dozens of candles. A floral centerpiece was sprawled across the dining table filled with asters, zinnias and sunflowers. There were so many pieces of silverware at each setting that no one but His Honor and Mrs. McCann could imagine their purposes. The sweet smell of burning cherry wood from the giant fireplace in the foyer and wafts of allspice from the kitchen perfumed the intimate room. The table majestically accommodated all thirteen. This was the room where, historically, many important deals had been struck. How appropriate.

The bride, the groom, the two families, the elegant room and the well-behaved children could have been a scene from a Norman Rockwell painting except for one thing. My mother was nervously tapping her foot under the table like she does when she's upset and trying to keep something under control. Tiny jiggles were going up her leg right into my womb, kind of like hiccups, unpleasant. I hear her say to someone who must be a waiter "and I'll have a Harvey Wallbanger." Someone else at the table challenged her choice, saying it's not a good idea to drink when you're pregnant but she reminded them she is now 18, old enough to think for herself and certainly old enough to drink.

Somewhere between my mother's first Harvey Wallbanger and her second, as all the adults in the room harrumphed their disapproval, I float in a state of bliss. I feel something, someone nearby trying to get my attention. It feels like someone from my spiritual side. Then I recognize her, my mentor. She wants to talk.

"Here? Now?" I hazily ask.

"Now," she says then adds that she's looking at the broader picture and just can't stand by and let it happen.

"Let what happen?" I ask.

"Let you get hurt," she said. "I'm fairly sure your McCann family will be in and out of your life. It could be very troubling for you. You've already learned what Mrs. McCann thinks about native Americans."

"Hates us," I affirmed in my own boozy state.

"Here's the irony," mentor continued. "Mrs. McCann is herself part Native American. She had a Mayan mother and to this day, doesn't know it. Her father never told her."

"What!" I howled. "Her mother is native! You've got to be kidding!"

"I'm not," mentor went on.

"Fill me in, the Thompsons are going to love this!"

"Well," mentor began, "Margaret Mary's father was Colonel Conan O'Sullivan, an Irish immigrant. At age seventeen he emigrated from Tipperary and followed some cousins to the states. Because there was plenty of canal building, road and rail construction, Conan quickly found work. When the Spanish American War broke out, he joined the army. He was smart, charismatic, handsome, a brilliant negotiator and he spoke fluent Spanish. By age twenty-nine he was a colonel in the United States Army.

"The war lasted only a few months and in its aftermath Colonel O'Sullivan became a point man for the US government and traveled frequently to Cuba. That's when he met Kip's grandmother, a Mayan, with whom he fell hopelessly in love. Soon she was pregnant, but like your Oona, she wouldn't leave her home, not even for the handsome, charismatic O'Sullivan. He was torn between going on with his military career or retiring his commission to be with her.

"The decision of whether to go or stay came to a tragic conclusion when your great grandmother, A'mari was her name, perished giving birth to Margaret Mary. Heartbroken, devastated, the Colonel sent his new baby to live with his sister in Poughkeepsie until he could resign from the service and figure out how he could raise a little girl, a thought that terrified him more than battle.

"In time he met someone new and married. The Colonel and his new wife raised Margaret Mary and their next two children as if there was nothing unusual about their family and no one ever told Margaret Mary her true parentage or her cultural heritage. I'm surprised she never asked about it especially since she didn't look at all like her siblings. The Colonel loved all his children but he always favored his little Mayan. She was Daddy's girl.

"The Colonel never got over his longing for Ireland. He still sang the songs of his homeland, still held tight to his superstitions, still spoke with his brogue and always put his hat to his chest whenever he mentioned the old sod. To please him, little Margaret Mary became as Irish as she could. She learned all his songs and superstitions until they became hers as well, and she turned his partiality for all things Irish into her intolerance for anyone, anything not Irish."

Mentor finished her tale saying, "Those high Irish cheekbones that everyone admires, they're not Irish cheekbones, they're Mayan."

Ma! Ma! I tried to yell upward. *Ma, guess what? Your Irish mother-in-law isn't Irish. I knew it! I knew there was something about her I recognized. If she hadn't been so snobbish about her Irish heritage, I would have felt her indigenous spirit right away. Ma, she's like you, like me, like Oona.* This new information tickled me no end. I'm really excited about this turn of events. It's going to make life so much easier. Margaret Mary is my Mayan grandma, well, half Mayan. And somehow I'm going to let her know it. But it looks like my mother is going to beat me to it.

It was either my telepathic message about Margaret Mary or my mother's second Harvey Wallbanger that loosened my mother's powers of native intuition, or we were just drunk. Mom leaned into the table and studied her mother-in-law's high cheekbones for a full thirty conspicuous seconds then blew a harrumph through her nose. It wasn't very polite. I hoped nobody noticed her behavior. This would not be the best place to make a scene.

Between the salad and the main course, Margaret Mary picked up her peau de soie clutch and excused herself for the ladies' room. Connie waited thirty seconds and followed. I knew my mother wasn't going to let this 'Indian' episode pass.

I heard the whole ugly thing in the ladies' room. It started out calm enough...Connie asking Mrs. McCann what she would like to be called. "Should I call you Mother or Mom or Margaret Mary?" she wanted to know.

"Mrs. McCann will be just fine," Margaret Mary said to her own lips in the mirror as she applied more Russian Red lipstick. Shortly after that part of the conversation I heard the plinking of pearls as they hit the bathroom floor one at a time, and then "you bitch," then silence. Five minutes later both Mrs. McCanns returned to the table, the elder poised but piqued with the string of pearls she wore to the ladies room now loose in her clutch; the young Mrs. McCann, foxy-faced and jubilant.

No one acknowledged the electricity the women brought back to the table but eyes darted from one to the other as if they all felt it, except for the kids who had just received their third Coca Colas and were busy sucking them up through their straws.

Stilted cordiality at the table continued through dessert until someone brought up the topic of 'tomorrow'—Thanksgiving. Each family apparently had the same immutable law—Thanksgiving is always at 'our' house. Kip and Connie looked at each other perplexed. Their first conflict materialized while they were still at the wedding table.

The parents went round and round trying to accommodate the newly-weds into each family's traditions. They spoke of dining hours, relatives arriving, college football games and the Macy parade. The conclusion was the McCann family would integrate the couple into their celebration from Thanksgiving morning until 4 p.m. at which time the couple would hurry to the Thompson's for a second dinner with Oona's sisters and their children. Oona reminded Connie how much she counted on Connie's help in the kitchen for what was the Thompson's biggest celebration of the year. A sense of disloyalty washed over Connie

Margaret Mary worried if the turkey and trimmings she had already ordered from the Colony House Restaurant, where she always bought her nicely browned, fully cooked fifteen pound turkey, could be ready earlier than she had requested but she didn't stress about it for long. She had already made a mental note assigning the unpleasantries needed to remedy the situation with the Colony House to Mortimer. Kip cringed at the new plan knowing full well his mother can't get her day going before noon, let alone get the table set by two.

While the adults were ticklishly ironing out the details of tomorrow's events, the children managed to get triple cokes and desserts from the wait staff. By the time everyone put their soiled napkins on the banquet table and pushed back their chairs the McCann youngsters and Connie's little sister, Janet, concluded this was a very good blending of families. From their point of view, in-law life was going to be full of triple fudge brownies.

GETTING TO KNOW YOU

The crisp, early winter wind blew right through my mother's lightweight wool A-line coat and she snuggled into my dad's body as we crossed the parking lot, still wobbly from the Galliano. Now, alone in the truck as the heater began warming us up, Dad wanted an explanation.

"What happened in the ladies' room?" he said firmly and not too kindly.

"Nothing, really," Mom replied dreamily. "Apparently your mother didn't know I'm Native American and I had to enlighten her. I explained that my family is just like everyone else's. Irish, British, Polish, what's the difference? Your mother kept saying 'you're an Indian, you're just an Indian' as if it were a terrible thing. I think she finally understands we are all the same under our skin. I made it perfectly clear."

"My mother's very sensitive about her Irish. I hope you didn't offend her," Kip responded as sure as night follows day that she had.

"I may have," Connie replied. "Wait. There's more. I bet your mother's not even Irish. She looks Native American to me."

"You're crazy," Dad said with a sharp edge in his voice.

"Haven't you ever suspected?" Connie's tongue was still very loose. "I bet I know more about your grandfather, Colonel O'Sullivan than you *and* your mother know."

"I know all about him," Kip shot back. "My grandfather rose through the ranks during the Spanish American War serving in Cuba. At the end of the war he was part of President McKinley's team to normalize Cuba after Spain was ousted. I know a lot."

"Well, Mr. Know-it-all, apparently you and your mother didn't know that Colonel O'Sullivan fell in love with a Cuban Mayan woman during that reformation and had a baby with her. And that Mayan woman was Margaret Mary's birth mother."

"What are you smokin'?" Kip retaliated. "My grandmother's not Mayan."

"You're the one studying anthropology," Connie added, "look it up for yourself."

"Where do you get this nonsense?" Kip wanted to know.

"I'm very in tune with my native side," Mom explained, "I can feel the spirits of those who have gone before. When I listen carefully I can know things."

I rolled my eyes. I couldn't believe my mother said that. She was always too gabby, too busy, too flighty to listen to spirits. At least she's listening now...to mine.

Kip fumed and Connie got sleepier as they pulled into the hotel parking lot. She was clinging to his arm when he unlocked the door to the honeymoon suite on the tenth floor of the Crown which Mortimer had reluctantly reserved for them.

My mother kicked off her shoes, dropped onto the bed and was asleep before Dad got the suitcases through the door. The new Mrs. McCann's day was so over.

Nine o'clock the next morning Dad was still sitting in his wedding suit minus the jacket and tie, he hadn't been to bed. "Wake up, wake up. Get up if you want breakfast before we check out. We have to get to my parents," he said as I somersaulted.

Mom was slow to stir. The bed we were in was the most comfortable bed she and I had ever been in. We could have stayed put for the day. But no, Dad was rattling us by shaking Mom's shoulder. "Come on, get up."

Mom was grouchy from being rousted and Dad wasn't talking except for "hurry, hurry."

The McCann household was in its typical holiday routine when the newlyweds arrived. The Thanksgiving Day newspaper with all the toy ads was strewn over the living room floor and the kids were studying every ad. Margaret Mary had yet to make an appearance downstairs. Mortimer was trying to find the section of the paper that told the start time for the football games.

"You kids have breakfast yet?" Mortimer called out as they came through the kitchen door, not that he had intended on getting up and making something. He pushed the paper aside to make room on the couch for Connie. She looked at her watch as she found a space to sit. It was already noon. In four hours she was going to be home, her home, with her family and her Thanksgiving. There was nothing to indicate a holiday was underway in this household. No scent of pies baking, nothing roasting in the oven, no one peeling anything in the kitchen.

"Can I help with anything?" Connie volunteered hoping to keep the holiday schedule on her timetable.

"No, we're all set," Mortimer said. "I was able to get ahold of the owner of the Colony House and he said he could get our turkey order out early. I'll be picking it up at one."

Connie looked at her watch again. "Maybe I should set the table."

"No," he replied. "Mrs. McCann will be right down. She likes to do things her way."

The phone rang and Kip grabbed for the receiver. "Hey, Mooney, long time no see. How are ya man?" This was the most enthusiasm Connie had noticed in her husband all weekend.

"No, I'm only home until Saturday. No, nothing much new." He felt Connie's eyes searing into his back. "Well, I shouldn't say 'nothing,' " he continued, "I got married yesterday." Pause. "Yeah, that's the one." Long pause.

"Really! A GTO? You got rid of the Fairlane?" he said reviving his enthusiasm, "Hey, I'd love a ride." Kip turned toward Connie to ascertain what her reaction might be if he said he was going over to Mooney's for ten minutes. Her reaction was a look that said I'll kill you if you do. "Maybe I better not," Kip continued, "we're having Thanksgiving dinner here in a few hours and then we're going to Connie's parents. Don't crash it before Christmas," Kip said ending the conversation. "I'll get a ride then."

We never got to Oona's until 5:30. Thanksgiving was well underway and smelling scrumptious to Connie. All the scents of her childhood enveloped her. This was home.

She turned to Kip hopeful that he'd realize *this* is what Thanksgiving is all about. Dozens of cousins darting through the rooms, aunts in the kitchen stirring and tasting and talking, uncles out on the porch, leaning against the rail drinking and kibitzing and laughing, food sizzling in the oven, and two tables set, one for grown-ups and one for kids. Kip took the beer someone handed him as men folk slapped him on the shoulder, congratulating him, welcoming him to the family.

As heads became unbowed after Will's short grace, memories from former Thanksgivings were passed along with the peas and potatoes, subduing the tinkling of soup spoons that were hitting the sides of bowls. Each new course came amid *ahhs* and *ohhs* and compliments to the cooks. Dinner and desserts went on and on. It was well past eight when the men announced they'd clear and clean up and do the dishes. The children were all given dish towels and set about drying everything that got handed to them.

At ten o'clock the food came out again. Sandwiches were constructed with leftover dressing and cranberry sauce and take-home packages were prepared.

Voices streamed from the kitchen, "you're putting too much in that container," and, "you know how much Uncle John loves your dressing, Oona." It was almost midnight before the last hugs were squeezed and the house emptied out. Oona fell into her club chair, exhausted, put her feet up on the ottoman and declared "this was the best Thanksgiving we're ever had," the same exact words she says every Thanksgiving around midnight. Connie agreed.

The phone rang.

The phone never rings in the Thompson house after nine. That's the rule...unless, God forbid, it's the unthinkable. Kip watched as terror froze on the faces of his in-laws. It rang and rang until Will had the courage to pick up the receiver.

A communal exhale was audible as Will turned to Kip and said, "It's your mother." Kip took the receiver and tried to corner himself in the spare space at the foot of the stairs away from the others. In silence the others stared at his back, curious, listening.

"Yeah, Mom, I'm still here." Pause. "I don't know. I have no idea what I'm doing tonight. I have no idea what I'm supposed to be doing." Long pause. "Mom, I'm married now, it's not like I can...yeah, yeah, I have a key." As they spoke he could visualize the smoke streams coming out of his mother's nose as she puffed her words, he could sense she was pacing.

He hung up the phone and stood in the living room doorway facing his newly acquired family and bride. It was past midnight of the first day of their married lives. The family looked to Kip as if he was the man with the plan.

"I guess you and I had better find a hotel," he suggested to Connie when he realized they were all expecting a brilliant idea from him.

"At this hour? You won't find a room at this hour," Oona said incredulously. "We'll figure something out here. Let's see," she said to no one in particular. "The younger girls sleep in twin beds and Janet's already in Connie's old room. So that won't work. I guess you and I can give up our double, Will, you take the couch and I can squeeze in with Janet."

"No!" Will boomed. "We are not giving up our bed." Shock waves ricocheted around the room. No one had ever heard my Grandpap so emphatic. Nor had anyone ever heard him say no to Oona.

"The simplest solution," Kip quickly replied, "is for me to go home and Connie stay here in her own bed. Then in the morning I'll come back and we can make a plan." There were no dissenters, not even Connie. Everyone just wanted to get to bed.

DAD BOLTS

It might have been the turkey from the Colony House or maybe the dressing. The Thompsons asked each other "what else could it be? No one in our family got sick, just Connie." My mother was up half the night retching. Each time it happened I'd push my body against the walls of my womb hoping I wouldn't be ejected. Finally at daybreak, Oona and Grandpap bundled Mom up and drove us to the hospital.

Grandpap spotted a pay phone at the far end of the waiting room and dialed Kip's number. "Your wife's in the hospital," he said into the receiver, "we're at the General. You'd better come."

Kip sunk onto the arm of the couch when Mr. Thompson said your wife, that's all he heard. He now had a wife he didn't want, a life he didn't want, a child he didn't want, in-laws who were handing off responsibilities to him that he didn't want. He couldn't respond; he was paralyzed.

"Hello, hello, are you there?" he heard Mr. Thompson repeating.

"Yeah, I'm here, I'm just taking in your news. Tell me again. She's where?"

Kip mumbled into the phone about getting to the General right away or as soon as possible or during visiting hours or something like that. Will didn't know how it got left. He hung up bewildered. Kip was still staring at the receiver when his dad came down the stairs. "You okay?" Mortimer asked, sensing something was different.

"I'm fine."

"Then would you mind going to Donna's Doughnuts and getting us a dozen, mix it up some, peanut sticks, a couple of fritters, you know what the family likes. I'm going to make one of my rare but delicious family breakfasts. Change is in the air. Not a bad change, of course, just different. Soon there'll be more of us. This'll be our end-of-the-old-era breakfast."

"Sure," Kip replied glad to have a mission that seemed more important than sitting all day in the hospital. Mortimer padded to the kitchen in his leather-bottomed wool slipper-socks and started rattling the pans while Kip grabbed his pea coat from the front hall.

Donna's Doughnuts was busy. A long line of people saying "I'll have one of these and three of those, no, I mean two of those..." slowed the wait process to a crawl. While he was waiting, thoughts of *how do I get out of my life* kept creeping into his head. He tried concentrating on doughnuts but the predicament seemed to override everything.

As Kip returned with his box full of doughnuts he heard a loud wolf whistle and spotted the orange GTO through his truck's rear view mirror. Mooney was passing by. "Mooney, you fool," Kip called out as the Pontiac came to a stop at the end of the drive. "What the hell, Mooney, how on earth did you afford this thing?"

"You'd have one, too, college boy, if you got paid what they pay me at the plant." Mooney bragged through the rolled down window. "You've got to see this machine in action, get in," Mooney sang.

Torn between what he should be doing and what he wanted to be doing, Kip hesitated but only for a second. "Let me drop these doughnuts off, I'll be right back."

"Ten minutes, Dad," Kip said to Mortimer as he slid the Donna's box across the kitchen table. "I'm going for a ride in Mooney's new GTO."

"But breakfast's almost ready," Mortimer said to Kip's back.

"Ten minutes, that's all I'll be," and he was gone.

The GTO sped around Turner Mills searching for old high school buddies to whom Mooney could show off the car. Girls spotted the orange from afar and started whistling and waving for Mooney to give them a ride. When he tired of using gas on the girls, Mooney pulled to the curb and lifted the flashy hood to expose the big-ass engine for the guys to admire. It took most of the day. At three thirty Kip started making noises about getting to the hospital.

Reluctantly Mooney ended the joyride, calling it the best day of his life, and headed to the hospital to drop off Kip.

At exactly five minutes to four Kip was arguing with the volunteer lady who manned the reception desk and handed out room passes. "Visiting hours are over in five minutes," she said as stern as clerks usually are, "you can't go up."

"You don't understand, I have to get up there, it's my wife. I've been at the steel plant all day and didn't get out until three thirty, I rushed right over."

The reception lady looked Kip up and down.

"You don't look like you've been at the steel plant all day," she said catching a whiff of the Old Spice cologne that had followed him in through the revolving door. The look on her face said she doubted if he even had a wife.

"Look," he insisted pulling out his driver's license. "I'm John Patrick McCann, my wife is Connie McCann. Check on your list. Look under' M,' McCann."

Just then the voice of God came over the loudspeaker. "Visiting hours are now over. All visitors must leave the hospital immediately."

"Sorry," she said pointing to the loudspeaker as she reached under her desk for her purse and lunch bag, "come back at seven. Seven to nine."

At seven on the dot Kip was back at the General, the first in line to get a patient pass. He made sure he got there before Oona, and was still trying to think of some plausible excuse why he wasn't there earlier, when the elevator lurched to a stop on the fourth floor. 425-435, that way, the arrow pointed. Connie was hooked to an IV, her eyes red rimmed when he tapped lightly on her room's door and entered. She was relieved it was Kip. Mom had spent the hours between four and seven thinking Dad was about to bolt. She asked me time and again what we should do if that happened. I had no idea. I'd be happy just to be born and said so but she didn't want to hear that. She lit up when she saw it was Dad and made room on the bed for him to sit. She needed him close.

Every time she looked into those big dark eyes of his she melted. I could feel all her tension evaporate. Her whole body went into love mode. It heated, it softened, it ahhh-ed. I've got to remember what love is supposed to feel like. I was surprised when we pressed up against Dad's body in a big hug on the hospital bed that I didn't feel his heat, his ahh. He was more like— ahem. Now I'm confused.

Oona walked in. She was relieved to see Kip sitting on the bed for she, too, had her doubts about how all this would play out. She had cheery news. She had run into Dr. Morgan in the hall. "He wants to keep your overnight," she reported, "but you and the baby are fine. He said he'll release you at eleven tomorrow. You'd better come home with me, Connie," she added looking at Kip, not willing to give decisions about her daughter and grandchild to this kid. "What do you think, Kip?" she added trying to deflect the possibility of animosity. She didn't have to deflect. Kip was relieved.

Connie was hoping her mother wouldn't stay until visiting hours were over but she did. When the omnipresent voice of God crackled over the loudspeaker, Oona kissed her daughter on the forehead, patted her tummy and my bum and backed out of the room with a little wave. "Time to go," Kip said leaning into the bed, tangling himself in the IV tubes as he gave Mom a good night kiss. He said he'd see her at Oona's and mumbled "before I leave for school tomorrow."

She caught it. Mom's sharp like that. "Tomorrow?" she yelled, bolting upright. "Tomorrow's only Saturday. You can't leave tomorrow! I'm counting on you being here until Sunday. We haven't had ten minutes together since we got married. We need to sit down, like married people do and plan." I could hear her heart thumping as her blood tried to squeeze through it.

"I can't, honey," Kip replied and wrapped her in his arms. "It's my ride. He has to be back early. He's an RA. I'll tell you what. I'll call your mother tomorrow morning and then I'll spend as much time as I can with you." A nurse filled the doorway tapping her foot. "Got to go," he said acknowledging the tap. "Get some rest, Mrs. McCann," he added giving Connie the smile she always fell for.

"Mrs. McCann. Mrs. McCann. Mrs. McCann." The words stuck in his throat as he walked toward the elevator. He was not smiling now. In fact, he thought he was going to pass out as he stepped into the empty cage. Trapped. He was having a panic attack.

"I can't do this."

I burst into being on love's Big Day, February 14, 1964. My mother named me Kateri which means pure in the language of the Mohawk, my father gave me McCann which means screw you.

PART 2

Humankind has not woven the web of life.
We are but one thread within it.
Whatever we do to the web, we do to ourselves.
All things are bound together. All things connect.

Chief Seattle 1859

KATE MCCANN

Ever since she was thirteen Kate wanted to be a model. What else can you do with a body that is long and lean, so long in fact that on graduation day she was taller by three inches than the boys in her class. She worried that her eighth grade teacher, Mrs. Dietrich, would put her last in the graduation procession even behind the boys.

She hadn't realized she had grown so tall until one day in the spring of '77 she clunked her head on the three-quarters-opened garage door. She always passed easily through that door without ducking. Now, bang! A goose egg was swelling on her head. She looked around to see what had changed. The door was still three-quarters open as it always was because the garage is so full of bikes and boxes that her dad, not her real dad, Carl, her mom's second husband, had no choice but to leave the car on the street. She remembers that day rubbing the goose egg wondering how tall she was going to become.

At thirteen she finally began growing into the exaggerated features of her face—enormous eyes, big teeth, broad smile, high cheekbones—all set on the pedestal of a long neck. She stood five foot ten with a mane of strawberry-colored coily curls that bounced around her shoulders like bunnies on a hillock. Caribbean-blue eyes were set perfectly symmetrical on a vibrant face. Kate McCann turned heads. She could be a model, not any model, a supermodel, like Twiggy whose pencil-shaped body was still emulated ten years beyond her contagious, androgynous runway slinks. All Kate needed to do now was grow two more inches.

Kate and DeeDee, her best friend since third grade, spent hours sprawled atop Kate's bed weekend afternoons turning the pages of the latest editions of *Teen* and *Seventeen* magazines.

Every fourth Saturday at twelve noon, as the Angelus donged from St. Basil's Church the girls raced to Becker's Pharmacy to buy the latest issues. Mr. Becker could set his watch by the jingling bells that bumped against the door when the girls pushed their way in. If Becker didn't have the girls' magazines set aside by noon they'd pester him by rooting around the store looking at and touching everything until he unwrapped his magazine delivery. It made sense to be ready for them and, like clockwork at twelve noon Kate and DeeDee plunked their two dollars and twenty cents on the counter and dashed for Kate's house to turn those magnificent pages.

After studying all the pictures and reading some of the copy, Kate would start practicing her model struts in the full length mirror that hung on the back of her bedroom door.

"Stop walking like a prostitute," the five-foot-two-with-no-hopes-of-becoming-a-model DeeDee would say. DeeDee's main job was to critique her best friend's poses and sometimes she couldn't help but be negative.

Although Kate never outgrew her five foot ten frame she packed all seventy inches of her magnetic field with runway swivels, wide toothy smiles and way too many hair tosses. DeeDee liked to remind her that her teeth were too long and her mouth much too wide for a modeling career but nothing deterred Kate.

She begged her mother for modeling lessons when she was fourteen and Connie eventually give in, reluctantly, handing over the thirty seven dollars and fifteen cents to enroll in Vincenzo's Modeling School downtown. Kate began to finesse her struts. Her hips and long legs learned to play off each other in a sexy wiggle but the Vincenzo School turned that wiggle into a respectable slink. Kate could now slink like a real model. She practiced her new strut all junior year which made the girls talk behind her back and the boys find solace in a bathroom after she walked by.

Her grandmother, Oona, wasn't very happy when she heard Kateri was auditioning for the Miss Moose title in the upcoming Loyal Order of the Moose beauty pageant.

"Connie," she would complain to her daughter, "do something about that girl. Modeling is all she ever thinks about. She's getting D's in everything except dance. She's heading for trouble."

Oona definitely saw how headstrong her oldest grandchild was. When Kateri was five Oona began telling her of her Mohawk heritage but Kateri didn't want to be Native American. Then, when she was seven, Kateri decided she didn't like the name Kateri anymore, she said it sounded too Indian.

"My name is Kate now," she announced one day. "Everybody has to call me Kate or I won't answer." She was true to her word and soon she was Kate.

When she was ten she discovered she was Irish and she loved being Irish. Everybody who was anybody in Turner Mills was Irish. She made Connie tell her all about her Irish father and when she learned her grandfather was the charismatic Judge McCann, her self-image became gargantuan.

Before the end of her senior year Miss Moose of 1982 eloped with Chucky Jiglowski, captain of the basketball team. He had caught scent of her pheromones in the hallways between classes and she was wild enough to take him up on the dare he had whispered into her mane as they passed in the corridor. "In the gym...boys' locker room...after team hours...I have a key" was what he said into her hair. Two or three trysts later, forget modeling, all Kate wanted was Chucky. Eloping sounded sexy, grown up and happy ever after. It was already too late when DeeDee ran to Kate's house to tell Mrs. Warner what was rumored in school.

Connie Warner was actually relieved with the news. This McCann child, this whirlwind, this poltergeist in a threshold of calm and obedient Warner children, had brought years of turbulence to her life. Daily, Kate reminded Connie *of the bastard*. Kate had Kip's ready smile, his loud mouth, his insolent wit and his penchant for mischievous fun. Worse yet, with her red mass of curls, her brilliant blue eyes and her long, slender frame, she was the spitting image of her Irish grandfather, The Judge, the asshole who days after Kateri's birth, orchestrated the divorce, gratis... no charge...and poof! Connie joined the growing legion of single moms.

There was nothing easy about raising this child. The high school graduation party Connie had been planning for Kate since April was turning into shambles. Now Connie didn't know whether the party should have a graduation motif or a wedding theme and she had already purchased paper plates with caps and gowns on them. Oona could only shake her head at her daughter's dilemma. She wondered how Connie's priorities had become so skewed.

Oona had her own dilemma. For the nine months Connie carried Kateri,

Oona thought she had shared an ethereal bond with this special fetus. She could swear they spoke to each other in feelings, a language Oona had almost forgotten, a Mohawk language. Together they had understood what it was like to be Kip, to be Mortimer, to be Connie, to be Margaret Mary, especially Margaret Mary for some weird reason. Together they seemed to comprehend the passions and frailties in the bonds that these people were forming.

Oona didn't get it. What had happened to the spiritual connection she was sure she was going to have with this grandchild. Why hadn't it continued outside the womb? How strange.

She gave it one last try. "Think about what you're doing," Oona begged Kate as the graduation party got underway. "What about your modeling career?" Oona continued to coax, hoping modeling might supersede this ridiculous marriage. But Kate would have none of it. Instead she turned to her guests and announced that she and Chucky had secretly eloped. None of this was news to the people on the porch, especially her aunts, who had been on the phone with each other since the news hit the grapevine.

"Kate!" Oona pled taking hold of Kate's shoulders as if to shake some sense into her. "Look at me! Look into my eyes. Look into my spirit. Concentrate. What do you see?"

"I see you Oona," Kate had laughed, putting her arms around Oona, swooping her into a dance. The boom box on the porch rail was playing Kate's favorite group, *Foreigner.* She tossed her hair back and belted out the song in unison with the radio. *I want to know what love is. I want you to show me.* "Get it, Oona? I want to know what love is and I'm going to find it with Chucky. He wants to go to California for our honeymoon," Kate bubbled on. "Chucky has a cousin there. Santa Cruz. I'll write you from Santa Cruz. Promise. I love you." She twirled her grandmother away and continued dancing by herself.

Oona's heart sank. Kate hadn't felt the vaguest communion with the Mohawk spirit. "All's lost," she murmured and headed inside just as Chucky pulled into the yard.

"Hey, Grandma," he boomed as he popped out of the new red Honda CR-X his grandfather had just co-signed for him. The gullible elder Mr. Jiglowski thought Chucky was going to keep clerking at the family's athletic shoe store after graduation. He should have known better. Chucky was going to be *outta here* as fast as Grandpa's signature dried on the loan papers.

He leapt to the porch and finished the dance Kate had started with her grandmother. "Ta Da!" Chucky beamed using the sweep of his arm as a pointer to the CR-X he had just parked so obnoxiously in the middle of the Warner lawn when he couldn't find parking on the street. Oona felt like saying "I'm not your Grandma," but instead she waved without turning.

"Know what this means, darlin'?" he was saying to Kate, "we can leave tomorrow if we want, on our honeymoon. What do you say? Tomorrow?"

Kate hadn't thought about tomorrow. They'd been married almost three weeks according to the license Chuck carried in his wallet proving he had won the voluptuous Kate McCann, although he was hard-pressed to describe married life since she still lived at home.

"Tomorrow? So soon?" She hadn't even counted the loot in the unopened graduation cards her aunts had just given her. Did she want to leave so soon? She gave it her usual ten seconds of thought which resulted in her usual unexamined approval of anything that smacked of adventure. Kate glanced at the car on the lawn with its tires just kissing her mother's newly planted begonias, then looked at her guy, hot and handsome. Tomorrow was as good a day as any.

The bombshell news of a California honeymoon put a chill on the party. Her aunts asked and re-asked, "Why leave so soon? We wanted to give you a shower. We wanted to celebrate." Disappointed, Oona found her sweater on the bed in Connie's room and left for home. Kate's sisters cried, except Janet who wanted Kate's room. Carl and Connie pretended they were okay with the plan. After all, they had done the same thing themselves, eloped twelve years ago.

Carl knocked on Kate's door as she was throwing things into her suitcase. He pulled an envelope out of his pocket with ten one hundred dollar bills in it. "I didn't realize our time together was going to end so abruptly," he said. "There are things I've wanted to talk about with you but the timing never seemed right."

Kate sat down on the edge of her bed wondering what was coming next. She thought he was going to scold her for eloping instead he followed up with words she could hardly believe. "I don't know if you know I love you," he began. "You've always been your mother's child. She kept you for her own. I couldn't break into your circle of love. I tried. In retrospect," he exhaled sadly, "I should have tried harder."

He told her how sad it made him feel to think the twelve years they spent together was coming to an end. "It just dawned on me," he added, "that I blew my opportunity to be more than 'Carl' to you." He said he wished he had known how to be 'Dad.'

Fumbling with words he tried again to explain how he felt. Kate had never heard him talk like this, certainly not talk about his feelings. "Your mom and I, both of us, we were parents together to the other girls," he continued, "but not to you. She was your only parent. I was excluded. Up until today I thought I was the one being left out. Now I'm realizing you were the excluded one. I had it all backwards. I'm so sorry Katie. I screwed up. I've watched from the sidelines as you became this fascinating, vivacious woman right under my nose. I want you to know," he added, "I've always loved you only I couldn't find a way to show you."

Kate's jaw dropped. Everything he had just said made perfect sense. She wondered if she had ever called him 'Dad' even once, and she couldn't think that she had. He was just Carl.

She thought about the times her three younger half-sisters were sliding off the back of the couch onto Carl's stomach while he tried to watch his favorite TV shows. She could still hear them giggling as they crawled all over his body tumbling to the floor when he lifted his giant legs or when he snatched one of them with his strong arms and tossed her into the others. She remembered thinking that if she joined them, if all four of them had worked together, they could have strapped down their Gulliver and handily conquered him but not once did she climb on the arm of the couch to try. He was theirs.

"Well," Carl said, trying to think what to do next, "that's all I really came in here to say...and to give you this safety net." He handed her the envelope.

By now they both had tears in their eyes. "Is it too late?" she asked as she got up to give him a hug.

"For what?" he responded.

"To call you Dad?"

"It's never too late," he replied. "I take that back. Sometimes it is but not this time." Then he reminded her to be safe and to let him know if Chucky didn't treat her right. He said all the right things dads say when a daughter leaves home.

THE ROAD TRIP

The first fourteen hours of the road trip were the best fourteen hours of Kate's life. Between Turner Mills and Chicago they yelled over the blare of the car radio about California, their mecca, how they couldn't wait to see the waves crashing on the coast, walk through the redwoods, learn to surf. They reminded each other of how stifling and boring life had been in Turner Mills, how glad they were to be 'outta there.'

They talked of their dreams. Kate could model or become a movie star. Chucky said if they liked California enough to stay he might go to UC something or other and get on the basketball team, become a star, make the NBA. Opportunity seemed endless.

"How much money did you bring?" he nonchalantly asked. She pretended she didn't hear. He asked again.

"Two hundred," she lied, "how about you?"

"My folks gave me five," he replied.

Five what? she wondered. Five dollars? Five hundred? She hoped it was five thousand but he was from the Fourth Ward so she doubted it.

The next leg of the trip was Chicago to Reno. It was an entirely different view and viewpoint. Wheat, wheat and more wheat blurred past the car window except for the interruption of corn. Too much sameness, they were grumpy.

Grumpy because they'd been up most the night. They had made so much racket in the motel room the manager called to say "keep it down in there."

They laughed hysterically imagining the old fogies in the room next door with their ears pressed to the common wall, amazed or perhaps disgusted. "What they could learn from us!" they bragged and buried their laughter into their pillows. As dawn peeked through the crack in the thermal drapes they finally fell sound asleep in each other's arms only to wake to the maid pounding on the door. It was already past check-out.

Chucky was amazed at how long it took Kate to get those curls of hers going in the right direction. He had thought they just stayed put, stayed perfect. He was already grouchy when she finally came out of the bathroom all perky, awaiting a compliment from him that wasn't forthcoming. "Cripes," he complained, "what takes you so long? Get in the car."

Pouting, she slammed the car door. "What's with *you?*" she sneered.

Eggs and coffee at an all-day breakfast joint a few miles into Day 2 cured the teens of their snarly-ness; the thrill of adventure renewed.

At first I-80 seemed exciting; straight westward and into blue skies. They were making good time, shouting woohoo! at each other every time Chucky dared to top 100 on the speedometer. But, jeeze, it got boring. With not much to see and nothing to do Kate's eyelids began to droop. Her mind wandered to the events of the past few weeks.

Her mother's face filled the daydream. Kate thought there'd be lots of tears as departure approached. There were some, but not lots. Connie seemed excited for Kate's new adventure, maybe even jealous. Kate wondered if her mother felt she'd been cheated by Kip McCann out of the adventure Kate was now having, but as they parted, Connie's vibe was you go girl and Kate felt it. She thought of herself and her mother as two peas in a pod. Together or apart they were attached by heartstrings, each being an extension of the other. Unlike the blues that came over Kate when she thought about leaving DeeDee behind, her heart went ba-boom when she thought of her mother. "Love you, Mama," she said in her daydream.

The thought about DeeDee spread a smile across Kate's dreamy face. Poor DeeDee. All that modeling stuff she had to put up with, then the time Henry Moore walked Dee home from school leaving Kate to follow behind and how jealous Kate felt. That was a new, unexpected feeling because Kate was usually the center of attention. She could still hear DeeDee warning "don't do it," when Kate told her about her trysts with Chucky. An overwhelming longing washed over Kate and she wondered why in the world she didn't realize this might be it for their friendship. Kate hadn't even called her to say goodbye.

Oona's review came up next. "What's with my grandmother?" Kate frowned. "She got all weird on me the last couple of days... I mean, staring into my eyes and grabbing me by the shoulders, what the heck was that all about, Oona," she said to Oona's image as the corn fields blurred by, "are you trying to tell me something?"

Suddenly her body jolted as if someone had slapped the back of her head or yanked on her ear. "What the hell was that?" Kate cried out, now wide-eyed. "Did we hit a pothole or what?"

"I didn't feel anything." Chucky replied as he looked in the rearview mirror. He couldn't see anything in the road behind them and he hadn't seen anything in the road ahead to avoid.

"Maybe it was an armadillo or something," he figured. "I probably squashed it."

"Hmmm," Kate responded, not convinced, still bewildered, "or did I just dream that?"

"Lunch time!" Chucky declared. "What do you want, Mickey D's or The King?"

"Whatever comes first," she replied.

"My turn to drive," she declared after lunch.

"Nah, I'm good," he said with authority.

The unending parade of wheat and corn and asphalt put Kate back in her trance. She fumbled through her purse for her lipstick. Her hand landed on Carl's envelope. "Damn," she said to herself, "I'm still calling him Carl."

Kate never missed not having a father. Her mother, Oona and Grandpap were the center of her universe, no father required. Fingering the envelope brought flashbacks of Carl, incidents that had gone totally unappreciated.

She thought of all the times she called her mother from the modeling school downtown to see if Carl would pick her up so she wouldn't have to take the bus home and miss dinner. He always came, even in five o'clock traffic.

"Mom," she'd say on other occasions, "the ski bus gets back at midnight, do you think Carl can pick me up in the school parking lot?" There'd be Carl sitting in the car with the defrosters blasting. She wondered now if she had even said thanks.

"The house party! Oh my God! How old was I? Fourteen? Fifteen?" she pondered. There was a rumor around school that some kid's parents were out of town and there'd be a party. The grapevine invitation was short: 12 Walnut Street, 2 bucks to get in. Saturday.

Teens she didn't even know showed up, so did the beer balls and she drank her two dollars' worth. Things started to get broken, cigarettes got dropped on the carpet. She sneaked upstairs and found the parents' room, luckily no one was using the bed. A pink princess phone sat on the nightstand. *This must be the mother's side,* she noticed thinking how acutely one becomes aware of things when one is trespassing. She kept an eye on the bedroom door as she picked up the receiver. "Carl," she whispered when she heard his voice. "I'm at this party and kids are getting drunk and things are getting broken. I'm scared."

"Where are you?" he asked. "Get outside. Now! Stay out of sight until you see the car. I'll be there in ten minutes."

Without so much as a scold he told Kate she had done the right thing calling him. He said he'd give her a pass this one time. "Don't do it again."

Connie was still at her pinochle club when they got home. For two days afterward Kate waited for the shoe to drop, for her mother to announce the punishment, the length of the grounding, the lecture. It never came. Carl never told.

Suddenly she pressed her foot to the floorboard of the Honda as if slamming the brakes on her thoughts. It wasn't the car she subconsciously was stopping, it was the infantile definition of her real 'Dad,' the one that she had conjured up as a child and tenaciously clung to until this very moment, the Hero Dad, the myth.

She had built a handsome knight out of the scraps of stories she had heard about the invisible man she always referred to as her real father. She thought she remembered a moment right after she was born, her mother was sobbing, telling Oona "Kip left me to become a Marine, a freakin' Marine, Mama, Special Forces, for God's sake!"

"How can I possibly remember that?" Kate challenged her memory. "I was an infant." Yet it seemed so real.

She had another crazy memory. In second grade Sister Thomas Aquinas told the class about Jesus. She said he was tall and handsome with soft eyes. She said he was the Son of God who cured the blind man and chased the 'fairies' out of the temple, gave food to the hungry and made sick people well again. Kate would draw pictures of Jesus. For reference she'd copy the Jesus whose portrait hung in front of her classroom above the clock but she didn't like his beard so she erased it from her drawing making her Jesus clean shaven. She then put a uniform on him and stars on his chest. "That's how a savior should look," she said pleased with herself, a man more like her father who was in Vietnam finding food for the children whose fathers were killed by 'gorillas.' She couldn't understand why her mother was so upset about a father who was fighting gorillas.

She folded her drawing in half, then in half again and again until she had a tiny wad that she could hide in the bottom of her dancing ballerina musical jewelry box. As she tucked it in she knew with her whole heart that she believed in her Dad Savior and would wait to the end of time for him to come home to her.

"I wonder if the drawing's still there," she mused when she thought of her silly idea to hide it from her mother. Then the obvious dawned on her and she couldn't believe her own stupidity. Carl had been a real dad all along and Kip, only an imaginary hero, "like an imaginary friend you're supposed to outgrow," she told herself.

Her eyes popped open and she scrutinized Chucky's face. "What's your dad like?" she blurted out.

"I hate my old man," he laughed without hesitation.

This was the first substantial thing she had learned about her new husband other than his proclivity for sex since the trip began.

"Did you know I have two dads?" she quickly diverted, not wanting to go where Chucky was heading.

"Figured as much," he replied, "you being a McCann and your mom being a Warner. How'd that go?"

She considered his question for half a second, "actually it went pretty well. The dad who loved me, Carl, is the nicest guy and I had a wonderful childhood." She winced as she said those last words because this realization had come as an epiphany just seconds ago. "My biological dad, Kip," she continued, "has long been my hero. Unfortunately he's imaginary. He left Mom a few days after I was born. But you know what's funny? I think I know him. I somehow think he knows me. I think we're destined to meet."

"You're not one of those clairvoyants, I hope," he replied.

She pondered his question as the cows and fences whirred by.

Des Moines, Omaha, Lincoln, more wheat, more wheat, more wheat. "I can't do this anymore," Kate bellowed scaring the bejeebers out of Chucky as she shifted in her seat. Her legs needed to walk or dance or hike, she said, or do something, anything. "Stop the car," she said jabbing his side with her finger then leaning into him, tossing a bunch of her curls into his face.

"Cut it out," he complained. "I'm trying to get as far as Cheyenne today."

She unfolded the map she had picked up at a rest stop. "Oh, God, Chucky," she whined, "look how far Cheyenne is. We'll be driving all night and then we won't be able to find a motel. Why Cheyenne? Why not here," she added, pointing to North Platte on the map.

The sun was getting low in the sky and blinding them. They pulled their visors down but somehow the sun was always where the visors didn't reach. North Platte was the next place on the map. The last time they had eaten was at a rest stop in Omaha. "Come on, Chucky," she begged, "let's get off at North Platte and see what that place is all about or I'm going to die of hunger or boredom and make your life miserable."

"Okay," he finally gave in.

"How cool is that?" Kate noted pointing toward Penny's, a 1950's diner straight ahead. "Let's do it." They both ordered meatloaf with mashed potatoes, gravy and peas. The menu declared it to be "just like Mom's" but it wasn't. While they waited for their order Kate went back to the kiosk at the door and perused ads for nearby attractions. She picked up one with information on the Union Pacific rail yards, wondering if that's all there was to do in North Platte. Another flyer caught her attention. "North Platte, Gateway to Mt. Rushmore and the Badlands."

She grabbed it with such haste she nearly toppled a senior citizen trying to manage his cane, his wallet and his exit from his booth. "Sorry, sorry," she said and hurried by. She slid into her own booth, pushing tightly to Chucky and kissing him on the cheek as if it were an exclamation point to the news she was about to disclose.

"Look at this! We're near Mt. Rushmore. I've always wanted to see Mt. Rushmore. *Always!* We read about Gutzon Borglum in 6th grade," she went on and on, "and how he started dynamiting parts of the mountain to carve faces of presidents into it. Let's do it! Let's take a side trip and see some of this country we're speeding through," she continued, reminding him they might never have another chance, ever!

To her surprise Chucky was not opposed. The next morning they headed north. Rushmore, Crazy Horse, the Badlands, herds of bison, Deadwood, Wild Bill Hitchcock, Calamity Jane, this was beginning to turn into a real honeymoon. They became enamored with the beauty of the landscapes they were exploring. No more waves of grain, just purple mountains majesties. They found streams to ford, woods to walk, hills to traverse. The grandeur of the western states elicited so much finger pointing that their index fingerprints were smudging up the windshield of the Honda.

The shards of sunlight piercing the steep ravines, the see-forever openness of the high plains, the starry expanse of the night sky combined to become one of their first truly shared and beloved experiences. A oneness was developing between them and they began to feel married.

"What about this?" Chucky asked handing her a flyer he had picked up describing the Battle of Little Bighorn at the Custer Battlefield National Monument. "It says we can walk the battlefield were General George Armstrong Custer and the 7th US Cavalry engaged the Lakota and Cheyenne, I want to do that," he added. "Do you know why?"

"Because you want me to visit my ancestors?" she laughed, not having a clue why that idea came into her head. She hadn't thought of her native-ness since that day when she was seven and told Oona and everyone else she was now Kate and not Kateri. She remembered a veil of sadness that came over her Oona's eyes with the announcement. She blinked a couple times to make the image go away.

"No, really, do you want to know why?" he persisted without addressing her response. "It's because when I was little I loved the US Cavalry," he excitedly told her.

"Toy soldiers," he rambled, giving her a glimpse into his childhood. Almost every day when he was six or seven, he explained, he played US Cavalry on his living room floor. He told her how he'd pull his shoebox full of plastic soldiers from his closet and spread them all over the living room. "I must have had five hundred little soldiers, some with long guns, some with bayonets and just as many Indians holding bows and arrows pointed to shoot into the hearts of the soldiers. He told how he'd place his Indians behind a mountain. "Well," he corrected, "behind one of my shoes," to ambush the Cavalry but the Cavalry always had an Indian scout on its side to warn them. He told her his play imagined all kinds of strategies and tactics for battle scenarios. "The US Cavalry always won," he added with a sense of triumph, "and that's how the US Cavalry preserved the United States of America," he concluded with a flourish. At least that's how he remembered it.

She remembered history differently. "Wasn't that Custer's last stand?" she said. "Didn't the Sioux win that one?"

"What's it matter?" he scoffed. "I want to see it," and they headed for Montana.

HAUNTED BY THE MASSACRE

They bought sandwiches-to-go at a corner gas station just outside the National Monument and turned into the battlefield. The road was flanked by tombstones of 7th Cavalry soldiers. Not a tree, not a shrub grew out of the steep grassy hills that encompassed them, except in the ravine where the Little Bighorn River meandered. They had expected to see a more dramatic landscape. They stopped to read some of the inscriptions on the weathered burial stones and Chucky wondered why there wasn't a Lakota or Cheyenne name among them. "That's odd," he remarked.

"It's because Native Americans bury their dead in sacred burial grounds. They took their beloved dead away from the battleground to bury them with reverence in order to send them on to the spirits properly," she responded. *How'd I know that?* she wondered.

A few other visitors to the park slowly wound their way along the battlefield's summit road and soon disappeared. Now alone on the ridge Kate suddenly cried out, "Stop. Stop here."

"Why? What do you see?" Chucky said goose necking in the direction she was looking.

"I don't see anything," she replied, "I feel something."

He pulled off the road onto the grass. "I feel something, too," he said, "hungry. This is as good a place as any to eat our sandwiches" and reached into the back of the Honda for the Cokes and subs. He spread the plastic bag for a blanket and popped open the cans of Coke. Kate sat on the grass, knees to her chin, staring into the ravine where the Little Bighorn River picked up glints of silver sparkles in the river's ripples, on an otherwise barren landscape.

The tree-line that followed the river's path was dense but she thought she could see little children running out into the open and frantic women darting out in panic pulling them back into the obscurity of the foliage.

Then she heard hooves, hundreds of pounding hooves reverberating through the ground. She turned and looked behind her. At first she saw the dust, then out of the dust, mounted men in grey emerged. She saw the flashes and then smelled the spent gunpowder. She turned back to the river. Pandemonium. Men on palominos, some with guns, most with bows were charging up from the ravine attempting to protect their women and children. She could see looks of horror on the women's faces and looks of resolve on the men's. The noise became thunderous. The green grass reddened. Chaos reigned. Her head pounded, she felt faint, sick to her stomach.

"Let's go," she said, "I have to get out of here. Now."

"Now?" he questioned. "This is a great place for a picnic. It's quiet and peaceful. Here's your Coke."

"Now!" she demanded in a voice that didn't even sound like Kate. "Didn't you feel that?" she added with tears rolling down her cheeks.

"ouOUou," he taunted imitating scary movie music.

Kate glared at him with a look that only wives can give their men and then got into the car slamming its door. Chucky wondered if he should finish his sandwich first. "Shit," he said and poured the Cokes into the grass.

They rode a half hour not speaking a word. Finally Chucky had to know and asked, "What was *that* all about? Back there."

Kate stared into the road ahead not even noticing the landscape had changed. Rolling hills had given way to the looming spires of the Rocky Mountains as the car pushed through the Bighorn Pass. She didn't notice the breathtaking overlooks that came with every S turn as they zigzagged their way to the summit. She couldn't stop thinking of what Oona had said at the graduation party: "Look at me, Kate, look into my spirit. Concentrate. Can't you see it?"

"That," she quietly replied, "was about my heritage."

"Huh?" he said but she didn't bother to answer.

She had seen it. She had seen the spirit her Oona had begged her to find, her native soul. She saw it while sitting on that ridge, knees tucked under her chin, waiting for her husband to unwrap the tuna subs. It came in the guise of a universal native memory, one where the Lakota and Cheyenne and other tribes of the Sioux Nation banded together determined never to be corralled onto reservations by the United States government. It came in the shouts of bravado, the blaze of gun powered exploding, the whoosh of arrows and the cries of anguish as warriors thundered around her, over her, and through her a hundred years ago.

As they drove farther and farther from the battlefield, the thundering hooves receded and she became introspective. Anxiety was beginning to be replaced by a sense of calming in this quadrant of the country. She couldn't quite put her finger on why she was feeling this way. Something seemed to be tugging at the heritage she had spent her whole life denying.

She pulled down the Honda's visor and looked into its mirror. A mass of red curls still framed her ocean blue eyes and ivory complexion. She leaned into the mirror for a closer look, peering, wondering if she could find a trace of Native American features in the image that peered back. She pulled her hair back. Nothing. She gave it a toothy smile. Nothing. Ah, she noted at last, the cheekbones. *Look at that will ya,* she said to herself letting her fingertips explore her bone structure. She questioned whether her paternal grandmother McCann, the one they called Margaret Mary, had high cheekbones like hers. She conjured up an ancient memory about this grandmother who was an only child of a Mayan woman and a United States colonel. She wished she knew more about her strange heritage. Where had she heard this story before? The memory was too vague; she couldn't retrieve it.

"I wonder what our kids will look like," she mused out loud.

"Like you I hope," he laughed. "At least they better look like you."

"Yeah," she laughed back, "I see your point. If they looked like you they'd have big heads, round faces, Polish noses and oh, yeah," she added, "thin lips." The thought of her having a brood of kids with big heads, round faces, Polish noses and thin lips made her snort with laughter.

"That's not what I meant," he retorted curling his lip.

"Is Chucky getting mad?" she jabbed and went on laughing.

"Allow me to finish," he said, "I hope they look like you...not like your grandmother or aunts." He wasn't laughing.

"And just what do you mean by that, Mr. Jiglowski?" she stiffened.

"Can you imagine me, Chucky Jiglowski, captain of the winningest basketball team in the history of our high school...me...with a houseful of Sacagaweas underfoot. What would people think when I'd pull up to the curb at the kids' school, the car door opens and a bunch of Indians jump out whooping 'bye Daddy, love ya Daddy.' No, no that'll never do. The kids have to look like you. Or me," he quickly added as he glanced into the rear view mirror and admired his teeth as if he expected a starburst to flash from an incisor.

Stunned, she began processing what he had just said. Her first thought was, *have I married a moron or worse, a bigot? Oh my God, what if I'm pregnant?*

Her Irish kicked in and in the split second it took to decide whether she should reach over and cuff Jiglowski on his big Polish head or slather him with expletives from her vast repertoire, she heard a voice in her head, or maybe voices, she couldn't tell. The voice called her by name. *Kateri.* She stopped short to listen, *Kateri, don't do it. Not here. Not now.*

"Kateri," she repeated under her breath. "Nobody knows I'm Kateri, nobody except..." She let her words drift into mid-air as her eyes considered the landscape they were passing through, dotted with houses that were few and far between, each with a pony or two in the yard, a propane tank toward the rear and a few old tires on the front lawn some holding flowers others just laying there becoming part of the landscape. A *reservation*, she concluded.

Did the voice mean she should beware a hot-headed husband on a desolate Wyoming road? Did it mean give the guy a chance to grow into his big head? Did it mean a spirit might be looking after her? Did she really hear a voice at all? Her head was spinning.

In that same split second the old Chucky was back, laughing and saying "April Fools, only kidding. Just wanted to see your reaction."

Miffed, she said it wasn't funny; he said her comments weren't funny either. "We were being stupid. I think we've been on the road too long. Our first fight," he said, "I'm glad it's over. Come on, give me a kiss, right here," he added, pointing to his cheek.

Not here, not now, replayed in her head so she leaned over, gave him a kiss...and a pass.

ONE THOUSAND DOLLARS

Reno, just after twilight, dazzled in lightbulbs. They entered the city under an arch proclaiming it to be the Biggest Little City in the World. Harrah's and Harold's and the Silver Dollar solicited their business with wiggling fingers of neon pointing to this door and that.

"So this is how the other half lives," Chucky whistled not having seen anything this opulent in his life. He was in a fine mood, suggesting they hurry to their room, put on their best stuff and head out for a night in this mecca of the rich and famous.

"I am hurrying," she called from the bathroom as he became annoyed at what could be taking her so long to put on a little black dress and a pair of heels. At last she opened the bathroom door and the most gorgeous woman he had ever seen stepped out. The only time he had seen her this beautiful was prom night when he strutted in a tux with the prettiest girl in the school clinging to him. Tonight was different. Tonight, standing there, framed by a chipped bathroom door jamb in a hotel with an exterior that promised more than its interior delivered, provocative in a short black sleeveless dress, towering in four inch heels, tempting with one tiny diamond barely visible on a gold chain seductively hanging at her décolletage, my God, he was proud. Chucky Jiglowski, make that Chuck Jiglowski, was going to turn heads tonight with this chick on his arm.

They stepped off the elevator more confident-appearing that either one of them felt. She looked older than eighteen in that little black dress, and, maybe with her on his arm, he, too, could pass for twenty one. They headed for the slots. No one gave them so much as a glance as they selected what they referred to as their lucky seats. A scantily dressed cocktail waitress handed them each a drink. Chucky tipped her generously, maybe too generously. He looked around to see if he had raised anyone's suspicion that he was under age. No glances came their way. They pulled a few one-arms and easily won a hundred bucks. Chucky was hooked. He wanted to move on to the roulette table. She wasn't so sure

"How are we going to collect our winnings?" he wondered.

"No problem," Kate said pulling a phony ID out of her purse.

"Where'd you get that?" he asked admiringly.

"I used to sneak into the Tomb when I was sixteen," she answered. "You needed ID to get in. I got myself an ID. I can't believe you don't have one."

"Coach kept us on the straight and narrow," he admitted. "You're my lucky charm," he added, "cash in those chips and I'll take you to dinner."

Two Kamikazes and a bottle of Mateus later, she pushed her chicken cordon bleu around her plate while he quickly downed his king portion prime rib with a couple of Coors. Her eyelids began to droop and a feeling of exhaustion overcame her. Nothing seemed more elegant at the moment than to crawl into bed in this fancy hotel. He, on the other hand, was stoked by his recent luck at the bandits. His foot was already hyper-tapping under the table, unwittingly pulling the white linen cloth and all its accoutrements ever closer to his lap. Anxiously he waited for the check to arrive. All he could think of was the roulette table he had yet to try.

He begged her to come with him, to be his lucky charm, but by now she could barely stay atop her four-inch heels. "I really need a nap," she slurred. "Give me an hour."

From the bank of elevators in the lobby he could see into the gaming room with its strobing lights and dinging bells. Casino, elevator, elevator, casino. Which way to go? He couldn't decide. "Damn," he finally shrugged as he reluctantly pressed the up arrow.

The hour nap she had promised seemed to take forever. He flushed the toilet a few times, called the front desk hoping his voice would wake her, turned up the TV and paced. Here he was pigeon-holed in a stuffy hotel room, bored out of his mind, while all that action was happening four floors beneath him. He opened his wallet to see what he had left. He had spent most of what he had but thought he might be able to parlay his last fifty bucks into a hundred. He was feeling lucky. He was sure he could.

Kate's purse was at the end of the bed. He remembered she came with two hundred bucks and he knew she had only paid for gas once or twice and bought a few postcards. We're married, he told himself, what's hers is mine and what's mine is hers. *Should I go through her purse?* he asked his conscience. *Should I take a hundred? I'll double it for sure.*

Kate was breathing heavy, out like a rock. The purse on the bed happened to be next to his hand. It was so tempting. His fingertips trembled as they intuitively knew they should never plunge into the dark abyss of a woman's purse yet his desire overrode the warning. He eased his whole hand into the forbidden cavity, poking around for something familiar, a wallet. Still quaking, his fingertips explored what seemed to be an envelope and he thought, a letter. Who's she communicating with? He pulled it out into the light thinking he should read it. It might be important for him to know its secret. It was important, indeed. It contained beautiful, brand new, unwrinkled US hundred dollar bills.

"Liar, liar, pants on fire," he whistled under his breath realizing he had found his bonanza. He peeled the bills off one another and concluded there were ten. Ten one hundred dollar bills. A thousand dollars. He fanned the bills and then fanned himself with them wondering what he was going to do next. Would he just put them back where he found them and at some other time coax her into admitting she had more money than she had said. Would he tell her what he had discovered and throw her against a wall for lying to him, a punishment he figured she deserved and now he could understand why his dad sometimes hit his mother. Would he shake her awake to confront her and make her confess to him about the truth she'd been keeping from him. Or. Or. Should he just take it, now, before she wakes up.

He looked at her, he looked at the clock. It was early. He inched his body off the bed, put on his loafers, and carefully, oh so carefully, undid the chain lock. He slipped out into the hall and without looking back began walking fast, almost running, to the elevator. Once inside the Otis he let out a sigh of relief. He was about to double their money. If he doubled it, they'd be rich and, he told himself, he'd put her thousand back into her envelope, nobody being the wiser. If he lost the thousand, well, he'd deal with that later.

Of course, he lost it...all except one hundred dollars.

Was the casino getting hotter or was it just him? His shirt was soaking up the perspiration that oozed out of his armpits. He could smell it. It smelled like loser. It smelled like big trouble. It smelled like divorce. Bells were still dinging for others at the one arm bandits, ladies were still blowing on their guys' die for luck at the tables and clinging to them as the men pulled stacks of chips toward their chests. Everyone was having a heyday. "Oh, God," Chucky exclaimed to the whirring room, "how could this happen?" He had felt so lucky tonight how could this be?

His pocket still bulged with one hundred dollars' worth of chips he had yet to bet. He needed to know whether it was a better idea to see if he could win back some of his losses or just take what was left and get out of there. As he pivoted toward the tables a best case scenario came to mind. He wiped the sweat from his brow with the back of his sleeve, ran his fingers through hair that was now soaking wet and headed for the cashier window.

"I want to cash these chips in," he said to the top of a bald head with the green visor that concealed a face. The man in the cage scooped the chips to his side of the window without looking up. "I want ten brand new ten dollar bills," Chucky instructed. That got the cashier's attention. He pushed his green visor further up his bald head to get a look at the idiot making such a request. "You think I'm the Bank of Nevada," he said, then mumbling, "you think I haven't heard this one before."

"What did you say?" Chucky asked through the glass. "Nothing," the cashier replied and handed him ten fairly new ten dollar bills.

Now all that stood between Chucky and divorce was figuring out a way to get the ten bills back into the envelope, back into the purse, without her noticing. He put the key in the door as silently as possible hoping Kate would still be asleep.

"Where the hell did you go?" she called out from the bathroom when the lock turned.

"You were zonked so I decided to see what the streets of Reno looked like."

"I'm not feeling so good," she called through the bathroom's door. "I'm going to barf. Again," she added.

"Can I do anything for you?" he solicited.

"No," she replied, "just let me get through this."

Where's the purse? Where's the purse? He frantically thought scanning the room. It wasn't on the bed where he left it. *There it is, on the floor. Did she notice the money gone? She couldn't have,* he correctly assured himself. *She's too drunk.*

He picked it up off the floor and this time, not so tenuously, plunged his hand into its black hole scooping out the envelope. As quietly as possible he slipped the ten tens into its opening. He tested the envelope to make sure it felt as thick as it had felt when it was full of hundreds. It did.

She surprised him by catching him holding her purse as she emerged, gaunt, from the bathroom and gave him a look that said what are you doing?

"It was on the floor," he said quickly, "I thought it might get kicked under the bed and we'd leave it behind tomorrow." Kate's handbag was never out of sight and she knew she would never have kicked it under the bed leaving it behind but she thought it sweet that he was concerned.

"You really look shitty," he said without malice, changing the subject. "I don't think we should go out tonight."

"I'm good with that," she replied still holding her gut. "We can stay in Reno one more night and go out on the town tomorrow. I won't have a thing to drink. I promise. I want to make it up to you."

He brushed off her idea as not necessary saying he was getting itchy to get to California. They were so close now, "just the other side of the Sierras. Besides," he told her, "Reno's no big deal, trust me." She climbed under the covers once more, glad it was settled.

Daylight did no favors for Reno. She, who had been such a seductive temptress under neon last night, was nothing more than an old lady by day. The Jiglowskis were amazed by the transformation. The town looked down on its luck. "Goodbye," sang Kate as they passed the END 30 MPH sign on the road out of town. "Good riddance," waved Chucky and meant it.

DESTINATION: SANTA CRUZ

The exuberance they felt on the first leg of their journey between home and Chicago returned with a passion as they twisted their way through the Sierras. They high-fived as the signposts proved their progress. A mere four hours more would have them on the coast.

From time to time Kate would unobtrusively slip her hand into her handbag. You doing okay? she'd telepath to the envelope that leaned on its lining. That's good she'd reassure herself. Chucky often caught the movement out of the corner of his eye wondering how the hell this thing that he had done was going to play out.

"When'd you talk to your cousin about our coming to California?" she asked as they neared Sacramento.

"Around graduation," he replied.

"Around graduation?" she shot back. "You didn't make a specific plan? Does he even know we're coming? I mean isn't that the whole point of our road trip? I thought you were going to ask them if we could stay with them for a bit."

"Yeah. Hub said he'd ask Phoebe and let me know."

"Did he?"

"Well, no, not exactly. I mean we left right after graduation and there wasn't time for all the details. I'll just have to call him."

"How about now," she insisted. "Call him from here. We have to know where we're staying tonight."

Will you chill out," he reprimanded. "They're expecting us. Trust me."

"Where do they live?"

"I told you, Santa Cruz."

"Like what street? What's the address?"

"Will you shut up!" he said with exasperation.

"Call. Call now, junior," she shot back.

He was not about to be pushed around by a woman, he told himself. He'd call when he was good and ready. Within the next few minutes he spotted a gas station with a pay phone. He decided he was good and ready. He dialed. Nobody picked up.

They called from every pay phone between Sacramento and Santa Cruz. Tensions mounted. Finally a woman picked up.

"Phoebe?" Chucky said, hopefully, into the receiver.

"Yeah," she replied hesitating as if she was deciding whether or not to hang up on the caller.

"It's me, Chucky."

"Who?"

"Chucky. I know we haven't met. I'm Hub's cousin. Hub's expecting us."

"I doubt that," Phoebe said as she stepped away from the phone. "Somebody for you," he heard as her voice trailed off. Chucky waited for what seemed like minutes before his cousin said, "Is that you, Ski? Where the hell are you?"

"The Safeway parking lot, at a payphone. Where the hell are you?"

"You're so close you could spit to here," Hub said with enthusiasm. "On Dufour. Come on over."

Dufour was only a few blocks down Mission, the main drag. They found it easily although the house confused them. For starters it was tiny, very tiny. Bewildered, Chucky looked from the house-door to what was once a one-car-garage door, now sealed off, and replaced by an insignificant man-door. Both doors had welcome mats. Both had doorbells. He decided Hub wouldn't be living in the garage, he'd be in the main house. They rang that bell.

A lean, fit, older woman with a singular salt and pepper braid came to the door. "Phoebe?" Chucky said extending his hand thinking Hub must have married a cougar.

"You must want the couple in my garage apartment," she pleasantly said pointing toward the man-door.

The man-door opened as she was speaking and Hub came roaring out with the clumsiness of a Bigfoot. He snatched Chucky from the ground and twice twirled him around, then began their secret handshake, an elaborate ritual ending in chest bumps, cuffs to the ears and high-fives before falling into each other's arms. All this falderal went on before they had even looked at each other's face. Having worn themselves out in the greeting, Hub suddenly took notice of the lithe sprite standing by. "And the pretty lady is?" Hub finally said.

"The pretty lady is Mrs. Chuck Jiglowski, first name is Kate," Chucky said puffing out his chest.

This was the first time she had heard her new name spoken so matter of factly and she didn't like it. It sounded choppy and foreign to her ears. Other women were keeping their own last names in marriage and she wondered why she hadn't thought of it. She had a pretty name, a model's name, an actress name, Kate McCann. She had always loved its ring.

Why did I agree to Jiglowski? she asked herself. She knew why. It was because of those basketball games when Chucky was the immortal one on the court. He had become the hero. Students had idolized him, teachers had bumped up his grades, the principal gave half days off after every tournament win and when the team took the trophy, March 30th was re-named Jiglowski Day.

She could still hear the yells thundering from the bleachers, "Ski! Ski! Ski!" It was more than a name now, it was a chant. "Ski! Ski! Ski!" It roared out of the mouths of hundreds of spectators. It shook the bleachers. It coursed through the maple floorboards. It electrified Chucky and he could bring down the house. The word Ski meant invincible. Kate flushed even now remembering him saying into her hair as they passed in the corridor between classes "I want you."

Hub's plump wife was now filling the welcome mat evaluating the situation, eyeing her husband's enthusiasm for the pretty lady. From the eyes in the back of his head that some husbands are known to develop, Hub could see Phoebe position her hands on her generous hips and could feel her hot breath scalding the back of his neck. He ignored the warning. With the sweep of a gesture he said, "Phoebe, honey, meet my cousin Ski and his wife.

"Well, don't just stand there, people," the gregarious Hub continued, "come on in." Phoebe had to quickly decide whether she'd hold her ground on the welcome mat and prevent the visitors from entering or move aside inviting trouble into her home. Too late. Hub took hold of her waist and directed her in. Kate and Chucky followed.

Kate's eyes grew huge as they surveyed the apartment; it was all one room with the exception of a ceiling to floor box, a partition, with a door that had two robes on hooks hanging from it. *The bathroom?* she guessed feeling her nose wrinkle in disbelief at the tiny jut in the otherwise rectangular space. The far wall pretended to be a kitchen with a stove, an old Kelvinator and a sink lined up in a row. A bed pushed against a wall occupied another corner while the dark brown velour couch with its large overstuffed arms prevented the front door from opening all the way. A TV squawked from the top of the highboy the couple shared. She hadn't noticed the old cat on the couch until it stretched out one leg and started to lick.

Hub threw the cat off the couch and with two beers in his hand, one for Ski and one for himself, told everybody to grab a seat. Chucky and Hub took the middle of the couch where they got into animated conversations about basketball, football drafts and who from the old neighborhood survived their youthful shenanigans. Kate had had enough and suggested it was getting late but Chucky, enjoying his beer and his cousin, took Kate by the wrist and pulled her down next to him into the depths of the brown velour. Her eyes watered and began to itch from the cat hair that took to the air. Phoebe was pissed and turned up the volume on the TV set.

"Come on, Chucky, let's go. We've stayed too long already," Kate said when the conversation allowed for an edgewise word.

"Well...well," Chucky said stumbling over his wells. He was confused by the mixed messages flying around the room. Kate was insisting on leaving. Hub seemed to want him to stay and Phoebe was downright rude concentrating on CHiPS, the TV program now filling the room with sound.

"I thought we were staying here for a bit...until we found a place...I mean, did I misinterpret your welcome, Hub?" Chucky said, finally realizing a few pleasantries on the phone with his cousin a few months back was not an invitation to an extended visit.

"Hubbb," Phoebe intoned putting a dramatic emphasis on the b as if the word had a dagger where an exclamation point should be. "Hubbb," she repeated sternly letting the word fall from her lips onto the floor, its meaning now occupying the entire room.

Now Hub was confused. His wife was giving him definite signals to end this reunion. He couldn't remember what he had said on the phone to Ski a few weeks ago. He thought he was just chit-chatting with his long lost cousin. Did "yeah, man, it'll be great to see you again," mean "come to my house, stay as long as you want, bring your new wife?" Apparently that was the interpretation.

Four pairs of eyes moved about the room, each pair sending a specific message. The eye noise was louder than the TV. One pair said *get me out of here,* one said *I thought we were invited*, another said *leave* and the fourth said *sorry*. Feet shuffled and the door mysteriously opened, it had to be Phoebe, she was the closest.

"Great seeing ya man."

"You, too."

"Call me when you get a place."

"Will do."

"Nice meeting you, Kate."

"Now what, asshole?" Kate said slamming the door to the Honda.

PLAN B

"Now we do Plan B."

"As if you have one," Kate countered.

"Plan B is Santa Cruz without Hub," he said.

"Plan B is Santa Cruz without Hub and without Kate," she warned.

"I have a plan for our immediate future," he was quick to reply. "We're going back to Safeway and buying ourselves some subs. Then we're taking them to the ocean, sitting on an outlook bench and enjoying every bite."

She was hungry. It would do.

Kate was beginning to think she would need the reserve she carried in the envelope in her handbag to get her out of what she was beginning to think of as her *situation*. When Chucky suggested they look for a motel room she asked what they had left, money-wise. He pulled out a twenty. Bypassing her envelope, she opened her wallet. "Eighty," she said.

"That's enough for tonight," he proclaimed with cheer. "We'll figure out tomorrow, tomorrow."

"I don't like living like this," she grumbled, "it's out of my comfort zone."

"I don't believe that for a second," he was quick to reply. "I mean how long did it take you to accept my invite to the boys' lockers? Ten seconds? Two seconds? How long did it take you to wiggle out of your panties? I thought you were a sport, a wild one, anything goes."

True, she did wiggle out of her panties pretty quickly, too quickly perhaps. That was the first and only wild and crazy thing she had ever done other than renounce her Mohawk-ness in front of her grandmother. For a short time after their trysts, spontaneity with sex pumped her with adrenalin. She had embraced her *bad girl*, liked the way it felt and thought it was permanent, *the new me* she called it.

Chucky licked the pickle brine from his right fingers having just scooped the last of the dills into his mouth and pulled a 'home rental' flyer out of his back pocket. He began reading in earnest. Kate stared out onto the Pacific and watched as a few evening lights began to flicker on in the hills of Monterey fifty miles away to the southwest. She was thinking of her options; her options, not necessarily their options. *At least I have options*, she told herself, adding *thank you Dad.*

"Here's one," Chucky announced, "cheap, too."

A room was available at Davenport Landing.

"Nine miles north," the voice at the other end of the line said, "go through Davenport, turn at the first left, we're the only house on the road, can't miss us." Now, at least, they had a place to stay.

"Who knows," Chucky said with optimism as they drove out Hwy 1, "we might love it there!" It wasn't as easy to find as the guy on the phone had suggested, besides it was pitch dark. The only house on the road was a swayback, old farmhouse framed by a toothless picket fence. Tilting white balustrades on the porch were draped with black carcasses.

"Spooky," said Kate, "it's probably haunted."

"Wouldn't that be fun," Chucky added, meaning it.

A shard of light broke out onto the porch silhouetting a figure in the doorway. "I see you found us. Come on up. Don't mind the wetsuits," he added noticing Kate's trepidation at the leggy blobs spanning the rails. "Awesome waves today."

A surfer house, Kate realized.

They were directed to small, dingy room in the back of the house. A mattress on the floor had a box spring beneath it which made it seem okay to Chucky. Kate knew better. Floor mattresses were guy things. *One night maybe*, she told herself, *I am not going to live like this.*

She pulled some of the dirty clothes out of her suitcase, things she had been wearing since the trip began and carefully spread them out on the bed exactly where her body was going to spend the night. *Chucky is not going to get some tonight*, she told herself with conviction, *not on this mattress.*

She could hear Chucky and Mike talking in the kitchen. They would settle things in the morning regarding the room....*how long do you think you'll be staying...do you surf or windsurf?* On and on.

Kate positioned herself on top of her dirty clothes and said to the ceiling, *oh Mama, if you could see me now. You'd have a cow if you only knew where I was putting my pretty red curls tonight.* What was taking Chucky so long? She really wanted to get this night over, wake up tomorrow and figure out what the hell she was doing with her life. Her eyes closed and she never even heard Chucky getting in beside her.

He was already in the kitchen having coffee with Mike when she inched her eyes open the next morning. She felt luxurious. This was the best sleep she had ever had. A blue Turkish towel tacked to the small sliding window ruined the reverie. *Oh, yeah,* she remembered, *the surfer house.*

A cat meowed at the door. She got up and opened it a crack. "You sleep here, too?" she asked the little black panther with its white puss-in-boots paws as it squeezed in through the crack. "Did I sleep in your space? Is this your bedroom?" she asked it, cooing. The cat liked being talked to and twirled around Kate's ankles as if they were best friends. They both got back into the bed and Lupita happily kneaded her claws into Kate's body. "Ouch," cried Kate throwing the little monster off the mattress. She was back in reality. *Should I throw him out, too?* she pondered tossing a head full of curls in the direction of the voice in the kitchen.

A female voice from the kitchen caught her attention. Maybe this house isn't a den of men surfers after all, and maybe the surfer boy they had met last night wasn't the equivalent of Hell's Angel. She popped a dirty tee shirt over her head and stepped out of the room into the kitchen.

"Hi, I'm Jenna," the voice Kate recognized from the bedroom called out as the tiny blonde extended her hand across an island that consumed the kitchen, happy to see another female.

"Kate. Kate McCann," she answered reaching out for Jenna's hand.

"Whoa there girlfriend," Chucky interrupted turning away from his surf conversation with Mike. "You used to be Kate McCann, now you're Mrs. Chuck Jiglowski, don't forget you're married." The two women looked at each other as if Rodney Dangerfield was in the room. "No respect," Kate mouthed to Jenna on the sly.

The blonde turned to Mike telling him her plans for the day. Apparently she was Mike's girl. The plans included a stop at the old Wrigley bubble gum factory on Mission. A casting crew was renting some space in the now defunct warehouse and holding auditions for some TV commercials, she informed him. She thought she'd try out, she said, before she drove over the hill to her real job. "Go for it, girl!" Mike enthusiastically replied leaning over the island to give her a smooch.

"What's on your agenda?" Jenna said turning to Kate, almost as an afterthought.

Kate had no agenda. She couldn't even tell you the name of the town she was in. If that wasn't bad enough, it sounded from the bits and pieces of conversation she was picking up from the boys, Mike was about to teach Chucky to surf. It seemed to Kate that she'd be hanging out with the cat. Jenna was already on the staircase leading to her room when she called back, "Hey, Kate, come with me to the audition, try out, it'll be fun. I'll drive you into Santa Cruz after. Chucky can pick you up later."

Jenna was truly beautiful Kate thought. Tiny, bronzed, blonde, dimpled, very California. Kate imagined all the girls trying out today would look exactly like her. California girls had a look, a good look that was clean, bubbly, wholesome. Chucky and Mike were busy talking wetsuits and boards. Kate now had a choice, the unknown with Jenna or the boring unknown watching Chucky avoid drowning.

"What time are you leaving?" Kate asked.

"In an hour," Jenna replied.

"I'll be ready," Kate called up the staircase.

Plans were taking form. Mike would take Chucky down to the cove and give him a few pointers. Kate would go with Jenna. After the audition, she'd drop Kate on Pacific Ave to check out downtown Santa Cruz. Chucky would meet her there at the bookstore at two and they'd go to lunch.

Kate fretted that she'd need more than an hour to get her mop of bed hair presentable. She'd have to work fast. She was not about to miss her ride to town and her opportunity to detach from Chucky for a few hours.

Jenna did a double take when Kate bounded off the porch toward the car parked along the fence. "What big hair you have, Grandmama," she laughed as Kate's red curls bounded into the car. Kate liked her a lot. As Jenna did a U-ee on Davenport Landing Road Kate got her first daytime glimpse at the little swayback farmhouse with its toothless fence from which she had just emerged.

"It's haunted, you know," Jenna offered glancing at Kate's face as Kate was observing the details of the decrepit little building.

"G'wan! How do you know?" Kate quickly replied.

"I don't know from personal experience," Jenna added. "The boys say they've seen her a few times. Not often."

"Her?"

"Yep. They talk about apparitions at breakfast some mornings but they are not too interested in ghosts. All they do is eat, drink, sleep and surf. Why? Does it scare you?"

"No," Kate answered truthfully, "somehow it interests me. I'd like to meet her."

"Well you probably won't," Jenna continued, "a lot of women have lived here with various guys over time and none of them have seen her. Mathilde likes men."

"Mathilde?" Kate laughed. "She has a name?"

"Not really. I think one of the guys started calling her that and it stuck. I don't really know."

"Hmmm," Kate mused.

As they drove, Jenna pointed out the Cash Store at the top of the hill on Hwy 1 and the few other shops that formed the heart of the little community of Davenport. Within minutes they were looking for a parking spot on Mission in front of the old Wrigley building.

The cavernous factory echoed their footfalls as they entered. Their eyes were adjusting to the darkness when they noticed a woman with piercings sitting at a long folding table strewn with forms and pencils. "Must be the sign in," Jenna remarked nudging Kate in that direction. They each picked up a pencil and started filling in the blanks.

"What commercials are we auditioning for?" Kate asked the young woman. The woman glanced up at them over a stud protruding from her eyebrow as if she'd been asked this same question a million times already and was not about to engage in small talk. "Wait over there," she pointed with her head. An area on her left was full of wannabes.

"I can't hang around that long," Jenna said as she scanned a section of the warehouse packed with would-be actors. "I'll be late for work. Sorry, Kate, let me know how it goes. See you back at the house."

An hour went by before Kate heard her name. "Kateri McCann."

She was slow to respond. *Did I write Kateri on that form?* she asked herself. *I can't believe I did that. I must have.* Her heels clipped on the concrete floor turning heads like a filly might in a barnful of stallions. A spotlight lighted the floor. This must be where they want me she decided because the rest of the space was so dark she couldn't see. She approached the lighted disk on the floor and stood there for what seemed an eternity. No one spoke. Nervous now she wondered if there was anybody in the abyss in front of her. Finally a male voice said, "Kateri?"

"Yes," she answered.

"Are you Irish?" it asked.

"Yes," she said again.

She was then asked to read a short script, walk the pretend stage, give a look of demur, now coy, now happy. "Can you be back here at ten tomorrow morning?" someone asked. She thought she overheard a muffled voice say she was perfect for the part.

"Sure," she said, "I can be here."

Kate stepped out of the cave into the sunshine. "Yes, yes, yes!" she told the guy painting the chain link fence next to the factory. "Yes, yes, yes!" she sang across the street to the lady coaxing a determined-to-stay-put poodle out of the car at the veterinary clinic.

Miss McCann, I do believe you have the part. I do believe you're going to be an actress! she announced to the sky tossing her hair with her hands and throwing her hips first left, then right, as if she had just stepped out of a limo at the Oscars. Sunlight caught her watchband and she looked at the time. Euphoria drained out of her. *Oh my God it's two o'clock. Where the hell am I? Where the hell is downtown Santa Cruz?* She knew Chucky would have a fit. That was another thing she had learned about her new husband...he didn't like to be inconvenienced. Suddenly she was in a hurry, wishing she had brought her sandals and a map.

TEN TENS

Downtown Santa Cruz was right-sized. A main shopping district that was not too big to stroll in an afternoon and not too small to carry designers like Lilly Pulitzer and Desigual. Shoppers popped in and out of eclectic boutiques or pressed their fingers to windows filled with lacy corsets, silk blouses, fishnet stockings and other objects of femininity spawned by Madonna. She walked past old men sitting at sidewalk cafes their hands cupped around mugs that were sending contrails of coffee steam into the air who seemed to be ogling the window-shopping UC Santa Cruz students milling about. It was well after three when Kate maneuvered herself around the college kids, the skateboarders carving paths between shoppers, and the chairs jutting out from the sidewalk cafes. Downtown Santa Cruz was a fun discovery.

A tiny flower market kiosk on the sidewalk in front of the bookstore elevated her spirits and she bought Chucky an enormous sunflower as an apology for her tardiness. She was sure he'd be right inside the door waiting for her as he didn't like books all that much. But he wasn't. The bookstore was huge with nooks and crannies everywhere. Surely he'd be in the magazine section. No Chucky. She increased her speed and her frenzy as she scurried around the bookstore looking in all the reading chairs and couches. No Chucky.

I'm late and he's mad, she decided, *I bet he's left me here to figure things out for myself.* Kate fumed as she plopped her body into a couch, mangling the sunflower, breaking its top heavy neck.

Shit. Now what? she ruminated. She pulled her handbag close, *thank God for you*, she said to the envelope in her purse, hugging it, patting it, petting it. *I think I'm going to need you sooner rather than later; I can't keep carrying you around like this,* she told the ten one hundred dollar bills inside. *I need to put you in a bank or at least hide you someplace in the room. If somebody swiped you I'd be up shit's creek,* she affectionately said to the envelope and she decided to take a peek at the babies inside. She hadn't looked at them directly since she left Turner Mills but knowing they were in her purse in all their glorious crispness filled her with a sense of security.

She cautiously pulled just the tips of her one hundred dollar bills out of their envelope in case somebody was eavesdropping. There they were, all ten, but wait, she remembered them being more crispy and new; the money she was handling now seemed flimsy and worn. She pulled them out a tad further. No extra zeros were hiding in the depths of the envelope. The number on each bill stopped at ten. She recounted. *Ten tens? How can that be? Where'd you go?* her inner voice panicked. *Who took you? Who stole you? Who? Who?*

She sunk deeper into the couch. Perspiration formed on her upper lip, her stomach flipped, the lights began to flicker and the couch closed in around her. *Where'd you go?* she agonized. *You've never been more than two feet from my body.* She began reviewing the past four weeks, meticulously going over the care she had given her purse. She knew she had it with her at all times, she never let it out of her sight. Not even once! Not for a minute! *Except...except for a few hours in Reno when I got sick.* Then she remembered. *Chucky had my purse in his hands in that hotel room, said he didn't want me to forget it. No! He wouldn't go through my purse. He just wouldn't it. Or would he?*

"Are you all right, Miss?" a voice belonging to a bookstore clerk was repeating. "We close at five. You need to check out." She looked at her watch, 4:55. 4:55 and no sign of the thieving bastard. What if he was outside waiting, should she haul off and change the shape of his broad Polish nose? Should she walk out of here and go straight to the police station? Would the cops even believe her? Should she find the Greyhound station and see where ten tens would take her?

Inconsolable, Kate pulled herself off the couch. The bookstore was closing, what should she do about Chucky? Which way to turn on Pacific?

"Oh, Miss," the clerk called chasing after her with a sunflower in hand, "you forgot this."

"No I didn't," she replied without turning, her heels making a resolute statement on the terrazzo floor.

The five o'clock sun blinded Kate as she emerged from the bookstore. *Now where?* she wondered, looking right and left. Earlier in the day she had peered into the elegant foyer of the Shalimar Hotel as she wandered the shops on Pacific. To get back to the Landing, if that's where she decided she was going to go, getting a cab at the Shalimar was probably her best bet. She turned left in its direction.

The Shalimar's uniformed bellhop was busy unloading the trunk of a Cadillac. Kate paused a minute hoping to catch his eye to ask if he'd get her a cab. But no, the bell hop was fawning over the elderly couple with scads of luggage emerging from its vacuous trunk, not unlike how a silk hankie gets pulled out of a magician's sleeve. Instead she pushed through the revolving door and stood a moment talking in the spectacular foyer...marble floors, crystal chandeliers dripping from ceilings and walls, stepped platforms with highly polished brass handrails leading travelers upward toward elegantly uniformed receptionists who stood sentinel behind black walnut counters handing out time-worn room keys on chunky brass plates. She had never been surrounded by such elegance. She thought the historic Rose Grove at home where senior prom was held was the most magical place on earth and she recalled how Cinderell-esque she felt in its grand ballroom. This place was even more magical. She was awed and at the same time intimidated. Turner Mills had not prepared her for California's opulence. Happy now that she didn't have on her sandals, she threw back her shoulders, tossed her red mane and clicked her heels toward the front desk like a movie star.

"Kateri," a voice rang out across the marbled room from the direction of a Victorian settee. "Kateri!" it rang again with no reaction from Kate. "McCann! Over here." She was so unused to her given name, Kateri, that she didn't even recognize it, McCann she recognized. She pivoted, lit up her smile just like Vincenzo's Modeling School had trained her to do and pretended she knew the guy who was bounding toward her with the widest smile on the tannest face she had ever seen. At first she thought it was the Marlboro Man but that seemed ridiculous. How would the Marlboro Man, whom she knew only from TV ads and billboards back home, know who she was. Then it struck her. It's the guy at the casting. The dark factory with its one spotlight had been so blinding earlier in the day when she approached the lighted disk on the factory floor that she couldn't possibly have known to whom the voice from the shadows of the bubblegum factory belonged...but this was that voice. She recognized it.

Scott Bainbridge had already transgressed her aura as if they were long lost friends. At first she thought she was going to get tackled or at least hugged by the handsome stranger skidding toward her.

"Are you staying at the hotel, too?" he was saying, breathless from his sprint and near crash. "I forgot," he was now apologizing, "you don't even know my name. I'm Scott Bainbridge, the casting director...from this afternoon."

"I'd know that sexy voice anywhere," she cooed thinking cooing wouldn't hurt her chances of getting the part, whatever the part was. "So," she said, "did I get the part?"

"You not only got the part," he blurted out, "you, my friend, are the new Dublin Aire Girl."

"I'm the new what!" Kate bellowed, her voice bouncing around the foyer turning heads in her direction. "The new Dublin Aire Girl? You've gotta be kidding!"

People nudged their companions, pointing and buzzing: "That's the new Dublin Aire girl." Kate leaned really close to Scott's ear and whispered, "What the hell's a Dublin Aire Girl?"

Scott laughed. "You did know you were trying out for a soap product commercial, didn't you? You must've! We've been blitzing the central coast with ads for casting calls for the past week." He looked around the lobby for a quiet spot to continue the conversation and not finding one said, "Do you have time for a drink?" then lightly touching her elbow he directed her toward the Candlelight Lounge. She went willingly.

Over cocktails she learned that Scott Bainbridge owned a casting company in LA. His new client, Dublin Aire Cosmetics, wanted a US presence to compete with Colgate Palmolive's wild success with Irish Spring soap. She learned he had decided to cast in Santa Cruz so he could avoid all the tiny 5 foot 2, blonde, bronzed, look-alike valley girls from Southern California who'd be auditioning. It was a fluke he said that he had found the old bubble gum factory in Santa Cruz available for short term rent without a lease. She also learned Scott Bainbridge liked central coast girls, "they're more outdoorsy, more natural, more authentic than LA girls." He needed a real girl for the Dublin Aire commercials, he added.

Here's what he learned about her: she was married.

"Oh, that," she said responding to his surveying of the ring on her finger. "It's temporary," she noted surprising even herself with the words that had recklessly slipped over her tongue.

"Temporary?" he questioned. "That's a new one. Want to talk about it?"

"No," she answered. "But I do want to talk about Dublin Aire."

She was picking the olive out of her martini when he said he'd order another round, but she hadn't eaten all day and didn't want to find herself in a repeat performance of her Reno experience. As she was declining the drink Scott was already coming up with a plan.

"Let's finish our conversation over dinner on the Wharf," he said "or do you have to get back, wherever back is."

She said she didn't have plans and sure, why not, she hadn't been to the wharf. "I've only been in Santa Cruz a day," she told him.

"And what a lucky day it was for me," he was telling her. He knew the minute she stepped into that spotlight that she was perfect for the part. He said he held his breath while she read the script. Perfect. Then held it again as he asked her to cross the makeshift stage. "My God, yes! Look how she owns the stage," he had whispered to his assistant.

"Where are you from?" he was now saying, positive it wasn't anywhere in California.

"Turner Mills," she replied, suddenly embarrassed by her nowhere-ness, "but enough about me, more about this Dublin Aire Girl gig, before the clock strikes midnight and I go back to being a small town girl...and to Chucky."

Chucky. The temporary husband had a name. Scott made a mental note as he launched into the job details. "We were looking for a girl exactly like you. Lots of red hair, impish, someone we could make seem Irish. And there you were, the complete package without need for any special effects. The Dublin Aire Girl has to be able to commit to a shooting schedule that will be happening over the next few weeks either in our studios in LA or outdoors in San Francisco. By the way," he interrupted himself, "are you available to work in either place? Can you promise a month?"

She leaned across the table, took his cheeks between her hands and planted a full lip kiss smack on his mouth. Then, because he looked so shocked, she let out a raucous roar that small town girls seem to do so well.

"I really wasn't expecting that!" he sputtered trying to compose himself, first by smoothing his hair and then by following the line of his unbuttoned collar with his index finger as if he was unloosening an imaginary tie. "I take that as a yes."

"Uh huh," she said, "that's how we say yes in Turner Mills!" she laughed, telling herself *ain't that the truth.*

He got back to the details. She was to return to the casting station tomorrow morning at ten where she would sign a contract. She'd be given the full script and they'd explain what was to be expected of the Dublin Aire Girl. If all went well, there might even be commercials in the future, a lot more work. If it didn't pan out, she'd be paid for the initial work.

"How much?" she asked. She had an amount in mind. She wanted ten new one hundred dollar bills. He said the job paid more than that. She said they could talk about that later but for now, to start, she needed ten new one hundred dollar bills.

That's quirky he thought but said, "okay."

He introduced her to oysters at Stegnaro's on the wharf. She trusted his recommendation and slurped one down, not bad. Surprising herself she took another, dousing it with cocktail sauce and horseradish. She ate more than her share of the dozen. Scott was an easy conversationalist and soon the sun was slipping behind Steamer's Cove. He suggested a walk on the beach after which he would drive her out to the Landing. She took off her heels and asked him if the Dublin Aire Girl walked in the water "like this..." she said, running ahead and twirling on the shore so her sundress fluffed out catching the orange shards of the setting sun and making her seem like a sea sprite. As far as Scott was concerned she was already the Dublin Aire Girl. He had nailed it.

GO. NOW.

It was after eleven when they pulled up in front of the house at the Landing. "Are you sure this is the place?" Scott asked as he surveyed the swayback house with its gapped-tooth picket fence.

"It's not as bad as it looks," she assured him. "The people we're staying with are awesome, they're surfers. I hope someone's up."

"I'll come in to be sure," Scott volunteered.

"Better not," she replied. "I'll be okay. See you at ten, thanks for the ride."

Scott could barely see her ascend the steps in the dark but then a beam of light popped as she opened the door and the Dublin Aire Girl disappeared behind it.

Chucky was waiting in the kitchen...and drunk. "Where the hell have you been?" he slurred. "I looked all over for you."

"Really?" she replied curling her lip. "Did you happen to look for me at the bookstore at two o'clock, where and when we were supposed to meet?"

"Yeah, well, I was late. Mike took me to Scott's Creek. He said I'm a natural. Damn I am good. You gotta come watch me surf tomorrow. Anyhow time got away. I thought you'd be good in the bookstore a few hours, you like to read. When I got there at six the bookstore was closed...so, where were you? More to the point, who were you with?"

Not sure what was going to happen between them next, Kate spotted a landline at the end of the counter and picked up the receiver. She turned her back to Chucky and dialed. The phone rang and rang and finally a groggy voice said hello.

"Mama, Mama," Kate bellowed into the receiver, "Mama, guess what?"

"Are you all right?" Connie's voice jumped out of its grogginess into panic mode at hearing her daughter's voice. It was 2 a.m.

This was the first time mother and daughter had talked since the day Kate left. Kate was ecstatic. Connie was relieved and she had news, too. "Your grandfather's dead," Connie blurted into the phone without any tenderness.

"Grandpap is dead?" Kate gasped as her back slid down the kitchen cabinet onto the floor. She clutched her knees close to her chest and tears welled in her eyes.

"No, not Grandpap. The Judge," Connie quickly recanted. "That grandfather."

"Oh him," Kate said without emotion. The only thing she knew about her Grandfather McCann is that he was the reason she's Irish and she liked being Irish. What the heck, it got her this TV commercial. Kate wanted to talk more about being the Dublin Aire Girl but Connie, harboring her hatred for The Judge, kept turning the conversation back to her bastard ex-husband and his despicable family. In the background Kate kept hearing Chucky say "get off the phone, you and I have something to settle."

On the other end of the line Connie was going on as if floodgates had been opened. She couldn't stop bitching about the McCanns. "Oh, and guess what?" she ranted, "your father, The Loser, is supposed to be somewhere in California. The family can't reach him. They've got The Judge on ice while they try. The paper says they'll hold off the burial in hopes of locating his son. Leave it to your father to disappear, even from them."

California was the only word Kate heard in her mother's diatribe. "My father's in California?" she said into the phone. "Where I wonder?"

Connie reiterated, "Nobody knows. Maybe he's living off the grid. That would be just like him. And one more thing," she continued, "Mr. Jiglowski, Chucky's grandfather, has been calling me trying to find out where you two are. He says Chucky didn't make the first car payment and the finance company is after him. Then he said I should pay half, after all, you ran off with their pride and joy. You know what I told him?" Connie joyfully ranted.

"I know what you told him, Mama, you told him to go to hell."

Connie laughed. "Damn right I told him." Just then the phone went dead. Chucky had pulled the wire out of the wall.

"I said," he slurred, "where were you tonight?"

She looked at the receiver, then at the line Chucky held in his hand. "Out," she retorted, "and now I'm going to bed."

He caught her by the shoulder and twisted her toward him. "I don't think you understand," he commanded. "I asked you where you've been."

"Ouch, you're hurting me," she barked. "Let go."

He spun her with such force she fell backwards hitting her head on the corner of the counter as she crumpled to the floor. She saw stars. She went black.

"Are you okay?" he was saying, shaking her gently. "I didn't mean to...oh, God, are you all right?"

She rubbed the back of her head and could feel the swelling emerge. It hurt. Violence was new to her. She was shocked by it as much as she was by the flaring pain.

"Let me kiss it," he was saying, "let me make it feel better. Please, honey, please."

She let him help her up. "I said I'm going to bed."

He continued to plea for forgiveness as she steadied herself against the hall wall and headed toward their room. She opened the bedroom door and the last thing she heard from the kitchen was another beer can popping open.

She was furious mostly because she needed her sleep. Tomorrow was going to be a make-it-or-break-it day for her new career as the Dublin Aire Girl. She needed to look fabulous and her head was killing her. She buried her face in the previously owned pillow that had come with the room hoping to ease the pain. It smelled like wet hair and not hers. She willed herself to sleep but it wouldn't come. Tossing and turning, she was getting more angry at her husband by the half hour until at last she finally dozed.

Somewhere between the time when she dozed off and an hour before dawn she thought she heard a whisper. Her subconscious began to concentrate on it. *What? What are you saying? I can't hear you.* She tried to memorize the exact words she heard. She thought she heard *now. Now it's time. Act now and don't look back. Go.*

Kate's eyes flew open and she looked around the room to see who was talking. It was so real she thought there had to be someone else in the room. "Who's there?" she said aloud. Nobody was there, nobody, not even Chucky. She couldn't fall back to sleep now even if she tried. Something had just happened and she didn't know what. She looked over to the other side of the mattress. Chucky hadn't come to bed.

She pulled the blanket off the bed and wrapped it around herself. She padded out of the bedroom to the sound of snores and tiptoed past Chucky dead drunk on the couch. The house was quiet, not a creature was stirring as Kate opened the front door and slipped out to the porch. In the moonlight she could make out the mess of plastic chairs on the porch and plucked one taking it to a spot where she could look out between the wet suits that hung perpetually on the railing to dry.

The dark air was laden with dew and she breathed it in filling her lungs with the Pacific Ocean. The heavy fog obliterated the farm land and fence across the road and tempered the sounds of the night. *Was I dreaming* she asked herself over and over *or did I really hear that voice?* It had sounded like Oona's but older. Oona had a lovely voice with a sonorous timber. This voice had that timber but it was raspy. *So it couldn't have been her* she convinced herself and tried to forget. But it kept coming back. It said *GO*, I'm sure of it she brooded.

Just then something cold and wet pushed against the bare foot that was sticking out of her blanket. Kate jumped out of the plastic chair, tipping it over. "Oh my God, a coyote!" she cried as her eyes landed on the mangy animal

"That's not a coyote, it's Eugene. He won't hurt you," a woman was saying. "I thought he was sniffing the pickets as he usually does," she added. "I didn't notice he had gone up on your porch."

An elderly woman with long grey hair falling below her shoulders and a remarkable unwrinkled face was approaching the porch passing through the narrow opening where a gate once might have swung.

"I'm Maddie," she offered. "I walk Eugene here every morning before daylight. It's my favorite time. I love the quiet. I love the dewy smell of the ocean air. So does Eugene, 'don't you Eugie?'" Eugene bounded off the porch and twisted himself around Maddie's ankles.

"Thank God," said Kate, "I thought I was a goner." Maddie apologized. Kate tipped her chair upright and began pulling another one out of the pile. "Will you sit a minute?" she offered the stranger. "I could use a visitor."

"No," said Maddie, "Eugene has his rituals. He's an old dog and you know what they say," she added with a twinkle. "Every morning at this time we walk the road to the Landing, run around the beach...well, Eugene runs around the beach, I sit on a log. Then we circle out the other end of the loop and go back home. But you're welcome to walk with us."

"I think I will. Let me get my shoes." Kate quietly slipped in and out of the house. "I needed a walk," Kate announced as she and Maddie took off, "but I've never taken one in the middle of the night."

"This isn't the middle of the night," laughed Maddie, "it's minutes before the crack of dawn, the best part of the day."

"I used to love to walk with my grandmother," Kate reminisced. "When I was little she walked me to kindergarten holding my hand. With my hand in hers I felt brave. It felt like it feels now, walking with you."

Maddie reached over and took Kate's hand. A shiver went up Kate's back. Maddie's hand was so soft and tender and true, exactly like Oona's. Maddie held on a few seconds then let go to pick up a stick for Eugene.

By the time they reached the log on the beach Kate was telling Maddie everything: Scott Bainbridge and the Dublin Aire opportunity, her rash marriage to Chucky, their trip west, the vision she had at Little Bighorn, the ten one hundred dollar bills, the bump on her head and the voice in the night that sounded so real. "I don't know what I'm supposed to do," Kate said at last. "I'm so confused." Tears popped out of her lids cooling as they rolled down her cheeks.

"Nineteen," Maddie said softly, remembering how it was to be nineteen. "You're on the young side of big decisions. Unfortunately they don't wait for us to be ready for them. Looks like this is your watershed moment. It doesn't get easier. Decisions are always difficult when you can't foresee the future. All you can do is make your best guess. Cry your heart out, child, tears are sacred medicine. Then do what you were born to do."

Kate unwrapped enough of her blanket to put a share over Maddie's shoulders. The two stayed cuddled on the log, quiet, one wondering how to console, one wanting consolation.

"Good heavens," Maddie said jumping up when she felt dawn beginning to warm her back. "I'm expected back at the house. I've got to go. Come on Eugie." The dog happily bound toward the loop in the road eager for his breakfast and a nap. "Don't let yesterday use up too much of today," Maddie said giving Kate a hand-up from the log.

"Thank you," Kate whispered catching Maddie in a hug that surprised them both. "Just when I needed my grandmother I found you. I'll set my clock and meet your tomorrow," she added buoyed by the feeling of connection. "We'll see," Maddie called back over her shoulder and she and Eugene headed toward the rest of their walk.

As she walked back to the house Kate considered Maddie's words: tears are sacred medicine. She thought about that for a while and then said aloud, "I already feel better. This is going to be a good day for you Kate McCann."

The house smelled of toast and coffee when she returned. People she hadn't seen before were congregating around the island and discussing the wind and the swell. She was quickly introduced to the tenants she hadn't yet met. Chucky was off the couch and embracing a huge mug of coffee. "Hi Hon, where've you been?" he asked sweetly in front of the others.

"I couldn't sleep," she said just as sweetly, "so I walked down to the Landing. By the way, Chucky, I need the car for a couple of hours this morning. They've called me back for a second audition."

Chucky wasn't sure how he felt about his wife's demand for the car. He doubted she was a contender for the part. *No,* he thought to himself, *I'm not going to give up the car. Not today, not when I'm getting in tight with these guys.* "You know, Hon..." he started to say and she knew what was coming. Kate put everything she had into a leer she drilled into his eyes then lifted her hand and slowly but pointedly massaged the swelling on her head. He hesitated. "On second thought, take the car. If you get the job at least we'll have an income. It'll give us a cushion until we can figure out whether we'll be staying here in Santa Cruz or moving on. What time do you think you'll be back?" Kate, already on her way to the room, gave a wave with the back of her hand that told him nothing.

Chucky was pissed. Guys were already grabbing their wetsuits off the porch railing, their gear was already in their trucks. Nobody was saying, "Hey, Chuck, grab a board." Surfing was not a team sport, every man for himself.

"How the hell am I going to get to Scott's Creek," he brooded. He had already figured why Mike had been so generous with the loan of a wetsuit...it had let in the cold Pacific, it was junk, and the board Mike had resurrected from the stockpile of beat-out boards in the back of the yard, a no man's land of surfer flotsam, it, too, had been scrapped. Chucky realized he needed his own equipment and his own ride to Scott's or Steamer's or wherever the boys who studied the wind and waves were headed. And now she wanted the car, his car.

The house had already emptied when Kate stepped out of their dingy room looking like a Disney princess. Chucky was always awed when she metamorphosed like this into a Belle or an Arial. He had no clue how she could do that. He whistled as she approached thinking he was going to be delighted with a kiss, instead she asked for the keys. “Bitch,” he said as the door closed behind her. “Free,” she said as she put the key in the ignition.

The casting crew was packing equipment into the van when Kate pulled up. Scott was standing in the one ray of sunlight that penetrated the vacuous building. *He looks like a god in the ray* she mused. She studied him for a few seconds before turning off the engine. *This is my lucky day* she told herself.

He, too, was watching, waiting. One long bare leg then another materialized from the red Honda. He was enjoying her unfurling. Suddenly a gust of wind caught her mane as a mass of red curls spilled out over the roofline of the Honda. She could hear him laughing as she tried to control the tangle she had so carefully tamed into curls an hour ago. *She looks like a goddess* he told himself as he hurried to rescue her from the wind.

He pulled a bank envelope out of his shirt pocket. “For you,” he said as they entered the warehouse now empty except for a folding table with contracts on it. “Accept this,” he said handing her the envelope, “and sign that,” he added, pointing to a contract with her name on it, “and you’re officially the Dublin Aire Girl.”

“Are there ten of them in here?” she asked with delight putting her nose to the envelope to smell its bouquet. “You’re not tricking me are you?”

“Just like you asked,” he replied, “ten new one hundred dollar bills. That is the strangest request I’ve ever had. There’s got to be story behind it,” he concluded fishing for an explanation.

“Someday,” she said, “someday I’ll tell you. Where do I sign?”

“Don’t you want to read it?” he asked incredulously.

“No,” she said.

“You’re a strange one, Kateri McCann,” he continued. “California girls would have their lawyers all over this contract.”

“Whatever’s in this contract is all right with me,” she resolved.

“Even if it says you have to get in your car right now and head for San Francisco because we start setting up the shoot tomorrow.”

“Oh, no, I can’t do that,” she laughed. “I don’t have a car. Rewrite the contract. Make it say I have to go with you. Now. In your car. To set up the shoot tomorrow in San Francisco."

Scott turned serious "Actually you don't have to be there for two days. Thursday, that's when we start working on the project. Are you saying you want to come with me, now, today?" His eyebrows went up as he looked at her over the rim of his glasses.

The voice last night had said to her *Go. Now.* This is what it must have meant.

It seemed to Scott that Kateri was making a split second decision but she had had a feeling ever since the road trip that she wouldn't be staying with Chucky forever. The only thing she didn't know was how long it was going to take to unravel. If she hadn't heard that dream voice last night, that *Go. Now.* she might not have had the courage to do what she was about to do. She thought of what Maddie said as dawn broke over Davenport Landing *don't let yesterday use up too much of today.* It all made sense. She would go, now, with Scott Bainbridge and not worry about yesterday.

"And I thought West Coast girls were wild and crazy," Scott was saying as he walked her to the Honda. Instead of getting in it, she locked it. "He'll find it," she said and reached under the fender for the Hide-a-Key box. "Where are you parked?" she went on as nonchalantly as if she were asking for a lift to the market.

"Is this how a marriage ends?" Scott asked as they buckled their seat belts in his BMW.

"I don't know," Kate answered thoughtfully, "I've never done this before."

They rode pensively into Santa Cruz to pick up Scott's things at the Shalamar, each wondering what had just happened. She pulled her purse to her lap and started rummaging through it for pen and a scrap of paper. She resurrected an old receipt, turned the blank side and tried to compose in her head a way to say goodbye. *Dear Chucky,* no, she thought, just Chuck...she wanted him to know she meant business. *Chuck,* she began again, *what I have to say hurts me as much as it will hurt you* but as the pen descended on the receipt she scribbled "the car key is in the Hide-a-Key, you know where. I'm leaving you. Sorry. PS you missed a car payment. Your grandfather's pissed. Kate McCann.

"Come up to the room while I make a few phone calls," Scott was saying as the valet hopped off his high seat to whisk the car away.

"No," she answered, "this Dublin Aire Girl needs to pick up a few things for the trip. Meet you in the lobby in an hour." Sure as hell she wasn't going to pack up her things at the Landing where Chucky would be waiting for his car, breathing fire.

Yet as confident as she sounded about her decision, her ankles were wobbling in her high heels and she was pretty sure it was the odor of armpits, her armpits, she was smelling as she crossed Pacific toward the Gap.

She didn't know how to think about walking out on a marriage. *I mean do you just walk out? Can you do that?* she asked herself between deep breaths. *Yes you can,* she replied, *you don't want to get shoved again, do you?*

"No!"

Then just walk out.

"Are you sure?"

Positive.

PART 3

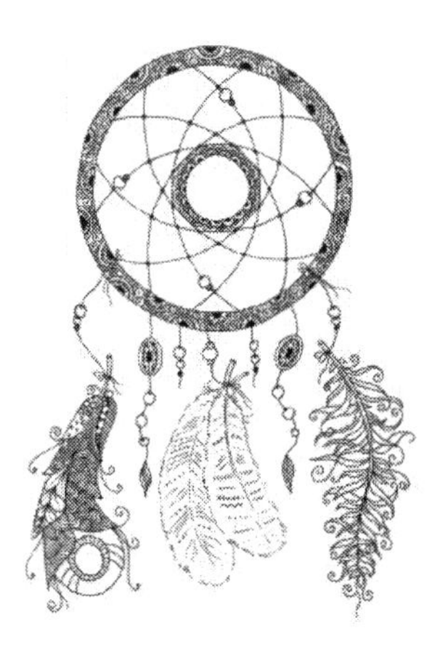

Give thanks for unknown blessings
for they are already on their way.

Native American saying

THE DUBLIN AIRE GIRL

The phone rang and rang in the Thompson house every time the commercial aired. Carl and the girls would lift the receiver and without saying hello call out, "Connie, it's for you," or "Mom, phone." Everyone Connie knew and many people she knew only because of friendly greetings Sunday mornings as she approached the steps of St. Basil's were calling to ask, "Is that your Kate on the Dublin Aire commercial?"

They wanted to know all the gossipy details. How Kate got into television? Does she know any important people? *My daughter's going out to Hollywood would you give me Kate's number?* A few even asked how much Kate was making.

Since Chucky Jiglowski was now back in Turner Mills and working in his grandfather's running shoe store, Kate and Chucky's relationship was also the talk of the town. Some folks implied Kate must be sleeping around. Whispers of *was she always this easy?* Or *did she just walk out on poor Chucky,* he deserves better, was often overheard in the supermarket as carts idled in the aisles. The grapevine inevitably went full circle as Connie got wind of the gossip.

"They're just jealous," she would tell Oona as she continued to fill friends and acquaintances with bit and pieces of news about Kate's good fortune. Oona would just shake her head, baffled by how easily her daughter and granddaughter had abandoned the spirit of their native roots.

Connie had to embellish most of the details of Kate's success because, truth be told, Kate didn't call home very often and when she did she always brought up Kip. "Did the McCanns find Kip's whereabouts in time for The Judge's funeral? Do you ever run into Margaret Mary?"

"What's *that* all about?" Connie would ask.

"I only have a minute," was Kate's pat answer, "I've got to be in make-up in two minutes, love ya, I'll call as soon as I can, we'll talk more then." Even as she hung up the receiver Connie would begin waiting for that next call, waiting for some news she could share with Turner Mills. Initially she dropped out of pinochle club thinking the call would come Wednesday evenings, then she stopped klatching with a neighbor Saturday mornings, waiting for the call, and finally she canceled her standing Friday night date with Carl at Cheesy's, in case that would be the moment Kate would call home.

Connie's consolation was the television. Kate would drop into the Thompson living room via soap commercials regularly. As least she could admire the screen and it seemed to Connie that her oldest daughter was even more beautiful on screen than in person.

Kate was no longer Kate. She had reclaimed Kateri. Bainbridge said it was a beautiful name and she should reinstate it. "It's unusual, more mysterious, more made for TV," he chatted as they wound their way up the coast road to her new life.

"It's Gaelic," she lied creating a version of her life that omitted any reference to her Mohawk heritage...and twinged.

The Dublin Aire Girl became the neighborhood celebrity in the Haight-Ashbury district where she now lived, and her fame fostered opportunities beyond her wildest dreams. At the neighborhood deli extra slices of roast beef got piled onto her sandwiches with a wink and a smile, and the surprise of a few extra tomatoes would tumble out of her bag from the farmers' market.

Scott came from LA most weekends and showed her the town. He wined her at the St. Francis and dined her atop the Mark, business meetings he called them. "Here's your next week's schedule. Did you get your passport yet?" He took for granted a standing invitation to stay the night at her place and waited somewhat impatiently for her to ask "come in for a nightcap?" He never once mentioned his wife and two children and she didn't ask although the little voice in her head that resembled a conscience kept dropping hints, especially when she found a receipt for tampons under the passenger seat of his car and the ruffle of a child's sock wedged into the upholstery in the back.

Every once in a while she imagined a tsk, tsk, a noise Oona used to make when she was not happy. Yet despite the tsk and the evidence, Kateri was not about to give up her weekend guy.

By the end of her first year as the Dublin Aire Girl she had banked more money than her mother made in five years at her job in the mall. Life was good. Kateri had scored an apartment in the up-and-coming Haight-Ashbury. The old Haight of the ’60’s had disappeared and was more a memory than a movement although it still had some vestiges of its former self. Hard rock and grunge still seeped out of the few music halls left standing and anyone could find weed or a cap if one knew where to look.

She scoured vintage shops to find pieces for a wardrobe that paid homage to the ‘60’s, floral frocks, Birkenstocks and Doc Martens began taking up space in her closet. “Born too late,” Kateri would lament as she’d follow the sound of fuzz from a heavy metal bass guitar and push through the door of a dive in her neighborhood. Even in grunge she looked gorgeous, although she never once let the stink of a dirty bar linger on her most outstanding feature, her mane.

The throwback wardrobe on this great looking chick caught the attention of the adrenaline pumping rock guitarists on stage. Every time a musician would slide to the edge of the stage in a frenzy of spit, sweat and music he would zero in on the jivin’ girl with the big, bouncing hair and intensify his pleasure and hers.

Meeting the boys in the band was becoming a passion for Kateri, looming high on her list of things to do before she died, higher even than making big bucks being photographed traipsing through green fields pretending to chase the scent of a man clad in white linen who had just bathed in a minty Irish soap.

Her resolve to juice up her life with rockers was facilitated by a thirty-year old named Cory, the bass player whose group, the Skids, commonly opened for the more popular bands that played the I-Beam those days. He’d watch from the wings as the leads would spot Kateri from the stage and play into *her eyes only* during the set. He’d watch as she danced by herself jumping to the music, while blowing kisses of admiration to the leads.

Each time Kateri showed up the club Cory’s hands would begin to sweat all over his strings; he could barely concentrate. As much as he stared into her eyes from the stage, she never looked his way. “That’s just how it is,” he told himself, “she’ll never know how I feel.”

One time in between sets Kateri did notice Cory. He was heading to the bar at the conclusion of his opener. She was looking right at him, coming directly his way. He turned to see if there was a more prominent musician behind him that she was about to engage. No. It was him. She was telling him her name and asking a question, "Would you do me a favor?" she was saying. He would do anything for her, he would go to the ends of the earth for her, he would marry her on the spot. "Sure," is all that came out.

The favor was could he get her backstage, after the gig that was now on stage, and introduce her to the lead. "Great!" she said, "I'll wait right here for you. By the way, what's your name?"

"Cory."

That's how it began. Every time Kateri went to the club, Cory would get her an introduction to the star performer after the last set. Often times Cory was left twirling his swizzle stick in his drink as she flashed her sparkle and left with the guy, her arm in his. The next time she would come to the club she'd give Cory the lowdown. "That guy was a jerk," she said on one occasion or "we closed every bar in town," on another.

A handbill in a smoke shop window announcing that Jerry Garcia was coming back to the Haight to "reminisce...for one night only" became a turning point. "Garcia! Here! In my neighborhood!" she squealed as she spun around the parking meter in delight. "I must've died and gone to heaven!" At that moment she vowed to quit her boring soap gig and get a real life.

Scott called. "Pack your bags, Sweetie, the brass wants you in Dublin."

"Ireland?" tumbled out of her mouth before she realized how dumb it sounded. He said she was to leave in two days.

"Can you be ready?" he said, adding he'd have a courier drop off the ticket "and when you get off the plane," he continued, "there'll be someone with a placard that has your name on it. That's your ride.

"Are you still there?" he was saying when she didn't respond. "Hello, hello"

"I'm thinking," she finally answered. She was hesitating, waiting, listening for the voice that comes at her crossroads, the one that says Go. Now. She couldn't hear it.

"Don't choke on me now," Scott was warning in a tone she hadn't heard before. "This is big. It could give you global recognition. We've done so well with Dublin Aire success here, corporate is thinking of putting me in charge of international marketing for the product line and you are the face of it. Did you get your passport like I asked?"

"Yes," followed by silence.

"What the hell is wrong with you?" Scott was demanding. "You signed a contract. Remember?"

She did remember but what did it say? She hadn't read it. Where, she wondered, did she put her copy. "There's something I need to tell you," she was yammering into the phone, finally blurting out, "I'm not going to Ireland. I'm quitting."

Scott was in LA so he couldn't do much more than swear and threaten into the receiver and he did both profusely. Not to be bullied she shot right back telling him he didn't own her. He said he'd see to it that she'd never find work in this town again and that his next call would be to his lawyer. She said she had met someone and her new beau was also a lawyer, "so there," she lied. When the call finally ended Kateri bolted to the box under the bed where she kept her papers hoping the contract was there. It was. The paper shook in her hands and she tried to read it, scanning, skimming, the words blending into each other until, at last, she came to the dates. "OMG," she whooped, "this contract has lapsed!" She didn't have to be the Dublin Aire Girl anymore. Legally. Then she started to shake all over, head to toe.

"Stop this," she scolded her quivering body. "Get a grip." But her body wouldn't stop. Her breath came in gasps as she tried to grab air, her heart started racing, her chest was now pounding. "Dear God, what's the matter with me. I'm having a heart attack!" Without thinking, hands trembling, she picked up the receiver of the Princess phone on the nightstand and dialed.

"Can I come over?" she cried into the phone. "I need to come over. I'm falling apart. I don't know what's wrong."

Cory opened the door to the mascara-stained unhappy face of a woman he might not have recognized had her red hair not been the giveaway. She didn't say a word, just grabbed him and hung on for dear life, her chin resting on the top of his head.

Oh God I'm short Cory said to himself as he held the sobbing woman. "It's okay, honey. It's okay," he kept repeating into her shoulder, inhaling the scent of Dune and thinking his knees might buckle out from under him in sheer ecstasy. He held her and held her and held her. It seemed like forever. He was in heaven. Eventually her body stopped shaking and she released her grip.

"You're such a good friend," she was now saying wiping a leftover tear. "I didn't know where to turn. I didn't know who to talk to. I saw my phone and I thought of you. I knew you'd know what to say," even though at this point he had said nothing but "it's okay, it's okay."

She explained everything...the mess she was in by quitting Dublin Aire, Scott Bainbridge and their weekend trysts and now his threats, she told him she had married her high school heart throb, Jiglowski, and how she upped and walked out on him in Santa Cruz, she told him she is such a fake making everyone think she was as Irish as St. Patrick. "I'm Indian, for chrissake." she blurted out and started crying again. Cory didn't care if she was Klingon. She was here, in his house, on his couch, without so much as an inch separating them.

Then it was over. She stood up, dusted herself off with the back of her hands and said, "Cory, I know exactly what I have to do. I have to go home, wash my face and go out and get a modeling job, I'm a model, that's what I was born to do and that's what I'm going to do now. Thank you for calming me down, for helping me think this through."

With that she plucked her handbag off the floor where she had dropped it in the doorway, blew him a kiss from the hall and told him he was the best. "I mean that Cory. You are a true gentleman. I've never met a man as nice as you except..."

The door closed behind her and he didn't catch who the exception was. He slumped into the couch. The ecstasy of her clinging to him, needing him, evaporated as he began to brood about who the exception might be.

"...except Carl," she was saying. "Dad."

When Kateri first walked through the door of Prestige Modeling on that fortuitous Monday five years ago she had no idea that this Prestige was the same Prestige out of Paris, the world's premiere modeling firm. Her timing was perfect. The universal look of the archetypical Parisienne model was giving sway to the look of multi-cultural heritage and Prestige was on top of the trend. Satellite offices had opened in Stockholm and Rio, Tokyo and Cape Town and now, this one in San Francisco. Kateri possessed the face and the form that Prestige was recruiting. She began getting calls for work immediately and now, because her closet was full of '60's vintage, she had to create a new style for herself on the fly, one that showed more breast, more leg, definitely more skin than the style she had when she was buried in gingham as the Dublin Aire Girl.

What she liked best about modeling was that every job was different. The scenes changed, the clients changed, her look changed. One day she'd be the femme fatale in a Valentine's Day matching bra and panties ad, the next day a teenager whose acne had vanished, or perhaps a forty year old whose newly dyed hair was now incredibly voluminous. But there was one call that caught the breath in her throat. An environmental firm needed a model to portray a Native American and had picked her photo from the portfolios.

"I don't see how anybody could read Native American in these shots," she complained to her agent as she flipped through the pictures in her portfolio. "Do I look native to you?"

"Hmm," the agent replied. "You certainly have a look that goes many ways. You possibly could pass for native. That's why you work for us. We represent models that can do it all."

Kateri's favorite shoots were for expensive perfumes and luxury cars, especially when clients would put her in gowns of gold that fell like soft seductions from her shoulders to the very small of her back with nothing to stop the viewer from wanting to follow the line of her vertebrae with the faint touch of a finger. Without even showing her face she could make love to the camera.

She called Cory once to tell him she had just posed with a cheetah, "like this," she said into the phone, *grrrrr*. He shivered at the throaty sound of it and tried to make small talk to keep her on the line longer but without much success. She was always just on her way out the door.

Having Cory in her life during these exciting days was a godsend and convenience. He'd drop everything to take her to the airport when she called pleading breathlessly, saying she was running late. He'd pick up her mail and water her plants when a shoot would take her to New Orleans or Toronto.

"Paris!" she screamed into the phone at a volume so loud all he could hear was sssssss. "Tone it down," he interrupted, "I can't understand a word you're saying."

"I've been asked to be a runway model for the spring collections in Paris! Me! I can't believe it! Can you believe it!" She was throwing names like Versace, McQueen, Herrera, Loubouti and Choo at him. "Who?" he was asking.

"The guys who make fashion for the world." she went on and on. "The world's first glimpse of this year's designs will be on my bod. I'm so nervous I could die. Oh how I could use one of your hugs right now. You make me believe in myself. I wish you were here. I'm so happy."

"I'll come."

"You know I'd love to see you right now but I have a million things to do. I have to start packing, I leave next week. Would you be a dear and do me a favor? Pretty please. I need a ride to the airport at two next Thursday. Can you possibly take me? And would you pick up my mail? And water the plants?"

Of course he would take her to the airport and pick up her mail mail and water her plants. How could he not?

THE STORYTELLER

She might have been too busy for a hug from Cory but she found the time for a brew or two at Chief's on Fifth. Ever since she discovered this Irish pub a few months ago, it had become her new favorite hangout. She remembered feeling weird the first time she entered.

Heads turned when she walked in that day, voices stopped their cacophonous hum and the singer with the ukulele on whose sad lips a soulful lament was streaming trained his eyes on her from his perch on the stool in the far corner. She would have turned to make a quick getaway had the bartender not shoved a customer off the stool near the waitress stand telling him he'd been there long enough, then calling out to Kateri "here's a spot, he was just leaving, what can I get you?" They laugh now about how Tillie kicked the poor guy off his perch because of a sense of connection she had felt for the girl in the doorway but, strange as it may seem, Kateri had felt the connection as well and a friendship began. Tillie was a year older than Kateri and a grad student at SFU, "anthropology," she said all the while with an ear to the waitresses' drink orders and filling one glass after another with beer from a spigot as she talked with Kateri.

"You'll feel right at home here," she was saying, and Kateri was feeling it already. Tillie showed her around the room by nodding her head. "The singer is Seamus," she nodded toward the corner. "His specialty is dirges, God spare us. Every once in a while somebody will call out, 'hey Seamus, lighten up, we're trying to get festive here,' and the best he'll do is Billy Boy.

"Over there," she nodded toward a table where seven or eight boisterous men were keeping their waitress busy bringing more rounds, "they call themselves the Choir Boys, all from St. Cecelia's. They just think they're boys," Tillie was laughing.

"Yeah," Kateri agreed, "the beards and mustaches are a sure giveaway."

"And they probably haven't seen the inside of St. Cecilia's since their first communions," Tillie chortled.

"One of these days," Tillie was telling Kateri, "the Storyteller will stop in. He hasn't been here in a while so I don't know if he's still around or even still alive. If you like characters, you're going to love this guy."

"Storyteller?" Kateri responded, wide-eyed as if Tillie was unwrapping a surprise package with the promise of a treasure inside.

"Some old Vietnam vet. We call him the storyteller...hey, Jimmy," she called to the guy at the end of the bar, "what's Storyteller's real name?"

"King Cong," Jimmy said laughing, "or John Pat or something like that."

"Anyhow," Tillie continued, "he comes in once in a while and that's his perch." She pointed to the last bar stool before the bar made a 90-degree turn and continued toward the mirrored wall. "Whoever happens to be on the stool gives it up out of respect for the Storyteller," she continued, "and he climbs aboard as if he owns it. He regales everyone with tales about the clans of Ireland, going back hundreds of years. Next year when I have to do my thesis, I'm thinking of writing on the Kings of Ireland and picking his brain but I don't know if he really knows his stuff or is just high on weed. It's hard to tell these days."

Kateri hoped Storyteller would come in before she had to leave for Paris. He sounded like a character.

On Tuesday, a few nights before she was leaving for Paris, Kateri stopped at Chief's to say goodbye and that she'd be back asap, when she noticed the stranger on the last bar stool before it made the right angle turn.

"Is that him?" she whispered tugging Tillie's sleeve.

"That's him," Tillie answered, "King Cong. King because of the stories he tells of the ancient High Kings of Ireland, he knows all the stuff, and Cong because when he's not talking Irish ancestry, he's enthralling the boys with tales from the jungles of Vietnam. I was going to call you but I thought you'd be packing."

Some of the Choir Boys had already moved close to hear his stories. Tonight he was Cong. With his back to her, Kateri considered Cong's long silvery pony tail and how straight and silky it seemed to be. *Unusual,* she remembers thinking, *most old guys never take their baseball caps off hoping to corral the grey wires they call hair.* Curious, she decided to become part of his audience and dragged her bar stool toward the area now packed with Choir Boys. Everyone moved his seat a few inches right or left as she wedged her barstool in and soon Kateri had a front row seat.

It was difficult to tell if Storyteller noticed the pretty redhead's arrival because he never stopped, never even slowed his story, he was in his zone telling what it was like landing in Da Nang in '67 gung-ho to roust the commies. He mesmerized them with his tales of guerrilla warfare, dropping out of helicopters behind enemy lines, slogging through rice paddies with seventy-five pounds of gear on his back. "Special Forces are long on guts," he assured them.

He was excited now, re-living the day. His breaths began coming in short bursts. He and his listeners' hearts began pounding, the mark of a good storyteller. His words sent shivers throughout Kateri's body but something was wrong. His stories, through dramatic, were not what was giving her goosebumps. It had something to do with his voice. She couldn't put her finger on it but she knew she had heard it before and the more she concentrated, the more frustrated she became. She couldn't place it.

Then someone asked if he had been wounded in the war. He reached into the neck of his tee shirt and pulled out a chain on which hung two amulets.

"See these," he told the Boys as they craned to see what he was displaying, "these saved my life. I wear them all the time."

The necklace held his old dog tags and a two inch metal disk on which a peace symbol was inscribed. He was fingering them slowly between his thumb and index as if they were prayer beads. The peace medal was one his brother had given him as a good luck charm on the day he enlisted. It was dimpled. "Saved my life," he continued as he pointed to the round indent pockmarking the jewelry. It was impossible to see the small circular dent from where the Boys were sitting and Storyteller reluctantly pulled the chain over his head and slid it across the bar for closer inspection. It got handed around and when it was Kateri's turn to inspect, she cocked the dog tags toward the light to better read the inscription.

Squinting, she could barely read the worn words, John Patrick, and when she moved her thumb to see the rest of the tag she realized what had been bothering her. The word McCann appeared. John Patrick McCann. Could it possibly be the Kip McCann her mother always called *the bastard,* her real dad. She had to be sure.

"I'm Kateri," she said drilling her eyes into his but he wasn't looking or listening. Instead he was panicking, watching his amulets as they got passed around the bar. He felt naked without them and now this kid was handling them like she wasn't going to return them.

"I'm Kateri," she said again.

"Would you mind passing them back," he responded. "I need them back."

"Here you go, Kip," she said tossing the chain into the air toward his outstretched hand.

Kip. He had disowned that name a long time ago when his father...*Oh my God!* he heard his soul scream.

Kip. He wanted to cover his ears. *Kip.* He felt the word pierce his chest, like a bullet, like a close call in Nam. *Kip.* He'd been found after all these years of running from the Unforgivable Disgrace. His eyes shot up from his amulet to hers and that's when he saw him, his father, The Judge, sitting there staring at him with her Solomon-like high forehead, her magistrative red hair, her adjudicating blue eyes. His soft brown eyes hardened as the flashback of his ostracization began to overwhelm him. The Judge, who had stolen his life, had returned to renew the curse.

They said he looked as if he had seen a ghost as they watched him back out of Chief's, tipping over a barstool in his escape. "I can't do this anymore. I just can't do this anymore," he muttered as he fumbled his way to the door.

Now she remembered the voice. *I just can't do this anymore. I can't do this anymore,* isn't that what she heard him say to Mom...the day he disappeared?

"Tillie. Tillie, help me," she cried out as a blackness filled her eyelids and her body crumpled to the dirty barroom floor.

The jovial drinkers stopped being jovial. Their revered King Cong had lost it. "Too much war talk" they said to each other. Quickly, as if they all had appointments elsewhere, they paid their tabs and emptied the room.

Kateri's face was now blackened by mascara rivulets as she tried, through sobs, to tell Tillie that King Cong or whoever he was pretending to be was her father.

"That bastard! He knew it was me. He knew it," she kept repeating. Tillie put her arm around Kateri's waist and guided her to a booth in the back. Kateri slid in and made a circle on the table with her arms then buried her head in them while Tillie searched for words to comfort her inconsolable friend.

"I believe you," Tillie was speaking so softly Kateri stopped sobbing in order to hear. She put her face into Kateri's mess of curls that now spilled onto the table and whispered into her hair. "Tears are sacred medicine." Kateri didn't stir, she completely stopped sobbing, she almost stopped breathing.

"I felt that when you tossed the chain back to Storyteller that a fuse had been lit and a bomb was about to go off, but it gets even stranger," Tillie was saying, "the bomb went off but it wasn't so much about you. I felt Storyteller disintegrate. It seemed to me in that instant when he and you locked eyes that all the glue holding him together for all these years, let go. It wasn't like an epiphany when at last he finds the beautiful daughter his seed has created and he realizes how wrong he had been and how punishing a God his father had been. No, it was as if he had been running from himself for so long all he could see was his father's face and all he could feel was the curse. It wasn't about you, Kateri, it was about his enemy within."

"How do you know this?" Kateri said lifting her head from the table.

"I don't know it," Tillie answered. "I feel it."

Tillie wanted Kateri to stay until her shift was over then drive her home but Kateri said no, she was fine, she needed to get home, pack, take her life to Europe where she was sure she'd forget what had happened tonight. She left the bar but didn't go home.

Cory was at the keyboard working on an arrangement for a musician friend when she knocked. He wasn't sure he even heard the faint rap or his name being whispered into the door frame. He could have been hearing things. Just in case it possibly might be her, he undid the short chain and turned the tumbler. There she stood, not unlike the first time she appeared in his doorway except tonight she looked even worse. She wasn't crying, she wasn't rushing into his arms, she wasn't talking, just standing there looking awful.

"I couldn't go home," she finally uttered. "I can't be alone." And finally, "I found him."

Him could only mean one thing.

"I'm so tired," she sobbed, "I just need to sleep. I just need to die. Please let me stay here. With you. Tonight." Without waiting for an answer she headed toward his bedroom.

A thousand thoughts ran through his head, not the least of which was how fortuitous it was he had gone to the laundromat earlier that day or she would have stepped all over his underwear on the way to his bed. She kicked off her shoes and fell onto his pillow. He grabbed the throw from his reading chair and, getting in next to her, wrapped her in it like a newborn and held her tight as a cocoon. With her back toward him, his nose was now in her hair, ah, her hair smelled so pretty. He held her so close her shivers became his shivers and her icy cold skin was thermally transferred. It was a long time before the shivers fell into a calmness and warmth and finally into an ease of breathing that let him know she had fallen asleep.

"If she only knew," he sighed and spent the night awake holding her tight.

PARIS

The modeling gig was only supposed to last three weeks, a month at most, but Kateri had become that 'new face, that not quite American, not quite European, perhaps more indigenous face' that every designer wanted to hire to showcase his wares. Three weeks in Paris became three months and three months became a small flat she bought in the Marais. She paid a small fortune for it but money was no longer an object. And she had met someone. He raced cars.

They had been dating less than three months when Alec Charpentier popped the question. His circle of friends, although much older than she, was incredibly exciting. Each was preoccupied with outdoing the other. They delighted in competing on every imaginable platform and celebrated their competitions with lavish dinner parties to which they wore tuxedos. Jean Paul owned a pharmaceutical company, Pierre owned a steamship line, Claude had several banks and sat on the boards of the most prestigious charities, Bisset probably had the most money (he was born to it). Alec, four times winner at LeMans, the most intrepid among them, had the youngest and undoubtedly the most beautiful soon-to-be wife. No wonder they were slapping old Alec on the back. He had just upstaged them all.

Kateri didn't know she had just become a trophy for Alec. He was charming, charismatic, handsome, thin, tan and confident. He was madly in love with poise, beauty and hair while she was sure he was in love with a nice middle class kid from a steel city who would adore him, give him pretty babies and do the forever wife. Yes, she was sure of it. She called her mother to tell her the news.

"He's a little older," she told Connie on the phone.

"By how much?" her mother wanted to know, concerned. "For God's sake! He's older than Carl!" her mother blared into the receiver..

"I've met Mr. Wonderful," she wrote in a note to Cory. "He's famous and rich, drives race cars."

"Since when was that important to you?" he tersely wrote back on a post-card depicting the Golden Gate Bridge.

She also called Tillie. "In some ways he's like a real father to me. And a lover. Does it get any better than that?"

"You don't marry your father, not even figuratively," Tillie warned in her reply.

Kateri laughingly told Alec their responses as she repeated the concerns from her friends and family.

Alec was 63. He said he didn't want Kateri to be surprised so he told her he had been married four times, and even though he couldn't remember the names of the last few kids he had fathered, he wasn't a scofflaw, he said, because he lavishly supported all of them, although his ex-es didn't always agree. Alec was fun, fast and enamored by her beauty. His honesty only re-inforced her love for him.

When Kateri told Alec her dream of going to Ireland to see the land of her McCann ancestors, Alec said that was a top-notch idea.

She winced at top-notch, thinking it was so old fashioned, like something Carl would say. Fleetingly Kateri pondered their age difference then decided top notch wasn't all that archaic. Coming from Alec it was cute.

For the trip, he said, he'd get his 1940 57C Bugatti out of storage, his prize possession, and have it shipped to Dublin. They'd run around Ireland in grand style. He told her he'd have his mechanic go over everything to make sure his baby, as he called it, was up for a big road trip, after all the car was over 40 years old and if it broke down parts would be impossible to find. He had babied this thing ever since he was lucky enough to find it in an old barn in the countryside on the outskirts of Paris. It wasn't cheap. The widow who had kept it in the barn for the twelve years since her husband passed, knew its worth even in its current condition. Alec had it restored and had only driven it to meets when the weather was perfect.

The prospect of taking his car on this tour put him in a state of exuberance. The two poured over a prospective itinerary, Alec looking at roadmaps while Kateri pinpointed cemeteries where McCanns might possibly be buried.

The Bugatti was buffed up and waiting for them when they arrived in Ireland. He covered his belt buckle with his jacket before hugging its hood and speaking softly to it. "We're going to find the McCanns," he told it, "it's all up to you. Don't let me down, baby." Kateri laughed as he whispered sweet nothings to this pretty piece of metal, then he opened the passenger door for her. She gingerly slid into this anachronism. She peered out the side window noticing her butt was just inches above the macadam. As he tenderly latched her door closed, she clutched its armrest hoping the door would stay shut as they drove through the narrow winding streets of Dublin toward the south towns of Ireland.

If she asked him to stop in a small town to investigate the names on the gravestones in the small cemeteries they passed, he'd say, "It's too nice of a day to waste in a decaying abbey cemetery" and he'd speed on. Yet when they stopped at a pub, which they did in each town, a crowd would gather around the car and soon learn that this was the Alec Charpentier from France. It helped that he wore his three-button baby-blue polo with the gold-threaded LeMans insignia sewn in. Alec knew how to play to a crowd.

As the Bugatti headed toward Crookhaven, the southwestern most point in Ireland, Alec gunned it as if it were LeMans all over again, the car leapt forward, unleashed, born to run. He laughed with glee at its eagerness to bolt and Kateri became giddy with its acceleration.

"What does that sign say?" Kateri asked pointing to a word in green calligraphy painted on the side of a yellow building as they approached Crookhaven. "Wait! You have to stop here," she suddenly demanded. "That word," she said pointing, "what does it mean?"

Alec stopped the car to see where she was pointing. He tried to pronounce the word: O'SUILLEABHAIN. He tried a few times, his tongue getting more twisted with each attempt, "must be Celtic," he said and quit trying but from his vantage point he could see the front of the building and the name of the establishment was over the door, it was a bar. "It says O'Sullivan's Irish Pub. O'Suilleabhain must be Celtic of O'Sullivan. Makes sense to me."

"That word, O'SUILLEABHAIN, just gave me goose bumps. Did it give you goose bumps?" Kateri said rubbing her arms, a chill rushing up them.

"No," he replied, "but what does give me goosebumps is you sitting here looking like you've just seen a ghost."

"Did you ever have a feeling that something you were seeing had some important meaning or message. I mean really important, something you shouldn't ignore and you are clueless, absolutely clueless as to what it should mean," she attempted to explain.

"No," he said, "unless you mean seeing a sign that says O'Sullivan's Pub and you suddenly get a subliminal message that tells you you're incredibly thirsty and the faster you can get inside the joint the better off you'll be."

Kateri pulled her point-and-shoot camera from her bag and said, "Be a dear and take my picture in front of this wall, make sure you get the whole sign in the shot. I want to remember this place and the feeling I got when I first saw it." She posed, he snapped, she shrugged, he offered his arm and they went inside.

She learned from the barkeeper that before the potato famine O'Sullivan's were all over this area between Cork and Kenmare. Some are buried in Goleen, he told her, others in Kenmare and those who managed to escape the famine by scraping up enough passage money, got on whatever ship was going west to the States.

"Those were real bad times," the barkeeper lamented, mopping the bar absent-mindedly around their drinks as if in reverie of the old days. The stories he was telling were stories that had been passed along for so many scores of years they no longer had any connection to him save the sod the pub stood on and the counter he had spent half a century mopping. "I keep the Celtic spelling on the side of my building," he added, "a nod to its history."

Kateri was still uneasy. Why did the name O'Sullivan interest her so? Why did the bartender mention the cemetery? Why did she have these strong feelings in this obscure place? And now this latest feeling, that she had to get to the cemetery in Kenmare.

"Hurry," she told Alec as his hands cupped around his half empty mug in a way that said he was getting used to this bar seat and becoming interested in the soccer game on the TV above the wine bottles.

"Finish it, let's go," she whispered wrapping her arms around his neck."

"Where to?" he asked coming back into the room from the mesmerization of the TV set.

"Kenmare," she answered. "Do you think your old jalopy can get us there before dark?"

"I'm so offended," he fawned, "Baby is not a jalopy. Please tell me we're not going to some old cemetery?" he winced.

"There's something I have to pay attention to," she replied, "a feeling that won't let go of me. So yes, we're going to some old cemetery."

"But all you and the barkeeper talked about were O'Sullivans. I thought we were looking for McCann's. Women," he mumbled to himself, "I just don't get them."

Alec really didn't care where they were going as long as they were speeding and stopping once in a while for ale. This was her dream and his holiday. He wasn't about to let weird feelings, old ghosts and lamenting bartenders complicate matters. Could he be at the Kenmare cemetery before dark?

"Get in, sit down, hang on, shut up," he bragged.

The cemetery wasn't on the main road and it took some time to find it. There was still enough daylight to read the headstones although dusk was setting in. Their toes were getting wet as the damp dew began seeping into their shoes. Alec would have much preferred the warm hearth of the pub he had noticed as they drove around Kenmare looking for cemeteries. "It's getting dark," he consoled himself, "this thing with the cemetery will end soon."

Mary, wife, 1822-1839 was etched next to *Seamus O'Suilleabhain, 1818-1860.* A small flat stone, barely visible in the sunken earth read *baby Daniel, cherished son, July 15, 1839-September 12, 1839.*

"Here," she said to Alec pulling the camera out once again, "take a picture." She positioned herself in the picture standing behind the stones. They walked around the cemetery for a few more minutes finding other O'Sullivan stones, each time pulling out her camera and having Alec take a picture. Finally it was too dark. They both felt the urgency to leave.

He was curious. "Why do you want photos of tombstones and why did you want to be in the pictures?"

"I don't know," she said.

As he drove back to the center of town Alec remembered exactly where he had seen the inn with the hearth. What luck, it was also a pub, not only could they get a Guinness but they could get cozy on the old couch in the lounge and toast their feet in the warmth of the stone hearth as well. There were rooms to be let on the second floor and they signed in as Mr. and Mrs. The crackling fire, the warm Guinness and the old timbered room was the perfect ending to a perfect day, they declared, and then they scuffed in their stocking feet up the narrow stairs, indented where many feet had gone before and they stayed the night.

The innkeeper's wife was a chatty woman who enjoyed travelers.

"They come in as strangers," she told Kateri the next morning over coffee at the bar, "and leave as friends." Mrs. Gannon was an in-your-face kind of busybody; Kateri could relate to that. Her mom, Connie, was like that, too. Connie could get anything out of Kateri even if Kateri was hell-bent on keeping some things private. The portly Mrs. Gannon reveled in the stories Kateri was telling, listening intently with her elbows on the bar, her chins in her hands, her eyes wide and round in enjoyment of the stranger's news.

Of course, the first thing she wanted to know, eyes twinkling in the mischief of the question, "is that gentleman you're with, the one with the fancy car, is that your father?"

"Yes," Kateri answered, playing to the mischief that was bubbling up between them.

"I thought so," said the innkeeper's wife, "he has your lying eyes."

"Do you have a problem with a young lass like me being engaged to such a handsome man?" Kateri smart-assed back flashing a large diamond ring under the older woman's nose.

"I'd be in hog heaven if my old man looked as good as yours," Mrs. Gannon replied taking Kateri's finger as if she could weigh the karats by holding the finger. "Is it real?"

The two women laughed as if they were old friends and found they could be as irreverent with each other as if they had been friends for ages. They were near hysterical comparing their *old men* and finally concluded their men had few similarities and that Kateri had probably gotten the better deal.

The scent of coffee that Mrs. Gannon was brewing while they teased each other began filling the room camouflaging the smell of spent embers from last night's fire. The two women were bonding.

"I've taken some great pictures on this trip," Kateri said, "do you mind if I pop my SD card in?" Kateri's head nodded toward the computer purring quietly at the end of the bar.

"Be my guest," Mrs. Gannon said pulling the computer toward Kateri as far as the cord would reach.

"Look at that!" she exclaimed pointing on the screen, "you've already been to Cork and O'Sullivan's on the Crook. You guys are certainly getting around."

The last few shots were in the old Kenmare cemetery. Mrs. Gannon noticed the smudge first. She stopped her running commentary. Kateri noticed it, too, but she thought it was dirt on the computer screen. She whisked her finger across the screen to see if she could wipe it away. No, it was in the picture.

"Let me see the next one," Mrs. Gannon said. There it was again, the smudge, only this time it was even more pronounced.

"I don't know what that's all about," Kateri said, "Maybe it's shadows from nearby trees, or Alec creating a shadow. I didn't see anything last night."

In the first picture the shadow was leaning into Kateri, rising from the ground to a height less than Kateri's mid arm. Part of the shadow's cloak-like extension covered Kateri's arm and shoulder bag. Kateri flipped back and forth between the cemetery photos. In the second photo the smudge was much larger, taller than Kateri, and wider with its own cloak-like extension wrapping around Kateri's shoulder and blending into the shorter smudge on the left.

"What the hell is that?" Kateri intoned, baffled, trying again to rub the smudges from the computer screen. Mrs. Gannon was uncommonly quiet.

"Why did you go to O'Sullivan's pub?" Mrs. Gannon quietly asked. "And why did you come to the Kenmare cemetery? And why did you have Alec take your picture in front of the O'Suilleabhain stone?"

"Because I remember the stories my mother told me about my father's family. I remember hearing the name O'Sullivan. I thought it would be fun to show my mom where my Irish grandmother might have come from. I was toying with my mom. You see, Margaret Mary O'Sullivan McCann was Mom's mother-in-law for all of fifteen seconds until the McCanns could get rid of us. Divorce. Oh, how Mom loathes that woman. I thought it would be funny to put the O'Sullivan name where she could appreciate it, on a tombstone. It's supposed to be a joke."

The convivial Mrs. Gannon was not as chirpy as she had been when the conversation was all small talk. She knew what she was looking at in those pictures and now had to decide whether to share what she had to say...or not.

"Has anyone ever contacted you before?" Mrs. Gannon asked gingerly.

"Contacted?" Kateri asked in bewilderment. "I don't know what you're talking about."

Mrs. Gannon was obviously in a dilemma. This wasn't the first time she was visited from the other side. If it was a gift, she hated it. In the past she was able to ignore the shadowy visitors. They were always fragile and she could easily make them disappear by hurrying to remind Mr. Gannon of something or another. They always vanished when Mr. Gannon came into view. Friendly as he was as an innkeeper, Mr. Gannon didn't suffer fools. Her talk of this enigma early on in their marriage had made him so angry he had shaken her by the shoulders threatening to put her out on the street if she dared to scare his patrons with that crazy talk.

He was right, of course, his patrons were all superstitious. They wouldn't walk under a ladder or cross the path of a black cat or, God forbid, break a mirror. Bad luck was everywhere Mr. Gannon told her, and he would not tolerate her inviting ghosts into their establishment with her crazy talk of visitors from the other side. "You keep your mouth shut, you understand me, woman." That was twenty six years ago and she hadn't uttered a word about them since. Today was different. She was overwhelmed with the urge to tell Kateri someone was trying to contact her.

The words had already begun sliding past her teeth. She could have easily stopped after blurting out "has anyone tried to contact you?" and Kateri would not have realized where this conversation was going. Mrs. Gannon could feel the cold underarm dampness beginning to saturate her blouse. She was going to do it. *Saints preserve me* she told herself.

"I think there's more to your pictures than you realize," she began. "You'll have to show me exactly where you were standing yesterday when you took your pictures."

"You want us to go to the cemetery? Now?" Kateri responded to Mrs. Gannon's strange request.

"It's now or never," Mrs. Gannon said pulling a jacket off the hook on the wall. "Mr. Gannon is in town getting supplies for the weekend and your Mr. Wonderful is probably having rashers and eggs at McPartlan's. I just saw him go in."

"Okay, let's do it," Kateri replied, her curiosity now at full tilt.

The two women were uncommonly silent on their ten-minute walk to Mt. Hope Cemetery, each wondering if this clandestine visit was a good idea. Mrs. Gannon hurried along in an uneasy step realizing this small act could put a set of circumstances into motion that might change her life and not in a good way. As for Kateri, although all her years of modeling prevented her from ever walking with trepidation or indecisive steps, she, too, was teetering with an uneasy feeling as the wrought iron gate of Mt Hope came into view.

VISITORS FROM THE OTHER SIDE

"The shadows in your pictures are from the other side," Mrs. Gannon started to explain, "someone wants to contact you. Now show me exactly where you were yesterday, maybe they're still here. Don't be afraid."

Kateri was not the least bit afraid. She had been having unexplainable other-worldly sensations ever since she stepped foot in Ireland. She was ready for an explanation, any explanation.

They hadn't gone but a few feet inside the cemetery gate when Mrs. Gannon tugged on Kateri's jacket. "They're here already. Let's find a spot where we can talk with them unnoticed. Over there," she pointed.

"They say they are your great-grandparents," she went on.

"I know," said Kateri, "I heard them."

Astonished, Mrs. Gannon peered at Kateri. "You can hear them, too?" she beamed. "Then I'm not crazy or weird or a witch? You really heard them? Prove it, what did they say?"

She wasn't looking at Mrs. Gannon now but at an evanescent figure on the cemetery landscape. "You said 'we are your great-grandparents,' " she repeated using exact words.

"Jesus, Mary and Joseph," said Mrs. Gannon, blessing herself three times.

Kateri was comfortable with the voices. She surmised she was talking to Oona's parents. It made perfect sense. Oona always had an aura of spiritualness and this wasn't the first time it had flashed across Kateri's mind that she might have inherited it. She could pinpoint it to the day she and Chucky were having lunch on the knoll at Little Bighorn when she visualized a replay of that awful battle.

"We're Margaret Mary's parents, John Patrick's grandparents," the voice was saying.

Kateri stiffened. She was no longer in the perceived warmth of Oona's people, she was in the enemy's camp, the McCann camp. Mrs. Gannon had stepped back wanting to leave the spirits for Kateri to handle but as she did Kateri grabbed her shoulder digging in with such force there would be no escaping the grip.

"You don't know us," the male voice continued, "you don't even know of us. That's the greatest travesty of my existence and the reason we have stayed so long in this intersect. Please don't run off."

Running off had crossed Kateri's mind but it would have put an end to this need to know that had been haunting her since the episode at Little Bighorn and even before that, she reminded herself. She flashed back to Oona taking her by the shoulders at her graduation party saying "look into my eyes, Kate, look into my spirit, concentrate, what do you see?" She winced now remembering she had pretended to Oona she didn't see anything but that was a lie, she had the inkling. Oona's quiet words that day were the invitation to Kateri's sacred side but it was no match for Chucky's spanking new car and hot young body.

There was one other thing. Something else that Kateri could never quite put her finger on. She had always felt she was part of a love affair yet she knew that couldn't be true. Chucky was her first encounter and she wouldn't call that steamy thing a *love* affair. *What was that memory?* she wondered. *Did she really remember the cooing of loving voices when she was part of a miracle. Did that miracle turn into an abomination? What horrible thing happened?* Or did she just imagine it.

The reverie ended. She was back in the moment. "I'm not going to run off," she told her great grandparents. "I want to know."

The woman spoke. "I'm A'mari, your great-grandmother. The Colonel and I had a wonderful love. Who would have thought that this dashing young soldier..." Kateri could feel the air move slightly and thought A'mari must be stroking his spirit as she spoke "...would fall in love with a poor Mayan. We met in the aftermath of the Spanish American War, in Cuba, and together we had a little girl. I never got to hold her, not even for a minute," A'mari said her voice disappearing in sadness.

"So here I am in tears," the Colonel picked up the story when A'mari couldn't go on, "a colonel in the US army, burying the love of my life while holding our newborn in my arms. I named our baby Margaret Mary, after my mother, it was the only name I could come up with at the time. Then I did the only thing I could think of. I took Margaret Mary to Poughkeepsie and asked my sister to take care of her while I disengaged from service.

"My sister spoiled her," he went on, "gave in to her every whim and by the time I was able to make a home for us, Margaret Mary was a most difficult child."

Kateri wondered what this story had to do with her.

"There's more," the Colonel went on.

"When she was six or seven I took Margaret Mary on a trip to A'mari's hometown in Cuba. I couldn't believe her reaction when she saw these wonderful people. She was so rude. She told me she didn't want to be Indian like *them,* pointing a finger from right to left across the faces of family who had gathered to welcome us. She said, "From now on, Daddy, I'm Irish. Like you."

Kateri gulped.

Their story continued. "Margaret Mary is an old woman now," A'mari said, "and even more entangled in the web of prejudice that she has spent her life weaving. Colonel wanted one more chance to talk with her. That's why we didn't move on. He has tried every way to reach her but she can't hear him. It's no use."

"I had all but given up," Colonel interrupted, "when we noticed that you and our grandson, John Patrick, were destined to cross paths in that bar in San Francisco. We plotted to interfere in your lives just enough for you two to recognize each other. We were so sure that when our grandson realized who you were and what a beautiful person this child of his has become, he would also realize that the sin with which my daughter and the Judge had cursed him was never his but theirs. We thought this might rescue him from the devils within. But he panicked and ran. We chased after him 'John Patrick, John Patrick' I cried until I was hoarse but it was no use. He couldn't hear."

While their story was unfolding Kateri had released the grip on Mrs. Gannon's shoulder and the older woman slowly and quietly stepped back until she thought it safe to turn and run. Tears began streaming down Kateri's cheeks.

"He couldn't get out of that bar fast enough," she told them, re-living the episode in the Chief's. "I know he recognized my face that night," she added, "and I recognized his voice."

She startled herself as she spoke those last words. It dawned on her that she recognized his voice but how could that be? She had never met her father.

"How *can* that be?" A'mari repeated her question. "You're talking with us right now and we're dead," she chided, "how can that be?" Kateri could hear the smile in her voice. A'mari went on, "relationships exist across time and space. There are no walls separating the living from the dead...or the unborn. Yet so few of us recognize the vast reach of our consciousness. You are one of the few."

The Colonel decided to shoulder her difficult question. He knew it did matter. She had been stoic all her life about missing her father. She deserved some kind of explanation. He attempted an answer.

"The voices you heard when John Patrick and Connie conceived you were the voices of love. Your mother and your father were truly in love, the kind of love A'mari and I have. Yet your parents' story ended as tragically as ours. Our love ended in A'mari's death giving birth to your grandmother, while your parents' love was crushed by prejudice, in that awful word...sin. It's a shame what we do to the ones we love in the name of love."

"Your father doesn't hate you," he went on. "He was only eighteen when you were conceived. What did he know of life except that he passionately adored Connie and that he trusted his parents. His parents unfortunately were so wrong. They told him his sin was so egregious that he had to be sent away to roam the earth and find his own path to forgiveness and to hide from the tongue wagging words, 'out of wedlock.'"

"At election time," A'mari coyly reminded him.

"I suspect it was more the tongue wagging that they couldn't endure," Colonel continued, "and your father can't forgive himself because, well, here you are, living proof of it. This awful sin that created you haunts his waking hours and even his dreams. Your father hates himself. He is lost."

A long silence passed before Kateri could say, "So am I." She held out her left hand and watched as the carats in her diamond ring threw speckles of color onto the leaves of the nearby elm. Pensively she told her great-grandparents, "I'm engaged." There was indecision in her voice and for the first time Kateri heard it. Hoping that spirits would know more than mere mortals, she hurried to ask her great-grandparents, "Should I marry Alec?"

"How should we know," they both answered, amused. "We're not prophets! All we've done is cross over. The only advantage we seem to have over mortals is we have a rich understanding of our personal history and have a strong sense of our spiritual side. Once you understand your own history, you can enrich the course your life takes."

"I could use some direction," Kateri admitted. "I don't want to get so lost I can't find my way back, like my father, yet it seems I'm always on the wrong path. How do you get to knowing yourself without having to, well, you know, cross over? No offense."

Her great grandfather thought for a moment and then said, "Be mindful."

Kateri frowned in a show of disappointment at his spartan response. She thought he could have come up with something more elucidating than: be mindful.

"You asked and we're telling," Colonel chastised in a grandfatherly voice. "Take it or leave it."

"But I am mindful," Kateri pouted. "I'm kind and I'm generous. I treat others as I would myself and I...I..." she searched her brain for more, "I recycle."

"I'll give you recycling," Colonel said. "When you decide to throw something in the blue box instead of the landfill you are definitely being mindful... about the earth. But that's the tip of the iceberg. Mindfulness is a way of life. If you choose it as your way of life you wouldn't have to ask us to prophesy whether or not you should marry Alec. You would know."

Kateri didn't see how this could possibly be true. "Is it true?" she asked looking to A'mari as if A'mari was the Guardian of Great Truth.

The great-grandparents looked at each other, distressed, as if they had just pried open and peeked into a Pandora's Box in which they saw a confused Kateri on the verge of spiritual knowledge but clueless on how to achieve it and realized they only had this one moment in all of eternity to make a difference in her journey.

Unfortunately," Colonel sighed, "we can't stay long enough to share with you the wisdom of the ages but," he added, "you will see we have many things in common with our journeys. We've been watching you run through your life chasing the dream of your father to no avail. Same for us. We've spent our eternity chasing after the dream of our daughter, with the same result.

"We had convinced ourselves that you, too, would probably flee from us if we made ourselves apparent. Quite frankly we are astonished you let Mrs. Gannon lead you to us."

"And thrilled," A'mari added. "By our being here today Colonel and I are released from our longing just as your finding us is about to change your journey going forward."

A breeze began to stir the leaves on the ground and swirl the two shapes into vagueness.

"Wait!" Kateri called, "don't go. Not yet. Give me something. Get me started. How do I begin?"

""Begin by recognizing and understanding what is actually happening in your life. Don't judge it, just see it. Be aware. Be aware. Answers will come."

The sun broke through a sky that had been speckled with clouds and made the landscape too bright to observe the shapes that defined the spirits of her great grandparents. Kateri could feel its warmth radiate through her jacket. She looked one last time at the surname inscribed on the tomb O'Suilleabhain then turned toward the gate. The sun stayed on her back gently nudging her toward the inn and Alec. "Be aware," she said to herself with each footfall. "Be aware. Be aware. Be aware."

As she rounded the corner Alec was leaning on the trunk of the Bugatti excitedly waving her toward him with what looked like a magazine in his hand, their suitcases at his feet.

"Look at this!" he was shouting even before she was within hearing distance. She picked up her pace. He was waving the latest issue of *Elle* magazine. "Do I know beauty when I see it?" he bragged, complimenting his own good taste in women as he opened to a full page spread filled with photos of her. When she realized the pages were filled with her image she squealed and jumped onto his torso, wrapping her legs around his hips, to hell with modesty, and he swung her around and around until he could feel his back going out. She slid to the ground and grabbed the magazine out of his hand. To the naked eye the model in the photographs was gorgeous, perfect, and the gown was exquisite but on closer inspection Kateri thought she should have tilted her head more to the right and noticed that the part in her hair was a little off and "good God," she winced, "is my mouth really that big?"

"No, really, you're perfect," Alec said as he took her elbow and edged her toward the passenger door. "Today we're driving the Ring of Kerry. I'm ready. I packed your stuff. Get in. Let's go." She thought for a moment he was going to put his hand on her head, like cops do, forcing her into the car. The words *be aware* sounded in her ear.

"Hey!" she countered. "I'm not ready. I have to say goodbye to Mrs. Gannon. I have to pee. Give me a break." He rolled his eyes and did that thing with his lips that she found so belittling. The pub door opened and she disappeared into its hollow.

Mrs. Gannon stopped sweeping. "He's not wasting any time," she noted giving her head a quick jerk toward the door and the car parked behind it.

"He was all set to whisk me away without me even saying goodbye to you, or more to the point, thank you," Kateri said.

I guess we're kindred souls, you and I," Mrs. Gannon offered. "We know each other's secrets. Mine that I'm clairvoyant and yours, who talks to spirits. It's me who wants to thank you. I've been locked inside my secret all my married life. You have helped me let it out. I feel we're not done with one another," she added, "I think you'll always be in my life." The realization was profound for Mrs. Gannon and she could feel a tear squeaking past her lids. Quickly she reached into her apron pocket and found the neatly ironed handkerchief. It had an M embroidered on it.

Kateri, used to seeing Kleenex, was surprised by such a pretty hanky coming out of a tavern apron. "I don't even know your first name," she said, "but I know it begins with an M."

"Jane," said Mrs. Gannon, "everyone calls me Jane. But yes, my real name starts with M, Mathilde. I hate it. My mother, God rest her soul, embroidered it for me. I always keep it close. Kateri stopped breathing for a second. The name Mathilde caught her by surprise.

"I'm sure Alec is running out of patience," Kateri finally said reaching around Jane for a hug that confirmed they were now kindred souls. "I won't forget you," she added, "ever." Jane admitted she didn't know the details but she was sure they would meet again. Kateri turned quickly toward the door as she searched her own pocket for a Kleenex.

Jane shook her head and clicked her tongue in a tsk as the scent of burning rubber wafted into the pub.

THE STORM

The day was awesome, sunny and warm, unusual for an Irish morning, a good day for a drive. Alec was taking Mr. Gannon's advice to drive the Ring counter-clockwise to avoid the tour buses, anticipating the next 180 km to be the most fun he could have in his precious car. Kateri had settled into her seat, distracted, pouring through *Elle*, maybe there'd be more photos. At last she looked up; the car seemed to be going too fast. Alarmed she pulled her elbow away from the opened window. The stone wall was nearly scraping the side of the car and it was the only thing separating them from a rocky abyss.

"Alec!" she yelled. "Slow down. You're going to kill us."

"I'm doing the speed limit," he shot back. "See?" A 100 km road sign whizzed by the window, confirming.

"Are they out of their minds?" she shrieked. "This road is way too narrow and winding for 100 km." Alec downshifted for a very tight turn and her body slammed against the door. "How do you lock this thing?" she asked reaching over her shoulder searching for the locking button.

"This is what I do for a living," he laughed. "I drive. Fast. Did you forget? You're perfectly safe, ma cherie. I know what I'm doing."

"Look," she said pointing to a little stone shop on their right with wisteria hanging from a latticed arch, "let's stop." He blew right past it.

"We'll catch the next one," he promised but the little shops, sea vistas, beaches and arched bridges kept flying by. It was all about the curves, the speed, the track. Alec was in his zone. He narrowly missed hitting a bicyclist on the next bend and that did it for Kateri.

"You have to stop," she demanded, "these turns are making me car sick. I'm going to puke." Alec didn't slow down.

"Should I puke on the leather seat or into the gearbox?" she asked, finally convincing him to pull onto a crowded overlook next to a tour bus. A chatty tourist approached Kateri expounding on the wonderful lunch she had just had about a mile back. "It overlooks the sea and the food is the best we've had so far in all of Ireland," she blathered. "Tell your dad, you'll both love it."

"I will," Kateri answered adding she appreciated the tip. She walked over to where Alec was admiring the vista; he put his arms around her and buried his nose in her scented hair. Out of the corner of her eye Kateri could see the woman pointing a wagging finger in their direction and a smug grin humored her lips.

The chatting tourist was right. Just as she said, the place overlooked the deep bay. The dark mountains away off in the distance were striped as the clouds ducked and dodged the sun in an otherwise chambray blue sky. It made the mountains look as if they were dancing. They ordered poached salmon with dill sauce, new potatoes, spring greens and a bottle of the house's best wine.

"We should get married here," Alec said dreamily reaching for her hand as he motioned for the waiter to fetch another bottle.

"You're quite the romantic," she softly replied curling her fingers around his hand, "but we can't just do that."

"Sure we can," he said, "we could find a Justice and get married right now, right here. This is such a romantic spot, I bet the maitre d would know one." No sooner had the words slipped out when he wished he could retrieve them. *What if she says yes? What was I thinking?* He had a secret he had neglected to mention. He had already made arrangements with Auclair, his best friend and lawyer back home, to draw up an iron-clad pre-nup. He wasn't going to marry her if she didn't sign it. He'd been down that road too many times before.

She had a secret too, a legal one. She was still officially married to Chucky Jiglowski and this is not how she wanted Alec to find out. She had meant to take care of this seemingly minor detail ages ago. *Soon,* she always told herself. *Real soon,* she had reaffirmed a few months ago when she accepted the diamond on her finger. Now she regretted she hadn't gotten her divorce before she started earning six figures.

The sky interrupted their thoughts by suddenly turning menacing. The faraway mountains stopped dancing, the wind picked their napkins off their laps and threw them on the flagstone, the sea started to churn and spew as the wait staff began hustling to get everything tucked away before the wind could join forces with the rain. Alec stood, poured the last of the wine into his glass, offered it to Kateri and when she refused, knocked it back as if it was a shot in a beer. They ran to the car.

He fussed with the roof. It didn't want to fall into place but finally did just as the first big drops splatted on the windshield. "Damn," he said as he turned on the wipers and watched them push grime all over the windshield. "I told my mechanic to change out these wipers. He must have forgotten."

Kateri suggested they wait out the storm but Alec would have none of it. He said it would take forever for the rain to stop in Ireland, "once it starts..." his voice trailed off as he tried to get the engine to turn over, dampness having made the ignition temperamental. It finally caught.

The car fishtailed out of the parking lot as he trounced on the accelerator. The road was greasy and the rain sounded like little rocks hitting the windshield yet Alec wouldn't slow down.

She awoke with a splitting headache and when Kateri tried to open her eyes she couldn't. In this bleak darkness a vision replayed. The car was going too fast, she was gripping the armrest with one hand while the other was braced on the dash. Through the rain-blurred windshield she saw blobs that looked like sheep looming toward the windshield on the road ahead.

"You're scaring me," she cried out. But it was too late. The wheels had already slipped off the narrow road and she re-heard the scraping of metal on rock and re-felt the nanosecond of weightlessness before the jolt and then the nothingness and the ultimate quiet that comes with death

As consciousness returned, the medicinal smells of a hospital penetrated her nostrils and Kateri realized she wasn't dead. As she reached to soothe her splitting headache her hand ran across the bristly cross grain of the bandage that enveloped her head and eyes.

Jane Gannon bolted out of her drowsy beside vigil when Kateri, in her awakening, screamed out "you're scaring me!" Jane had been sitting at the bedside for days, worrying if her newfound kindred spirit was going to survive. The crash had been the talk of Kenmare. Mr. Gannon wondered how a race driver of Alec's caliber could possibly have missed the turn. Animated opinions spread across the mahogany of the town's pubs. "Such a beautiful car, gone to junk," they were saying, "what a pity. And to think Charpentier walked unscathed, not a scratch."

"Yeah, but what about his daughter?" they buzzed. "I hear she was thrown and badly hurt."

"That's not his daughter, don't ya know, they say that's the girlfriend. She won't be modeling anytime soon."

"Sweet Jesus in heaven above," Jane said as she sprung from the chair, blessing herself. "Are you awake, child?"

"Jane? Jane Gannon?" Kateri questioned as she furled her brow in a painful frown. "Oh my God, Jane, everything hurts. I can't open my eyes." The more Kateri tried to put pieces together, the more her head pounded, with panic setting in when she couldn't move her left leg. "Jane!" she cried, "Jane, tell me this isn't happening. Oh my God!"

Jane could see a trickle of a tear escape the gauze. "I'm just going to leave you for one minute," Jane was saying over the panic. "I'm going to the nurses' station to tell them you've come to. I'll be right back. That's a promise."

"Don't leave me, Jane," Jane heard as she scurried down the hall.

Her injuries were extensive: broken femur, broken tibia, cracked skull, concussion, and then there was the worry about eyesight. The left leg had already been repaired with pins and rods and plates and she was being urged to walk a few steps on the crutches propped next to the bedrail. Little by little Kateri was able to inch her way first to the bathroom, then down the hall and back. "Soon," said the woman from PT, "we'll have you navigate a few stairs."

Her head was unwrapped each day when doctors came in with pocket flashlights they shone in her eyes. "Can you see this?" they would ask holding up two fingers, "or this?" holding up a complete hand.

"No," she would reply.

"Don't worry," they'd say, "these things take time."

In the first few hours after Kateri's awakening, Jane was sure Kateri would want to know about Alec. She didn't know how she was going to handle the answer to the inevitable question but it never came up. Kateri hadn't progressed that far in her discovery of losses.

Everyday Jane would arrive at eleven and stay until three when she had to get back to her duties at the inn. Mr. Gannon wanted to know how long this routine was going to interrupt their lives. "As long as it takes," Jane responded emboldened by her realization that she was destined to be in this young woman's life.

Then, at last, the inevitable question, "Where's Alec?"

Jane would rather have said he's dead, that he didn't survive the crash than tell her the truth. "Alec was lucky," Jane began, hoping her fury toward the self-absorbed deserter wasn't apparent. "He wasn't thrown from the car like you were so he didn't get hurt, just a few stitches. He sat with you here for a few days before you came to but had to get back to France 'on urgent business' he said. He told me to tell you he'll be back as soon as he possibly can."

"How many days have I been here?" Kateri asked trying to concentrate.

"Ten," Jane replied, wincing as Kateri responded with an onerous *hmmm*. Jane didn't believe Alec was coming back either.

Alec was gone for good and Kateri knew it. Staring into the darkness of her blindness, her mind's eye could see what her blue eyes could not, the truth about Alec. In reality, the truth about Alec became obvious that day in the cemetery when she had the eerie encounter with her great- grandparents. "Be aware," Colonel had said, "and mindful." At the time Kateri didn't give any weight to those words. She was in a hurry to get back to Alec who was in a rush to get on the road trip and she had become incredibly self-absorbed when she saw herself in the *Elle* article he had handed her.

Right now her mind's eye was the only vision she had and it was telling her a completely different story. Her mind's eye was recalling the time Alec was showing her off when he introduced her to his friends, gloating when their jaws dropped over her beauty, which encouraged him to pinch her butt through her emerald green dress as an exclamation point to his superior good taste and luck. She reminded herself she didn't like that at all.

Her mind's eye recalled how much more interested he was in negotiating those surprise hairpin turns on the Ring of Kerry than he was in stopping a few times so she could poke around those quaint Irish shops to get something to send her mom and Carl, *I mean Dad*, she chastised herself.

Her mind's eye revisited the times she burst into Cory's apartment, bawling, and as soon as he soothed her with his calming words and gentle hugs, she was able to pick herself up, dust herself off, and without so much as a thank you, get back to her unexamined life.

Her mind's eye even wondered how Chucky must have felt when she left him in Santa Cruz without so much as a goodbye. *That was mean,* she now admitted.

Her mind's eye was revealing a Kateri she hadn't bothered to know. She wondered how she could have been so blind when she actually had eyesight. "When I can see again," she told herself, "I'm going to do things differently. That's a promise."

The fact that her vision hadn't returned was baffling to her doctors.

"The concussion must have done something to your optic nerve," they guessed. "We think it will clear up in time." Of course it would. She was as sure of that as she had been of all the other good fortunes that had been her life.

Kateri was already learning to listen more intently to her world. She could tell the squish in Jane's orthopedic shoe that announced Jane was in the corridor.

"Good news!" Kateri yelled out as a puff of cold outdoor air preceded Jane's entry to the room. She waited for the swoosh the room's vinyl chair makes when a body descends upon it before adding, "The doctors said I could go home tomorrow." Kateri listened intently for any negativity coming from Jane, a sigh, perhaps, or an exhale, a gasp, a murmur, anything that might indicate Jane's unwillingness to help her get through the next few days but there was no hesitation in Jane's voice. She offered Kateri a room in the inn as if it was her idea in the first place and as if Mr. Gannon wasn't going to give her a hard time about having an invalid stumbling around his pub.

Despite the kind offer, days at the inn became interminably long. The pub smelled of all the fires that been allowed to die-in-the-night for the last hundred years along with a hint of stale, burnt Peterson's pipe tobacco patrons had tapped into the pub's ashtrays over the years. No matter how she tried to keep it clean, her hair always smelled like Mr. Gannon's pub and as a result Kateri tried to spend as much of her day as possible outdoors.

In the side yard where Jane kept a small garden, she could inhale the scent of chives as its buds became blossoms. She began recognizing things through senses other than her eyes and was becoming amazed at how much 'mindfulness' she had already learned from the Colonel and A'mari's brief encounter.

One afternoon a child about seven crossed from his yard to where she sat, curious about the lady with crutches.

"Hi lady," he called out, "what are they for?" he said examining them. "Can

I try them?" She laughed recognizing a child's voice, thinking only a kid would find crutches interesting.

"Now why would you want to do that?" she asked.

"Because I never tried crutches before," he answered sincerely, "and it looks like fun." She held the crutches toward the voice and he tried for a while to get them under his armpits to no avail.

The next thing she knew there was a blithe little body standing on the bench beside her. At this new height he could tuck the crutches into his armpits and swing like a flying squirrel from the bench to the ground. After a few flights he sat down on the bench, stared at her face and said, "How come you can't see me?"

She learned his name was Timmy.

TIMMY: A TURNING POINT

"You get out of my garden, Timmy McGurk!" the voice from the pub's side door bellowed. Kateri turned toward the inn. Mr. Gannon's large frame filled the door jamb. "If you're stealing Mrs. Gannon's radishes again I'll call the constable on you," he threatened.

"Leave the boy be," came Jane's voice from behind the hulking mass in the door frame.

"Do you steal Mrs. Gannon's radishes, Timmy?" Kateri asked turning now toward the boy.

"No ma'am," said Timmy, "I only take the little ones in between the big leaves just like my nana says to. She says it helps Mrs. Gannon so her radishes won't be so crowded and they can grow nice and plump."

"Is that so?" Kateri said, smiling at the child's innocent reply and imagined he was telling it exactly like his grandma put it.

As Mr. Gannon stepped out of the doorway onto the stoop Timmy was quick to turn and run.

"Come back when you see me out," Kateri called as the boy ran off. Timmy didn't stop to answer.

"What's with the little scenario that just played out in your garden?" Kateri asked when she had an opportunity to talk privately with Jane.

"Timmy, poor child," (every time Jane said 'Timmy' she added 'poor child' as if it was part of his given name). "Timmy, poor child, is caught in the middle of a long-standing feud between the McGurks and the Gannons. I'm not party to the feud, mind you, except by association," she was quick to add. "It's between my Padric and Timmy's dad, Ned."

As the story unfolded Kateri wanted to take Timmy in her arms and make his childhood a happier place. Jane said she would give Kateri the abridged version of the long-standing feud. She told how Padric and Ned were childhood playmates, best of friends, with Ned living behind the pub, where Timmy now lives with Ned's mother. Padric's grandfather owned the pub before Padric inherited it. All through grammar school and high school Padric came every day to his grandfather's pub to hang out with Ned.

"When Ned became engaged to Maureen after high school, he asked Padric to be his best man and when Maureen became pregnant, they started calling Padric Uncle Padric. Timmy's impending arrival brought great joy to their friendship.

"Everyone was stunned when Maureen didn't survive Timmy's birth and Ned blamed the infant. Ned wouldn't touch Timmy, wouldn't give him a bottle or a bath, wouldn't even look at him for that matter. Ned's mother had to take over raising the baby, either that or Timmy, poor child, would have to be given to the Sisters of Mercy."

Sad as it was, the story so far didn't include a feud. Kateri waited while Jane considered how she was going to paint Ned and her husband in the roles each played in the rest of the tale. Jane continued.

"Ned began drinking before Maureen was even cold in the ground. At first he drank in the parlor of his mother's little cottage behind the pub where he was now living. Every time Timmy would cry, Ned would cover his ears as if tormented by the devil himself. Ned would run out of the house, sometimes not returning for days. Mrs. McGurk was beside herself. She was not well even then, often suffering gout, and needed help with the baby. Sometimes I'd go over to give her relief so she could get to the grocers or to her doctor appointments. When Ned would show up again you could hear her shouts throughout the neighborhood, chastising him and him telling her to shut up with the baby crying all the while.

"Ned ran bar tabs all over town until he wasn't welcomed anywhere so he started frequenting our pub. He'd get drunk every night. Eventually he lost his job and became even more pitiful, begging Padric to let him run a tab until he got work again. Padric was a fool for a long time, years. Finally one Tuesday night he couldn't take it any longer. Padric had just refilled Ned's mug when Ned, stumbling as he passed the table where the mayor was sitting, accidentally poured the entire contents of the mug down the mayor's neck. The mayor was furious, mostly because he told his wife that on Tuesdays he had standing meetings in town hall with the planning committee," Jane added as an aside.

"Padric said: 'That's it. Ned, you're no longer welcomed here. Get out.' But Ned wouldn't leave. Padric took him by the collar and escorted him to the sidewalk. Unfortunately Ned tripped on the piece of broken sidewalk cement that Padric hadn't gotten around to repairing, despite the hundreds of times I'd told him to, and Ned broke his collarbone.

Ned hired a solicitor. He sued us and won. *Ten thousand pounds!*"

Kateri gave a long, slow whistle. "So where's Ned now?" she asked.

"Last I heard, prison," Jane replied, "Things didn't improve for him."

"So Mr. Gannon now takes his revenge on the boy?" Kateri asked, shocked.

"You don't know my Padric," Jane lamented, "he doesn't get over assaults to his character or to his wallet. He's the quintessential grudger, may God forgive him. Timmy, Ned, they're all McGurks. Padric doesn't discriminate."

As each day of recuperation passed, Kateri became more aware of Jane's quiet grace. Although she couldn't see Jane's orthopedic shoes or the worn apron strings that barely reached around the woman's thick waist or the lock of wiry grey hair that kept falling into Jane's face, Kateri began noticing the beauty of Jane through her mind's eye.

Every night Jane rapped lightly on Kateri's door and entered with a smile in her voice and a pitcher of water for her nightstand as if it was a last-minute thought to stop in and say goodnight and inquire if there was anything needed before she herself trundled up the stairs to her own bed.

"Oh here," Jane would say, again as an afterthought, "let me lay out your long sleeve tee and jeans for tomorrow. I've washed the tee. It was no bother. I was doing laundry anyhow."

In the morning, another light rap on the door. This time a teapot and cup quietly took the place of the water pitcher and the curtains were swished on their rods. It didn't make the room any brighter to Kateri's eyes but it filled her heart with sunshine.

"What are you bringing me?" Kateri inquired when the scent of a fresh-baked scone wafted toward her.

"Oh it's nothing," Jane replied, "just a scone."

"Just a scone!" Kateri sang out in delight. "That's not just a scone. That's what heaven must smell like."

Jane laughed. "I have angels in my kitchen to help."

"There's but one angel in your kitchen, Mathilde Jane," Kateri added, "and I am so lucky to know her."

Kateri was now wielding her crutches as if they were another set of legs. She could navigate the few steps to the side yard without Jane's help. On warm September afternoons she'd plan to be on the bench around three so she could wave to Timmy as he ran up the narrow sidewalk between the two yards after school. When Timmy was sure Mr. Gannon wasn't standing on the stoop he'd come over and sit for a minute while Kateri asked about his lessons. Kateri soon began saving her morning scone for the chance Timmy would visit and, of course, as soon as Timmy realized there was a treat at hand, became a regular to the bench.

Kateri was getting eager to explore her surroundings but didn't trust herself to wander away from the herb garden. The thought occurred to her that Timmy might be her eyes for a walk in the neighborhood.

"Ask your grandmother if you can go as far as the cemetery with me," she said as Timmy devoured his scone. The answer was yes.

For the first few walks they'd go as far as the cemetery and back but on one of their walks Timmy asked, "Are you afraid of ghosts?"

"No. Why?" Kateri curiously responded.

"Because I have a secret," he answered in a hushed voice as if someone might overhear him. "It's in the cemetery. I'll show you. But you have to promise not to tell anybody not even my nana." Kateri crossed her heart and hoped to die and the promise was set in stone. They walked through the gates.

"There's a bench over here just a little way. I'll show you," he was saying as he tugged on her scarf. Kateri's feet remembered this spot not far inside the gates.

"What's it say on the tombstone near this bench?" she asked as he guided her to its seat.

"O S U I L L E A B H A I N," he spelled, quickly adding he didn't know to whom the bench belonged but he always came to this one because it was close to the entrance. Shivers went up Kateri's spine.

"Do you think the family who owns this bench will mind us using it?" he suddenly worried.

"I'm positive they won't," she assured him. "I think they like it when people stop by for a visit." They sat in silence for a few minutes with Kateri wondering what the child was thinking. Finally he spoke.

"Mama," he said, "it's me, Timmy. I've brought someone to meet you, Mama."

As she wondered what would happen next, Timmy explained that he comes to the cemetery often to talk with his mother. He said she helps him figure things out when he doesn't know what to do.

"Like what?" Kateri asked.

"Like when I make my First Communion. I think there's supposed to be a party. All the kids in my class are having one. But Nana says we don't have enough relatives to have a party, so me and Mama talked about it. Mama said I should ask Nana to take me to the Chat-a-While after First Communion Mass and celebrate with a double order of French toast with butter, syrup AND whipped cream. My Nana said that was a splendid idea and that's just what we're going to do."

A big smile crossed Kateri's lips, *smart lady* she mused. Suddenly she felt Timmy's excitement as he jumped up from the bench. She sensed Maureen was near.

"Mama!" Timmy shouted, "Mama, I've brought someone to meet you and she's not afraid of ghosts so you can talk to her."

"Not everyone can talk with spirits, honey," his mother said, "so don't put your new friend on the spot."

"But you can, can't you Kateri?" Timmy insisted.

"I'm enjoying your son," Kateri said to Maureen. "He's a very sweet little boy and he's helping me recover."

"She can't see you, Mama," he said, "she's blind. She was in a bad accident."

Kateri and Maureen talked for a few minutes about Timmy, about life's twists and turns, about how they might have been friends in an alternate world. Timmy sat on the bench, beaming. He now had proof. He wasn't just imagining that he could talk to his mother or wishing for it so much that he believed it. It was true. His mother was not imaginary. His mother was real.

Every morning Jane came into Kateri's room and swished the curtain back on its brass rod but this morning was different. This morning, even before the curtain was fully retracted against the window frame a shard of light penetrated Kateri's eyelids. Was she imagining it? Was she seeing light? She held her breath and opened her eyes wide. Yes. There was light so bright she cupped her hand over her brow. This morning there was light.

"Sweetest Mother of God!" Jane squealed in disbelief. "Can you see me?"

"Not exactly," Kateri replied, "but I know where you're standing. In fact, you're blocking my light." Jane moved a little to the left and the sun struck Kateri in the face again. She jumped from the bed hobbling to the window hoping to see the streets of Kenmare but all she saw was more sunlight.

"It's okay," she consoled Jane who was expecting her to see more than just light, "sunlight today, maybe shadows tomorrow and who knows what after that!"

Later today Jane would be taking Kateri to her doctor's appointment, perhaps her final one. Kateri felt strong and healthy and was hoping Dr. Green would give her the okay to travel, to get her life back on course. Jane was fearful that is exactly what the doctor would say and thought about her own days ahead without the joy Kateri had brought to her life.

"You're a free woman," Dr. Green said triumphantly, "go home, see your Mom, get physical therapy and you'll be as good as new."

The ripples from Kateri's medical emancipation spread far and wide. When Padric heard, he gave her a hug wishing her lots of luck and offered to drive her to the airport anytime, today even. Jane's lip quivered as she tried to be cheerful about the good news. Connie was ecstatic on the phone call.

"Exactly when are you coming home?" she asked a dozen times making Kateri feel like she was still in high school.

Alec didn't pick up. Timmy cried.

"Will you stay for my First Communion?" Timmy pleaded dolefully when she told him the news. "It's only a month away."

She explained how she needed to get home to physical therapy so she could walk again and perhaps model again. He nodded as if used to disappointment.

"But I'll tell you what," she enthusiastically added, "I want to get you something really nice to celebrate your First Communion and I have an idea. Ask your nana if you can direct me to the shops on Main Street."

With Jane's directions she and Timmy walked to Mr. Handlebars and she told Timmy to pick out any bike at all. Jeff, the owner, took over the task as he moved the seats up and down so Timmy could try out the Giant and the Raleigh and the Cuda. After much discussion about color and cool, Timmy picked the Cuda. "You have good taste, my man," Jeff said, "that's the one I would have chosen, too."

"Can we ride to the cemetery. I mean walk to the cemetery?" Timmy beamed as they rolled the bike out of the store. "I want to show Mama. She won't believe it. Nobody in my grade has a bike like this. I'll never forget you," Timmy added looking up at her and they walked into the cemetery and past the *No Bicycles Allowed* sign at the gate.

"Nor I you," Kateri added tousling his hair, each realizing an impending loss.

HOME

Kateri was in a state of confusion. What to do first? Go back to France and settle her affairs? Go home to Turner Mills and reconnect with family, start physical therapy? Resume life in San Francisco, depend on old friends for the help she would need? They'd certainly be there for her.

Breathe she told herself, count to ten. That's when she remembered the words of Colonel O'Sullivan and A'mari and thought of those words as a gift from her gods. *Be mindful*, they had said, *be mindful.* She chose home.

Home was not the same as it was eighteen years ago when Kateri left it in a red CR-X with one hand waving like a flag from the passenger window. There were changes, too, in the family structure for Grandpap had succumbed to mesothelioma. Without Grandpap, Oona had slid into a malaise she wasn't able to conquer. Grandpap was her joie de vie and without him, when she was feeling sorry for herself, she told anyone who would listen that she was just an old woman, an old Mohawk who should be set loose on a slab of ice and left to drift off to the happy hunting ground.

"Stop it!" Connie would scold her mother more harshly than she had intended. "Stop that stupid talk right this minute. That's nonsense and you know it. You know I'll take care of you," adding under her breath, "even if it kills me."

"I heard that," came a frail voice from the living room. Then as if putting an exclamation point on her fury, Connie would slam the oven door on the chuck roast and remorse would creep in.

"How can I scold a mother I adore?" Connie would cry to Carl, berating herself for the ogre she was becoming. Carl would try to soothe her with his words but with his emphysema he hardly had enough breath to get his words out.

Though not officially a member of the Warner household, Oona trundled from her own house half way up the short block to the Warners each day to care for Underfoot and Shadow, Connie's aging cat and cocker spaniel dog, while the Warners went off to their jobs. The trio of cat, dog and Mohawk looked forward to their day together as Oona told the pets her Native American tales and they listened with sleepy eyes to her sonorous voice, moving their heads ever so slightly as her old fingers worked their way toward the secret spots behind their ears or under their chins as she talked. Ever since Connie's youngest daughter, Janet, got married a year ago, Connie, Carl, Oona and the pets had settled into this daily routine.

On weekdays, at exactly 5:30 pm, Connie's key went into the side door as she let herself into the house after her shift at the box factory. Tired, harried and impatient, she'd call a hello to her pets and, almost as an afterthought, to her mother, as she started onions in the fry pan so the household would get a sense dinner was eminent, harrumphing as she chopped, with the pets tangling around her feet.

Oona would begin inching her way out of Carl's Barcalounger knowing he would be home in a matter of minutes. At exactly 5:55 pm Carl would come through the door, hang his jacket on the peg in the side hall, peck Connie on the cheek and exhausted, drop into his well-worn Barcalounger as Dan Rather caught him up on the news. This was their routine day after day until the phone call.

"I'm coming home, Mom," the voice spoke so softly on the phone that Connie wasn't even sure she heard.

"She's coming home! She's coming home!" Connie shouted into the living room as Carl put the remote on mute. Oona scurried into the kitchen as if she didn't have any arthritis in her knees, hoping to catch any words that might escape into the room from the black receiver held tight to Connie's ear.

This was a difficult call for Kateri. She wasn't coming home a success. Her broken bones needed at least a year of PT, her modeling career was kaput, she wasn't getting married to Alec after all and she had no income except for the profit she had just made on selling her place in the Marais, which, thank God, would hold her for a while.

Details, everybody wanted details. "I can't hear her with you two butting in," Connie shushed at the others. "Will you please shut up? Yes, yes," Connie was affirming. "I'll be at the airport. Short hair? Really? You know I'll recognize you."

"My daughter's coming home," Connie told the chuck roast as she retrieved it from the oven. "She'll be here Tuesday," she sang to the dishes as she pulled them off the cupboard shelf. This was not an ordinary day. Kateri was coming home.

"Where are you going, Ma?" Connie called when, out of the corner of her eye, she caught the back of Oona scurrying down the hall stairs toward the side door.

"There's something over at my house I have to get," Oona answered, waving Connie off with the back of her hand. "I'll be right back," and she was. She was carrying two market bags with seeds and weeds, twigs and strips of leather overflowing their tops.

"Not that again," Connie cringed at the sight of Oona's bags. "Haven't you made and given away enough of your dreamcatchers?"

"They're not dreamcatchers," Oona insisted, "they're Sacred Hoops, and I'm going to teach my granddaughter not only how to make her own Sacred Hoop but to become acquainted with her Mohawk culture. I tried to teach her when she was a child but she wouldn't listen and I didn't insist. It's not often one gets a second chance. Now where can I keep these bags?"

Connie knew it was no use arguing. "I suppose there's room in the hall closet," she sighed, "on the shelf so Underfoot can't get at it."

For Oona the news of Kateri's return felt like the surprise of a warm sunny day at the end of a dreary winter, a harbinger of spring and good days ahead. She became lighthearted and cheerful, like she was when Will was alive, and chatted throughout dinner about Tuesday's homecoming. "Maybe Kate should stay at my house, with me," Oona ventured.

"No, Ma."

"Is she bringing the boyfriend?"

"No, Ma."

"Is she coming for just a visit or is she home for good?"

"Ma-a!" Connie answered louder than she meant.

Carl had lived with these two women long enough to know what would happen next: a mother-daughter Dance of Frustration was about to commence. In his wife's excitement, Connie was about to say something unkind to hush up her inquisitive mother; in Oona's excitement, she was about to retaliate with her own special effects and march out of the house. Carl would be spending much of the evening first assuaging his wife's remorse, then traipsing up the block to assuage Oona's hurt feelings.

"Ladies," he interjected, interrupting the first step of their dance. "I have a wonderful idea. Let's all three of us go to the airport to meet Kate and I'll take everyone to a nice sit-down dinner at a restaurant on the way home." The Warner budget barely accommodated dining out so Carl's invitation stopped the dance in its tracks. Carl's good idea became a conversation about restaurants and reservations and Tuesday couldn't come soon enough.

This wasn't the homecoming Kateri had envisioned for herself. There was no bravado in her demeanor as she walked past the airport's point of no return on the arm of a kind flight attendant who offered to see her to the welcome area. Her life was in chaos: blind, limping, her modeling career over, jilted, basically broke and thirty six.

She recalled the flight attendant asking her if "the short blonde lady and the Native American woman, waving and shouting 'there she is! I see her!' and the reticent man standing behind them was her family."

"I'm sure it is," Kateri laughed with embarrassment. The group hug in the middle of the airport's passageway reminded her how the prodigal son must have felt on his return—honored without cause. But the moment of defeat passed quickly as the hug turned to tears rolling down all four faces. They didn't move for what seemed like an eternity and then, one by one, started peeling away from each other's clutch to take in the whole visage. Last but not least Carl got his turn.

"Dad," Kateri whispered, "Dad, can you forgive me?"

"For what?" he whispered back as they both wiped their cheeks.

That was months ago. The four had now settled into a new normal. Connie and Carl left the house at eight for their jobs. Three times a week Kateri went to physical therapy and most mornings to the gym. Since she was determined to model again, she had to get her pivot back. Although Oona didn't dare drive on the interstate anymore, she still drove in her neighborhood and volunteered to drive Kateri to her appointments and the gym.

On one of those routine mornings while Kateri was fussing with the items in her gym bag as she got into the passenger side of Oona's Toyota, she neglected to buckle up. Within seconds, bam! a teenager on his way to school plowed into them at the stop sign. Kateri lurched forward hitting her head on the dash, hard. Instinctively she turned toward her grandmother asking if she was all right and saw Oona's face smushed into the air bag.

"Oona! Are you okay?" she cried out not realizing she was seeing her grandmother's face buried in the nylon bag. The shock that she was actually seeing Oona was more heart-stopping than the sudden crash. She looked through the front windshield and saw people at the bus stop with their hands to their mouths, aghast. She looked at the student who had rushed to the driver's door with a terrified look on his face, she looked at her grandmother dislodging herself from the airbag. She looked down at her hands, out at the crossing guard who was approaching, up at the tree limb hanging over the street. It wasn't her imagination, she could see.

Despite the huge goose egg swelling on Kateri's forehead and her grandmother's stiff neck, there were no complaints as the family rejoiced over the return of Kateri's sight. Had Kateri's airbag gone off, there would be no bump on the head, no jolt, no reason for a return of eyesight. As the jubilation wore on Connie came to her senses on the financial aspects of the crash. "We should sue Toyota," she proclaimed, "that airbag should have gone off."

"No, Mom, we won't be suing anyone. Things happen for a reason. Someone was looking after me. I really believe that," Kateri said firmly. Oona smiled at her granddaughter; she believed it too.

The crash set Kateri's physical therapy progress back but she didn't complain. "I'll be walking without a limp," she assured Oona on their afternoons together. "It's just going to take a little longer."

Oona wasn't going to waste a minute of these precious hours with her granddaughter. She had things to say that she meant to have said eighteen years ago. The market bag of seeds and weeds, as Connie called it, came out of the closet. Without saying a word, Oona began fiddling with a twig, twisting and turning it as her fingers carefully wound a slender piece of willow into a circle encouraging a new Sacred Hoop to emerge.

"Starting a new dreamcatcher?" Kateri asked remembering how her grandmother used to make them when she was a child. Oona would spend her evenings weaving them after dinner when she and Grandpap used to sit together watching the Lawrence Welk Show.

Nonchalantly, as if this emerging Sacred Hoop had no special meaning, Oona asked if Kateri remembered the one she had made for her. Kateri remembered. It had hung on her bedpost and would chase her bad dreams away.

"I remember it," she answered. "Then one day Mittens jumped at the feathers and pulled them all out, then broke the strings. I never did find the special bead you wove into it. When my mother saw the mess it had made in my room she made me throw it all out."

"Here," Oona offered, reaching into her bag for another twig of willow and a strap of leather, "make one with me."

Kateri watched Oona's fingers as they deftly twisted and turned the twigs into a circle which she bound where the ends met. "Like this," she demonstrated. As simple as the moment seemed, this circle now forming in Kateri's hands was about to become a journey to her soul. Oona wove and Kateri followed her grandmother's finger falls, catching on to the intricacies with ease.

"You're a natural at this," Oona said with delight. "You're a Mohawk after all."

As they worked their strings into an ever more complicated pattern resembling a web, Oona asked Kateri if she knew the story of Spider Woman. Kateri said she had no clue.

"Long ago," Oona began as her fingers spun the story, "there was an old Ojibwa grandmother who, for days, was watching a spider weave its web near her bed. Her grandson came in and, noticing the spider, picked up a rock to crush it. But Grandmother stopped him and when he asked why she just smiled.

"The spider thanked Grandmother for saving its life and promised to show her how to spin a web like hers. This web, the spider told her, could be used to snare the bad dreams that scare children at night. She showed Grandmother how to leave a small opening in the center of its labyrinth called the eye. Only good dreams can find the eye, she explained, and then can easily slip through the web allowing only sweet dreams to be remembered in the morning. Grandmother taught other Native American mothers how to weave the spider's web.

"As the Objibwa tribe grew and moved about North America, some of us became known as Cherokee, others as Navajo or Lakota or, as in our case, Mohawk of the Iroquois Nation, and the tradition of Sacred Hoops, or dreamcatchers as you call them, moved with us.

"Now this story has been repeated so many times," Oona concluded, "we don't call Grandmother grandmother anymore, we call her Spider Woman."

Kateri set down her hoop and hugged her grandmother. "You're beautiful," she said.

Oona went on to explain how a dreamcatcher can have either seven or eight points where the web is connected to the hoop. "Seven, if yours is about the Seven Promises," she said, "eight if you want yours to honor the spider because spiders have eight legs."

Kateri was mesmerized by her grandmother's story. As she rummaged again through the market bag looking for feathers to finish her project, she was deciding whether to tell Oona her secret.

"Oona, I have a secret," she finally began. "I don't understand it, maybe you will." She hesitated. "I talk to spirits."

Oona set her Sacred Hoop on her lap as her eyelids, which usually hung heavy over her dark irises, lifted to their full extension. She was quiet for the moment leaving Kateri to wonder whether or not it was a good idea to bring it up.

Finally, "Do they talk back? Are you communicating?"

Kateri nodded.

This was more than Oona could possibly have hoped. This grandchild of hers, this self-proclaimed Irish lass, this never-to-be-native, finally—finally could not deny her spirit. She quietly thanked Spider Woman for bringing Kateri back from that other, material world. As the floodgates of Kateri's secret places opened, she poured the stories of her recent mystical experiences into her grandmother's receptive ears.

In the long afternoons Kateri spent with Oona she began to sense that her grandmother didn't possess the *gift of harmony* but was the *essence of harmony itself*. As Oona spoke in her quiet way about things that matter, a feeling of comfort washed over Kateri, melting away the tensions that had become her life. Harmony was a new feeling. It was soft, sensuous, soothing, freeing. Harmony was grandmother.

Oona listened as Kateri blurted out the angst that framed her life—the worthless chase of a dream she called Dad, the cold-heartedness with which she ditched Chucky, the carelessness in the way she used her most trustes friend Cory, the few times she bothered to call her mother when she knew how her mother longed for her news. She decided she was no better than Alec and he was a pompous ass. "I'm a mess," she confessed. "I've made a mess."

"Hmmm," Oona hummed long after Kateri stopped berating herself. "There's a word for what you're feeling. It's *Eureka*!"

"Eureka!" laughed Kateri, "as in—I've just discovered something?"

Oona just smiled.

JANE'S NEWS

Kateri was tiring of her long recuperative days and getting itchy for more excitement. Where to start? she wondered and answered her own question with I need a job. Her resume always said in bold caps that she was the DUBLIN AIRE GIRL which always ended in interviews, and in no time, Lancôme had her managing the cosmetic counter in the mall. It was a start. Customers loved the expertise with which Kateri accentuated their eyes and refreshed their sallow skin. Her customers now had to call ahead for appointments. She was making a new name for herself in skin care and she might have had a fulfilling career, full of stepping stones with Lancôme, had another heart-stopping eureka not interrupted.

It came in the form of *The Observer* being tossed onto the driveway, as it usually was, one Thursday morning. As she retrieved it, pulling it out of its blue plastic sleeve, she unfurled its folds and there, looking out from the front page, was the obituary. Marine Corporal, Turner Mills son, Kip McCann, succumbs after illness in California.

She stared at the youthful picture of him *The Observer* ran, that of a handsome twenty-year-old Marine in a white tee shirt with sleeves rolled to show off a tattoo, in regulation trousers with a cigarette dangling from his lip. Dad. Her lips quivered as she waited for the tears. Nothing fell from her ducts. She waited longer, giving her heart a chance to reconcile the printed words with a feeling. Nothing. This Dad, pictured as a twenty-year-old, no longer held remorse for Kateri. She didn't even recognize him. She tried to relate the young face to the one that reduced her to tears in Chief's in San Francisco. Even the old bearded face that came to mind didn't stir her now. Dad was over for her and she read the rest of the obituary as a casual observer. Survived by Margaret Mary McCann, 90, son of the late Judge Mortimer McCann, brother of the late Thomas (Beaner), late Michael and late Charlotte McCann Golden. "All gone," Kateri mused, "this family is all gone except grandmother—and me."

She was still wondering about her Grandmother McCann and whether or not she should reach out to her in her old age. Surely she would finally be accepting of her son's only child. Surely she would want to know me, she thought, and surely she would want to know what I know about her parents, the Colonel O'Sullivan and A'mari. How could she not want to know? Kateri contemplated whether or not to pay Grandmother McCann a visit.

While she was debating the possibility within herself, her mother walked in the door, home from work early for a doctor's appointment.

"Why are you looking at me like that?" Connie could always tell when her daughter was hiding something. Kateri's elbow had curiously moved to conceal the Observer. Even before she was close enough to see the words, Connie spotted the picture of the young Marine in the white tee shirt and snatched the paper from under Kateri's grip.

Kateri watched as her mother fell on top of the page and began sobbing a torrent of tears that smudged the printer's ink making the words almost illegible. In the long minutes before Connie could gain control of herself, Kateri realized the awful truth. Her mom had never, ever, not even for a moment, stopped loving him. After all these years, after the life she had built with Carl, after three children with Carl, her true love was Kateri's dad. Her mother's grief broke the nonchalance with which Kateri had absorbed the front page story and the two fell into each other's arms shuddering uncontrollably, sobbing. Before the episode quelled, Kateri's Irish kicked in and she definitely decided she would have a word or two with Grandmother McCann.

But even that would have to wait.

Jane called.

"Oh my God," Kateri rang out on hearing the brogue she recognized. "Jane, Jane is that really you? Oh Jane how I've missed you. And your scones!" Then Kateri realized that Jane didn't make long distance calls lightly and that Padric would be scolding her when the monthly bill arrived. Jane was not going to spend his euros on small talk.

"Something's come up," Jane was saying. "I'm feeling so bad."

Kateri thought Padric must have gotten into trouble or perhaps died and Jane is scared or desperate. "What is it Jane? " Kateri asked, thinking the worst.

"No, no, it's nothing like that," Jane assured. "It's...it's Timmy, poor child."

Kateri's heart sank. Her sweet little Timmy, something awful must have happened to Timmy. Before Jane could explain, tears welled up in Kateri's eyes.

"Mrs. McGurk passed," Jane explained, "and there's nobody to care for Timmy. I can't take him in because of, you know, Padric, and all that went on with the McGurks. I'm watching him now but he'll be going to the Sisters of Mercy soon. An orphan," Jane's voice broke up. "Little Timmy, poor child, has no one."

The euros ka-chinged as the phone line went quiet. Jane was softy crying. Kateri was thinking *could I possibly take Timmy? Here? With mother and Carl and Oona?* She knew Oona would not have an issue but the others, well, their lives had just settled into a quiet comfort with just enough money to make them all happy. *But I don't have a place for him* she was thinking. *I really want to take him, to hug him, to give him a home. I want this little boy. He could be mine. I know I could raise him. But how could I possibly make it happen?*

She had to say something. Jane wouldn't be able to stay on the line much longer. "Tell the Sisters he has an aunt in the States who is willing to take him," her impulsive heart made her say. "Tell them and the police that I'll come and get him next week."

"So you want me to lie to the guard and tell them you're his aunt?" Jane said in disbelief. "We could both go to jail for this! You'd be a kidnapper and I'd be the accomplice!" she wailed, before adding, "God help us all. I'm in." They hatched a story they both would swear to if questioned, and planned the plot.

"I knew knowing you was going to be trouble," Jane laughed as they ended the call.

Kateri hung up the receiver. *What have I just done?* She circled around the small living room, sometimes running her hands through her hair, sometimes just shaking her head in disbelief. Was she adopting a kid or stealing one? What about Ned? Did he have a say in this? Is he even alive? *Where do I begin?* she asked as she walked to the phone and dialed Aer Lingus. *I guess I'm doing this,* she told herself when the reservation was complete.

The news put the household in turmoil.

"You'll go to jail," Connie cried.

"She will not," Carl assured, not sure he was right.

"Timmy!" Oona gleefully touted, "I always wanted a boy!"

In the final moments of this great, upsetting news everyone had come to the same conclusion: Timmy would be theirs—a son, a grandson, a great-grandson. Maureen would understand.

On the flight to Shannon Kateri was making a list of things she needed to accomplish: a passport, for sure, a talk with Ned, and perhaps a meeting with the guard and/or whoever else might get in the way of her scooping up Timmy and bringing him home.

Kateri was so in love with the idea of giving a beautiful little boy a much better life than his first seven years had provided that she never suspected her biggest challenge to accomplishing this feat would be Timmy himself.

Jane met her at the airport and the two fell into each other's arms as if they were sisters. They cried and laughed simultaneously as they hugged and Jane was amazed that Kateri had recognized her from a distance. "You really can see!" she exclaimed as Kateri came within earshot. "Padric's watching Timmy," Jane explained as they drove toward Kenmare. "Timmy didn't want to come. He was afraid you wouldn't remember him and he wouldn't know what to say. I told him to wait with Padric and I would smooth it all out with you on the ride home. What you're undertaking, Kateri, isn't going to be all that easy. Timmy has had a rough beginning. I hope you're up to it."

"I'm sure I am," Kateri responded. "My family is just like you, loving, caring, kind. They'll guide me through the rough times. Timmy will be happy. I promise."

Timmy clung to Jane's skirt, hiding in its folds, when they got to the pub.

"Remember me?" Kateri sang out as friendly as she could muster after seeing Timmy retreating into the folds of Jane's skirt. He nodded. "How's that bike holding up?" she added to the one-way conversation. He nodded. "Can you come out from behind Mrs. Gannon so I can see how tall you've grown since I left?"

Reluctantly the youngster inched his way to the front of the portly woman.

"Wow!" Kateri exclaimed, "you've grown a lot since I've been gone and I've been missing you a lot," she went on squatting to be on his level. "Did you miss me?" He nodded. Kateri wanted to scoop Timmy into a hug but she could see that he was not going to allow it. She abandoned the idea.

"You know, Jane," Kateri said pulling her frame up from her squatting position. "I don't think Timmy remembers me." The cat and mouse game continued. Jane asked Timmy if he remembered Kateri. Timmy nodded. She asked him why he was so shy right now and Timmy moved even closer into Jane's legs.

"Will you excuse us, Kateri?" she asked as she ushered Timmy behind the bar to have a private conversation. "What's wrong, Timmy?" she implored. "You know Kateri. You love Kateri. She was so nice to you and you to her while she was recovering. What's different? What's wrong?"

Timmy pulled her arm so her ear could be close to his mouth and whispered, "She looks different."

"How so Timmy? What's different to you?"

"She's looking at me," he replied. "My Kateri is blind."

"Oh!" Jane replied, "I forgot to tell you that her blindness went away and her broken leg went away. She's back to being a normal person."

"But she doesn't look the same to me," Timmy continued. "She had short hair and this lady has long hair. This lady isn't my Kateri. Please don't let her take me away from here. I want to stay with you."

"She is your Kateri," Jane went on, "didn't she ask you about your bike? How would she even know you had a new bike if she didn't get it for you?"

"You told her," Timmy replied.

"Well, I didn't tell her," Jane said firmly, "and to prove this is your Kateri, ask her what color your new bike is and what brand. Ask her anything you want and if she gives you the right answers, you'll know for sure. Will you do that Timmy, so you can be sure this is your Kateri?"

"I guess so," he reluctantly agreed.

The two came out from behind the bar and Jane nudged Timmy out in front of herself so he could stand alone. "Ask her," she instructed.

"What color is my new bike?" he blurted out.

"Green and black with a yellow stripe," Kateri replied. That answer was apparently correct but to be sure he challenged her to name what kind of bike.

"It's a Cuda, of course," she said. "Your favorite." That much was also true, the Cuda was his favorite among all the bikes.

When he asked about her long hair she carefully explained that she had always had long hair and that after the accident it had to be cut off to sew up her head injuries. She said she had let it grow again and it was getting long and curly. "Do you like it long?" she asked and he nodded.

"I heard about Nana," Kateri went on. "You must be so sad." Timmy stared at her eyes without blinking. "When I heard you were alone and might have to go to the Sisters of Mercy until a home can be found for you, I told Mrs. Gannon I could bring you to my house and if you like it there you could stay and go to school in America. What do you think of that idea?"

Timmy retreated into the folds as he shook his head side to side.

"Why not, Timmy?" Kateri asked. "You would love Turner Mills. There's a big lake for swimming in the summer, you can learn to ski in the winter, I could take you to New York City and we could go to the top of the Empire State Building or ride the ferry to the Statue of Liberty. Have you ever heard of the Statue of Liberty?" Timmy nodded affirmatively. Kateri was getting nowhere.

"Can I see how well you can ride your bike?" she floundered looking for a door to open. This he eagerly agreed to. The bike was leaning on the stoop at the side yard.

"I'll show you," he said, breaking out of his resistance. He slammed the kickstand up, pushed off with confidence and rode out of the side garden onto the sidewalk between the two houses. He went out of sight then returned to the sidewalk with both hands in the air and a huge smile on his face.

"All right!" Kateri chirped, clapping her hands as he turned back into the garden. "Remember how we used to go to the cemetery?" she asked. "Do you want to ride there now? Maybe we can talk to your mother."

Timmy was back to being the little boy she knew.

"Okay," he said eagerly. "I'll ride slow and you walk fast. Let's go to the cemetery." He stopped outside the cemetery gate and got off his bike, he needed to talk.

"I can't go to Turner Mills with you," he sadly said. "I can't leave my mother here by herself. She needs me." Now she understood.

"I think spirits can move around, Timmy," she responded, "at least the ones I've met can. Let's see if we can find your mother and ask."

Nothing had changed in the cemetery, nothing ever does. The bench was where they had last sat, the OSUILLEABHAIN tombstone was just where it was and had been for the past one hundred years. The grass was damp as it always seemed to be and the sunlight was flickering through the leaves of the trees.

"You ask," Timmy implored, "she might say no to me."

"Maureen," Kateri called softly, "Maureen, Timmy and I have a question. Are you near? Can you hear us?"

The response was quick. Maureen was always near; it was her fate, she said, to stand by her little boy. She would do it forever if need be.

"Do you want to ask or should I?" Kateri said to Timmy.

"You ask," he insisted.

"As you know," Kateri began, "Nana has passed."

"Yes, I know that and I'm worried about you, Timmy."

"Well, I have a solution," Kateri continued, "I would absolutely love it if Timmy could live with me. He's the sweetest boy and my whole family is counting on me bringing him home to America. But Timmy is worried. He doesn't want you to be alone here. I told him that spirits are free and can go anywhere even Turner Mills, but Timmy isn't convinced. We wonder how you feel about that."

"Timmy," Maureen answered as if her hands were on his shoulders and she was eye level with him, "spirits can go everywhere. And I will go anywhere with you. Kateri will help me find you again. It isn't so difficult for those of us who are spiritually connected. She will find the place where we can talk and be together, our special spot. Won't you, Kateri?"

"Then I should go to America and you promise to be there?" he asked for assurance.

"You have my word. And thank you Kateri. I was beside myself."

"Can I bring my bike?"

MARGARET MARY O'SULLIVAN MCCANN

It took a while before everyone in the Warner household got used to the new routine. Timmy was making friends at his new school and he was beginning to come home happy. Kateri took on more hours at the Lancome counter and was even contemplating getting a second job. Oona added one more charge to her dog and cat duties: that of overseeing Timmy when he got home from school. She'd have her market bag of twigs and twine out of the closet and waiting when he got off the bus, ready to show him how to make Sacred Hoops. Connie made room in the fry pan for one more pork chop or whatever was on the menu that night. Carl was buying matchbox cars and having floor races with Timmy before dinner. The two could be heard laughing over Rather's voice. Kateri had found a spot in the cemetery where Timmy could talk with his mother. The household seemed to hum with new energy in the boy's presence. The new routine elevated everyone's spirits and the euphoria lasted until Kateri decided to get a second job.

The ad in the classified section seeking a caregiver one night a week for an elderly person would fit into her schedule and give her a little more income for Timmy's future. She applied and within twenty four hours was on her way to the interview.

A cheerful woman opened the door of the small home in a neighborhood she was not familiar with and let Kateri into the kitchen to talk privately.

"You'll find Mrs. McCann to be very easy to care for, we all love her to pieces. Sometimes she's forgetful but she's sweet and grateful for anything we do for her. I'm sure you'll love her as we do," the person in charge of the interview explained.

Kateri had stopped breathing a few sentences back. "What did you say her name is?" Kateri responded.

"Mrs. McCann," came the answer.

"Margaret Mary McCann?" Kateri managed to ask without fainting.

"Yes, why? Do you know her?"

"No, not really," Kateri managed to say in what she hoped was a nonchalant voice. "I've heard of her. Isn't she the Judge's wife?"

"Yes, that's right," the interviewer responded.

Isn't this a coincidence Kateri told herself remembering how her mother was so heartbroken when she read the obituary of Margaret Mary's son and how angry Kateri had become. A feeling of something vaguely familiar from long ago crept into her consciousness. *What is it about Margaret Mary McCann that I'm trying to remember* she asked herself over and over. *Pearls,* she came up with, *something about pearls.*

The caregiver was already discussing the job description and Kateri had to blink out of her reverie and refocus.

"Are you related?" the caregiver asked as she became aware that the names were the same.

"No, there are a lot of McCanns in this town," Kateri replied hoping her lie was camouflaged in her voice.

"Well," the interviewer continued, "would you like to meet Mrs. McCann?"

"Of course," Kateri replied pretending to be casual while *oh my God, oh my God* was racing through her head. She was led into a small living room with well-worn furniture that included a turquoise couch and matching chair. Two blond end tables with gold circles for pulls flanked the couch and a blond kidney-shaped coffee table completed the mid-century look on which sat a plethora of pill bottles. The room looked as if it were still in the 1960's.

A fleeting thought ran through Kateri's head—this is the house where her father grew up, this is the living room where Dad and his brothers roughhoused, ate TV dinners and maybe even heard the Beatles for the first time on the Ed Sullivan Show. And this woman, serenely sitting in a living room whose furniture looked like Judy Jetson had been her interior decorator, was her grandmother.

"This is your night caregiver," the worker was explaining to Mrs. McCann, "her name is Kateri."

"How nice to meet you Mrs. McCann. I've heard a lot about you."

"You have, dear?" Mrs. McCann quizzically responded and because she couldn't remember too many things from the past, accepted Kateri's comment as a compliment without challenge.

The interviewer was now busy discussing Mrs. McCann's evening routine including the time a replacement would arrive in the morning. "We need the help, can you start tonight?" the interviewer was saying.

"Yes, of course," Kateri replied. "I just need to make a phone call, let them know at home."

This was her chance, Kateri thought, the chance the gods had given her to right the wrongs this woman had inflicted on her life and her mother's life. This was her opportunity to set the record straight. Within minutes the two women were alone until morning.

Not now Kateri told herself, fighting the urge to keep from pouncing. Be patient.

As old and as forgetful as Mrs. McCann had become, she looked at Kateri with a recognition she couldn't quite place. Kateri could see it in her eyes and thought for a moment she was looking into her grandmother's soul.

She recognizes me she thought and held her breath wondering what would happen next but the flame of recognition died before an association could be recalled. Gone.

"Be a dear," the elder McCann was saying, "I'd like some chamomile tea and a Lorna Doone cookie. I sleep so much better with chamomile tea. Can you get that for me?"

After tea, the routine was to assist Mrs. McCann up the narrow stairs and into the front bedroom that had been hers for seventy years, to be tucked in for the night. Mrs. McCann was a very compliant charge, thanking for every little effort made and as Kateri finally gently tucked her into the double bed, she said, "Goodnight Grandmother."

"Goodnight dear," the soft-spoken woman replied.

Margaret Mary slept soundly that night but Kateri, by her side, didn't dare close her eyes. The devil was still on her shoulder demanding justice once and for all, wanting Kateri to wait for the moment of her grandmother's lucidity and then pounce on Margaret Mary for the destruction of lives she had caused.

Not tonight Kateri told herself, not tonight. Dawn broke and as promised Kateri's replacement was letting herself in through the kitchen door. I'll do it next time she told herself as the morning worker entered. But next time didn't seem to be the right time either.

Four weeks had passed since she began taking care of her grandmother one night a week. She had plenty of opportunity to look around the house. The refrigerator in the kitchen was covered with pictures of babies and school age children, taken, no doubt, by school photographers. Kateri studied the photos trying to find similarities in faces that might resemble hers.

"Who's this?" she inquired one evening while Margaret Mary was taking her tea at the porcelain-topped kitchen table.

"I don't really know," she replied and Kateri assumed it was forgetfulness again. "I think that's Marcy's first grandchild," she suddenly remembered. "You don't know Marcy, she comes in at noon and gives me my lunch."

"You mean these are not your kids when they were young or your nieces and nephews?" Kateri responded, surprised that strangers had moved their family photos onto this treasured spot.

"They're my family now," Margaret Mary continued. "The women who care for me enjoy showing me their little ones. I ask them to put the children's pictures on the refrigerator so I can enjoy looking at their sweet little faces."

"That's very smart of you," Kateri replied. "I'm sure they are happy and proud talking to you about their grandchildren. Speaking of photos, I noticed one on the bookshelf in the living room. Is that your family? The woman certainly looks like you."

"Yes, that's all six of us," Margaret Mary explained becoming more energized. "A professional photographer came to the house and took the picture when my husband was running for judge. Bring it to me and I'll tell you who everyone is."

Kateri lifted the picture from the shelf staring at one of the faces for such a long time that Margaret Mary called from the kitchen asking if she had found it.

She took the framed 8x10 from Kateri's hand and with a trembling index finger began wiping the dust that had collected on the face of one of the children. "He's my precious," she said, "my firstborn. His name is John Patrick. My husband nicknamed him Kip. I like the name John Patrick so much better," she sighed. "He's the only one who looks like me. See? He has my eyes." Kateri looked at the soft brown eyes of the woman before her then at the eyes of the teenager in the picture and realized she, herself, did not inherit them. She studied the eyes of the other children in the photo then shifted her gaze to her grandfather's. All eyes were blue and large and laughing, like hers. Her gaze lingered on her grandfather a while longer as she noticed she and he had the same shape face, same fair skin, same nose even, and a smile broke out as she realized she also had his shit-eating grin. Of all his children, she—his granddaughter—looked most like his progeny. *It's no wonder my father recognized me in Chief's that night* she said to herself in amazement.

Kateri wanted to piece together a picture of her father as a youngster but worried that Margaret Mary's noticeable dementia would not get the memory right so she gave her grandmother a little test. "Where's John Patrick now?"

"He's in the Marines," her grandmother replied. "He wanted to join or maybe he had to join...there was an issue, a big brouhaha, oh I wish I could remember. He's in the Marines," she repeated, "he sends me cards once in a while..." her voice trailed off.

Another dead end. Kateri changed the subject.

"I'm going to Windex the glass on this picture so we can see the photo better," Kateri was saying as if she were just another caregiver. "Are you finished with your tea?"

She once again ushered her grandmother through the narrow hall and up the stairs to the front room with the evening ritual ending in the tender tuck in.

"Goodnight Grandmother," Kateri said as she smoothed the top blanket under her grandmother's chin.

"Goodnight dear," Margaret Mary tenderly replied.

The ritual continued, always the same, ending in *Goodnight Grandmother, Goodnight dear,* words that now seemed like vespers between them so Kateri was shaken to her core on the evening when Grandmother didn't return the usual Goodnight dear, but said, instead, "Goodnight Granddaughter." The two women looked deeply at each other and Kateri knew and Margaret Mary knew, there was no secret between them. Neither spoke another word. If it was her imagination Kateri didn't want the illusion shattered. She didn't want an apology, she didn't want tears, she wanted to belong and now she did.

On that very evening, tucked into the lower corner of the large mirror over the blond maple dresser in Margaret Mary's room, Kateri noticed a tiny, tattered photo of a man dressed in a military uniform, a photo Kateri had overlooked until now. It was of a soldier, Civil War era, no, maybe not quite that old, World War I, perhaps. The soldier was tall and lanky, his belt barely able to hold the gabardine trousers upon his narrow hips. He held a small child in his arms. The child was smiling, the soldier was looking straight into the camera, grim.

Kateri gasped. "Is this you, Great Grandfather O'Sullivan?" she asked the photo. "Is this what you look like?" She ran her finger over the small face hoping to erase the folds in the paper as she peered intently at the faded photograph, her mind going crazy with delight. Margaret Mary was breathing deeply, already asleep, so Kateri stayed in the room, staring. She wondered if there was more meaning to her noticing the photo on this particular night and hoped for some quiet words, perhaps some advice the Colonel might want to impart. She waited for the picture to speak but it didn't, it didn't have to. She already knew what its presence meant. He was reminding her that this aging, somewhat demented woman, shallow as she might have been in her youth and middle years, is Grandmother and if, in her old age and decrepitness, she could be forgiven by those she had harmed, she would be able to pass to a better place without languishing in the intersect, like he had, hoping for resolution. Tonight without prompting or hesitation, Kateri forgave her grandmother and the feeling of being able to give this gift to another was liberating, so liberating, in fact, that she pondered the prospect of forgiving her father, too.

THE INVITATION

Kateri turned the out-sized envelope around and around in her hands recognizing that it was a wedding invitation. Without hurrying to read its contents she began guessing from whom it might have come. The postmark gave a clue, San Francisco. That limited the guess down to three, Tillie Mulloy from Chief's, Cory, omg Cory, she hadn't thought about him in such a long while and Madeline, the front desk gal at Prestige Modeling who had kept Kateri on the top of her call list for modeling jobs. She eliminated Madeline because she didn't really know her all that well. That left Tillie and Cory.

Hmmm she purred as the pressure to open the envelope built. *It's Cory* she told herself as she slid a kitchen knife under the flap. Wrong. It was from Tillie. "Mathilde Mulloy and Josh Stevens to wed August 5," it read, "on Ocean Beach in San Francisco." The formal invitation continued on with the details but the handwritten script scribbled over the printed words were written in Tillie's hand saying she had met the man of her dreams and wondered if it was at all possible that Kateri would not only come out to the wedding but be her maid of honor. The note was so jubilant that Kateri wanted to rush to the phone and cry or laugh or hoot and holler into the receiver with Tillie doing the same on her end. But as she started dialing she remembered a small detail that could derail the plan, Timmy.

"Timmy. Timmy. What do I do with Timmy?" she pondered aloud and for the first time truly felt the obligations of parenthood. She set the receiver back on its cradle and began pacing back and forth in front of the phone tapping the invitation she still held in one hand onto the palm of the other. She re-read it, this time carefully. The wedding date was August 5. "August 5!" Kateri shouted to no one. "That's during summer vacation. Timmy can come. We can make it a road trip, a holiday!"

Kateri warned Timmy how long it would take to get from the east coast to the west coast, "at least four days," she said, "and that's if we don't stop along the way to look at things," but Timmy said he wanted to see everything. He wanted to see skyscrapers and mountains, corn fields and Mt. Rushmore, cowboys and Indians.

"Well then," Kateri mused, "it might take us a whole week or more. Promise you won't start saying 'are we there yet?' a hundred times." He promised and added he especially wanted to see cowboys and Indians because he used to watch Davy Crockett reruns on TV with his grandmother.

Oh great, Kateri sighed to herself, now I have to teach him the truth about those cowboys and the Native Americans. Little Bighorn will be an eye-opener for him.

And so it was that Kateri decided on the northern route she and Chucky had taken on their fateful honeymoon. They high-fived. The plan was set.

They arrived a week before the wedding at Tillie's insistence. Josh, a teacher with summers off, volunteered to show Timmy around San Francisco while the girls did "their girly wedding thing," he said, winking to Timmy. Timmy winked back.

"Is it okay if I go, Mom?" he asked.

"Sure, run along, have fun," Kateri responded not wanting to make a big deal out of the Big Deal that she had just been called Mom by a slip of Timmy's tongue. The boys set off in the direction of Powell Street and the cable cars.

"That's a first!" Kateri told Tillie, joyful tears rolling down her cheeks. "He actually called me Mom."

Tillie reminded her that the last time she saw Kateri was in Chief's when Kateri was tearfully wrenching her guts at the realization she had just confronted her father and he had fled from her like she had the plague.

"Now this," Tillie was saying, hugging her friend, "the antithesis of sorrow, tears of great joy."

"Oona says tears are sacred medicine," Kateri related. "Well, maybe it wasn't Oona who said it," she frowned trying to remember where she had heard it before. She was still pondering the point when Tillie suggested they go to Ocean Beach and work out the details of having a wedding on a beach. They needed to figure out the exact time of sunset, how to decorate the arch Tillie had bought that was now leaning against a wall in her apartment, how close to the shore line to put the arch and who'd put it there on the day of the wedding.

"Give me any job," Kateri said.

"Your job is to make me the belle of the ball," Tillie laughed. "I had second thoughts about asking you to be my bridesmaid," she continued with a sudden seriousness in her voice. "I didn't want to be upstaged by a beautiful international model."

"I will be beautiful," Kateri laughed, "because that's what I do best. And I'll put on my famous you-know-what-eating grin because that's all I got when I'm happy. But my face will only radiate my happiness for you, and everyone will know just by looking at me that I adore you. Promise!"

"Deal," Tillie replied.

"So who's all coming?" Kateri asked on the drive to Ocean Beach.

"Nobody that you know," Tillie conceded, "except Cory. You remember Cory?" Tillie ventured. "After you left for France, Cory came to the pub with some of your African violets. He said his dad had had some kind of a health issue and he had to move back to Los Angeles to help his mother run the furniture store. He wanted me to care for your violets. They were glorious. I don't know what he did to make them so beautiful. Within two weeks under my care they were deader than doorknobs.

"Cory was really sweet and on his second trip to Chief's with more of your stuff, he asked me out. We dated for a while and I really liked him but as time went on I realized he saw you in me. I was his connection to you. I think he was in love—with you."

"No shitting!" Kateri responded remembering how she had used the guy, barging in on him with her great traumas, always about her, never once thinking about him.

"I invited him to the wedding," Tillie went on, "and he's bringing a guest. Who knows maybe he's married. He didn't say, just put a number 2 on the RSVP card."

"It'll be good to see him again," Kateri said as they walked the long sandy span between the parking lot and the shore. "I bet he won't even recognize me without the black rivulet of tear stain from mascara running down my face.

He was my go-to guy, my comfort blankie, my teddy bear in those crazy days when I was chasing my ghost. *Hmmm,* she softly added under her breath, *did I even thank him for any of the nice things he did?*

"We brought our girls something," Josh was saying when they met up a little later at Tillie's apartment. Two small hands and two large hands each proffered a beautifully wrapped box from Cohen's Jewelers to the women. Beautifully wrapped gifts had been flowing into the apartment ever since the invitations went out so Tillie was nowhere near as excited to see her pretty box as was Kateri.

"What's this?" Kateri asked, taking her box from the small set of hands. "It's not my wedding." The boy beamed as the girls opened their boxes, slowly, together.

Tillie's held a necklace on a near invisible chain with a diamond off-centered on a gold heart. She swung her arms around Josh and said it was perfect, that she needed something dainty around her neck for the wedding, that everything in her jewelry box was from Macy's at best, "perfect," she kept repeating and slathering Josh with little kisses.

Kateri's box held a silver bracelet with one charm on it, a shamrock, "to remind you of me," Timmy said as he helped her with the clasp. She pulled him to her body and the warmth of the moment felt like mother and child. This feeling was new. *So this is love* she told herself *not at all what I was chasing for all these years. Not how I felt about Chucky in the locker room, not how I felt about Bainbridge when I was seeking fame and fortune, not how I felt about Alec as we jetsetted around Paris making his paunchy friends jealous. This is why Maureen can't say goodbye, this is how Oona loved Grandpap, how Josh loves Tillie. My God, this is the real thing.*

It was a perfect day for a wedding, no fog, no breeze, not a cloud in the sky. The Choir Boys had volunteered to set up the trellis on the beach and decorate it with the strands of plastic wisteria Tillie had bought. Tillie worried how the trellis would end up looking but the Boys actually had some artistic ability.

It was a stand-up wedding not even a folding chair. Wide satin ribbons were tied to bamboo stakes, topped by torches forming an aisle. Guests stood behind the ribbons on either side creating the ambiance of an aisle in a church.

Timmy was in khakis with a blue oxford shirt. The women guests wore long beach dresses and sandals with pedicured toes peeking out. Men were mostly in Hawaiian shirts and khakis but a few more conventional men had arrived in sport jackets which they now draped over their arms as the temperature on this unusual San Francisco day was approaching 85 degrees.

Josh stood confidently by the trellis with his brother on one side and the minister holding a well-worn prayer book on the other. At last the three-piece band began playing a song announcing the ceremony was about to begin and finally the Wedding March. Kateri stepped into the aisle of sand as all heads turned. She looked beautiful, radiant, model-esque, just as Tillie had predicted, but as beautiful as she looked, she didn't hold a candle to the radiance of the bride who followed her on her father's arm.

As Kateri approached the end of the aisle trying not to walk as if it were a runway, she glanced side to side at the guests and spotted the only person she could recognize, Cory. He was standing next to a woman who was leaning a little into his shoulder smiling and telling him something while pointing toward Josh and his brother. When Kateri saw him, she let her smile go full face and his face returned his joy at seeing her.

The wedding was simple and beautiful. The minister, though a little long-winded, talked personally of the bride and groom, telling stories mostly of Josh whom he knew quite well, as the guests chuckled at the tales.

The limo was waiting along the road and scooped up the wedding party, parents, Kateri and Timmy, while the guests lingered on the beach to watch how the sky would illuminate after the sun set, before dusting the sand from their shoes and heading to the reception downtown.

The dinner was over, the cake had been cut and the dancing began. Kateri was dancing with Josh's brother when a cut-in tapped the brother's shoulder.

"May I?" Cory queried, as his arm pulled her toward him.

"You may!" she said, surprised, "but first let me look at you." She pulled back a bit to study his face. Yes, he still looked like her go-to guy, her comfort blankie, the old Cory, and she reminded him of it. Small talk lasted only a few seconds before he pulled her close again and she was willing to let her body move to his suggestion. He buried his face in her hair as he had so often when she came to his apartment, crying. They danced without speaking.

"This feels like home," she finally whispered as the song ended.

He learned that she now had a son and that was disappointing to him until she explained the circumstances. She learned he wasn't with "a guest" as the RSVP indicated, that the woman who was going to accompany him to the wedding, a friend, had a dog that choked on a bone and needed surgery. "How can I leave my Bentley?" the friend said begging off the trip.

He learned of her blindness "and when my sight returned," she said knocking on wood, "I now see everything through a different prism. Everything!" she exclaimed excitedly. She told him that she had found love—for the first time—with a boy named Timmy.

He told her he had found love, too, but didn't elaborate.

"I'm not so famous anymore," she was saying admitting, "fame isn't all it's cracked up to be. I'm much happier now. What about you? You still got your chops?"

"In a way," he answered, "remember all those guys I used to open for?"

She remembered.

"Well, I started writing and arranging for them. You might say I've become famous—in my circle. I write and arrange music for a living. I mean, I'm still helping my Mom with the store but writing music is my livelihood...and passion. And I can do that anywhere. Best of both worlds."

Timmy came running to the table breathless. "Tillie is going to throw the bouquet. She says you have to be there. Come on. You'll miss it." Kateri rolled her eyes toward Cory, "Looks like I better go."

"I can see that," he responded laughing. Timmy tugged her arm as she reluctantly pulled herself away from the table. Tillie threw the bouquet exactly at Kateri and she caught it. This was splendid news for Timmy.

"You're going to meet somebody," he pronounced, "you're going to get married. We're going to be a family!"

"You're a funny one, Timmy McGurk," she said pretending to give him a noogie.

AUTUMN LEAVES

Summer ended on a high note and Timmy and Kateri settled back into their routines. Connie and Carl thrived having them both in the household. Timmy was a willing student to Oona's teaching of native ways and could now make dreamcatchers by himself. In fact, his dreamcatchers had special effects built into them. Oona told him that Spider Woman might not approve of some of the things he wove into his art forms but she was delighted with his imagination.

Mrs. McCann, Grandmother, had passed while they were in California. The dementia her grandmother suffered took the edge off the hostility Kateri felt toward her and she could now think of Margaret Mary as a gentle woman who had once said "Goodnight Granddaughter." She knew her grandmother recognized her and in those two words had given her back her birthright. She forgave the past, all of it.

October was splendid this year and Kateri was reveling in Indian summer. The grass in her mother's yard was buried under a coating of maple tree leaves.

"A good day for raking," she decided as she rummaged through the hall closet to find her old Buffalo-plaid jacket then went on to the garage where the rake was buried behind the snow shovel and bag of Halite. The sun danced on the red and gold leaves as she swished them into piles feeling like she was in the middle of a Norman Rockwell painting. When she had little piles of leaves everywhere she began pulling and pushing them into the center of the lawn into one gigantic pile. With each pull she imagined Timmy's astonished face as he got off the school bus. She knew he wouldn't be able to resist jumping into the leaves with abandon and this made her tingle in anticipation of his exuberance.

At last she heard the motor of the school bus as it neared the corner but when she looked up, a car was slowly approaching and she could see the driver rubbernecking in search of an address. It came to an abrupt stop in front of her house but the driver stayed in the car for what seemed like an eternity while she leaned onto her rake squinting to see if she recognized who was in the car. That looks like Cory.

The door finally opened and Cory emerged. He put his elbows on the roof of the car and with a sheepish grin called over the car's roof, "You caught the bouquet at Tillie's wedding. I'm doing a survey on the validity of wedding customs, especially the one of catching the bridal bouquet. You came to mind."

"Oh my God, Cory, are you crazy or what?" she called back as she dropped the rake and ran into his hug. Cory hadn't been all that sure how his impromptu visit was going to pan out but the warm welcome was a good sign.

"What's this?" he asked as he spied the pile of leaves in the lawn.

"It's for jumping in," she replied and before she could explain it was for Timmy, Cory detached from the hug, ran like a kid and dove into the center of the pile. Only his newsboy hat, the one he always wore even when she first met him, remained visible.

"Okay, smart ass," she called after him, "I bet I can dive deeper," and she belly flopped into the pile as the school bus rounded the corner.

Timmy was glued to the last step of the bus on seeing two people, one being his new mother, in what he thought was his pile of leaves.

"There's room for more," Kateri called out and Timmy dove in, backpack and all.

"Hi Cory," he said nonchalantly as if it was just yesterday they had been together. The trio splashed each other with leaves until Cory started wheezing.

"Allergies," he said, "now I'm screwed," and he ejected himself from the pile, dusting himself free of leaves. The spontaneous moment had ended. Timmy headed into the house to get the snack of apple slices and peanut butter Oona always had ready and Kateri and Cory sat down on the front stoop, basking in the warmth of the autumn sun.

"Okay, smart ass," she irreverently opened the conversation, "I take it you're not just passing through."

Cory reached into a pocket and pulled out what seemed to be airline tickets. "I happen to have a couple of tickets to Jamaica," he began, "and I was thinking, well, wondering if maybe you'd like to go to Jamaica with me next month."

"Wait a minute," Kateri responded completely confused. "Didn't you tell me at Tillie and Josh's wedding that you were in love with someone? What happened? Did you get dumped and now have a couple of tickets you don't know what to do with?"

That smarted. "Ouch," Cory replied. "Do you want to hear my real love story?"

She nodded.

"I fell in love years ago in a nightclub in the Haight. I had just finished opening for the No Names and was getting myself a drink at the bar. I looked up and saw this gorgeous redhead with hair bigger than God heading my way, looking directly at me. I said 'My God! what a creature! I'm in love.' My palms got sweaty, my heart started pounding and I tried to think of something very cool to say. Yes! She was deliberately coming toward me! That's when she said, 'Hi, my name is Kateri, would you be a dear and take me backstage after the next set to meet the No Names? Can you introduce me to Jordan, the lead?' "

It happened exactly as Cory had laid it out and that wasn't the only time she had used him. She'd have a fling with the lead, they'd be all cozy and go off together after the last set and then the next week, wait a minute, there's another band, a better one, and Kateri would clickety-clack in her stilettos over to where Cory was a having a drink and it would start all over. "Hi Cory, would you be a dear..."

"Why didn't you say something?" she winced recalling how she had treated him.

"Are you kidding me?" Cory responded, "I'm not that stupid. You were in love with fame and even though you were using me big time I couldn't help myself. I was in love. I used to hate it when you came to me with your tears time after time and all I could do was soothe your broken spirit and send you off to try again. When you went off to Paris I cared for your African violets as if you were coming back to me. Finally I got word that you were going to marry that Frenchman and I gave up.

"After that I got really serious about my music and let it consume me. I thought if I could be totally passionate about music I could live without you. I was actually getting on with my life—until," he slowed his story hoping to push back the tears that were welling in his eyes, "—that dance. I held you in my arms with my face buried in your hair and you whispered, 'This feels like home.'"

"So here I am," he concluded. "Home."

EPILOGUE

A mentor came by the other day. Her name is Mathilde. She wanted to know if I needed any help as I work my way into the world. I told her I didn't think so and she agreed saying she was so pleased with the way my mother had found her true self (as if she had doubts!) She said the moon and stars were in perfect alignment for me to be the most beloved child ever born.

I'm beginning to think we're someplace exotic. Jamaica, maybe. The sounds of steel drums are pulsating through my amniotic fluid. We are squished together...me, Mom and Dad. Mom says, "Stop rocking the hammock, Cory. I'm getting seasick."

Dad says, "Seasick? That's ridiculous. I'm hardly rocking, maybe you're pregnant."

Mom says, "Pregnant? So soon? I couldn't be."

Oh yes, Mama, I chuckle, *we are.*

Made in the USA
Columbia, SC
23 May 2021

38403037R00104